THE IRISH
BRIDE

THE IRISH BRIDE

Alexis Harrington

St. Martin's

*To the ladies who planted the seed
in my imagination to write this story
nearly ten years ago—*

*Sheelagh Kirwan Bandettini
Ferryl Dolph*

*You both helped with your friendship and
inspiration. My thanks to you.*

*To RIC and GLA, you turned Aidan and Farrell
into a very handsome couple.*

THE IRISH
BRIDE

CHAPTER ONE

February 1855
County Cork, Ireland

FEAR made Farrell Kirwan want to run the all the way home, but the road was slick with mud and she'd already fallen once. She hurried along as quickly as she could, her side aching with the effort, her throat burning from her dry, raspy breathing.

Now and then she glanced over her shoulder to see if *he* was following her, but in the pale winter twilight, she saw no one. She pulled her shawl closer against the chill, but it wasn't long enough to cover both her head and the ragged tear in the front of her uniform that reached from neck to waist.

The housemaid's job at Greensward Manor paid nine pounds per year, money the family was desperate for. But nothing was worth this humiliation. No amount could force her to endure Noel Cardwell's rough, proprietary groping, and at last she'd slapped him. It had been a spontaneous, foolish act on her part, she knew, but she had only to glance at her worn chemise gaping from between the raw edges of her bodice to know that given the chance, she would have done the same again.

It was bad enough that her brother Michael worked for Lord Arthur Cardwell and his son Noel, collecting rents from his own friends and family, and evicting them when they couldn't pay. But then Michael had talked her into accepting the servant's position. If she went to work at Greensward Manor, he'd told her, she could escape their cousin's overcrowded cottage. With time, hard work, and a pleasant smile for Noel, she might climb the domestic hierarchy to special assignments and privilege. Farrell was innocent but she was no fool. A smile alone wouldn't gain privileges from a man like Noel Cardwell. At least not the kind she wanted. As it had turned out, she'd been right. He'd begun baiting her with his lewd innuendos her first week there. These he'd followed with the occasional brush of a hand against her leg or her posterior, always with no witnesses. Despite her attempts to discourage him, the situation had worsened. This afternoon, he'd trapped her in the library and assaulted her. It had been more than she would stand. She realized now that she never should have accepted the position at all.

But in a tiny house overflowing with children and three adults, her cousin Clare had grown increasingly short-tempered. Her husband, Tommy, had muttered about all the mouths he had to feed, never failing to glance at Farrell when he said it. Until she and Liam O'Rourke could marry, Farrell had felt the servant's job was her only option, even though the family had raised a great fuss when she'd announced her intentions.

She turned again to look behind her. Was that a figure on the road behind her in the gathering nightfall? Maybe not. The purpling dusk played tricks on her eyes, making her heart thump even harder in her chest. Certainly, Cardwell would not let this offense go unpunished. She'd seen the cold look of implicit retaliation in his eyes as clearly as she'd seen the red imprint of her hand on his cheek.

Finally reaching the little valley that was home to what remained of a dozen families, she staggered to a stop when she came upon the pile of rocks and thatch that only yesterday had been the cottage her betrothed, Liam, and his brother Aidan shared with their father, Sean. It had been standing when she'd come home to visit on her half day off.

Farrell swallowed and swallowed, but her throat was so dry it felt as if the sides were stuck together. She stared at the ruins, stunned, disbelieving. A jumble of broken furniture lay amid the rubble. Scores of footsteps had churned the mud in the yard into a sucking morass. She'd seen this kind of destruction before, just last week in fact, when the McCreadys had been evicted—

When Michael had evicted them.

Michael's horse was tied to the bare-limbed tree in front of the debris. Please, no, don't let this be Michael's doing, God, please—She turned to run along the road toward home, her zigzagging lope like that of a panicked man drunk on poteen.

A gray, eerie stillness hung over the cottages she passed. Usually dogs and barefoot children scampered back and forth over the green, rocky turf. Here and there she saw a mouse or a bird, but except for the smoking chimneys, she would have thought the valley was deserted.

She ran to Clare's tiny house with footsteps that skidded on the mud. Gripping the torn edges of her bodice with a shaking hand, she pushed open the door. There she found the family standing in a tight circle with their heads bowed, as if in prayer. The bleakness outside turned to vaguely palpable tension in here.

She recognized the three O'Rourke brothers, Liam, Aidan, and Tommy. The last stood with his arm looped over Clare's narrow shoulders. Even their children were crowded into the circle in the corner. Sean O'Rourke lay on a pallet by the fire. As a group, they jumped at her entrance.

"Auntie Farrell," five-year-old Sheelagh wailed. Her thin cheeks wet with tears, the little girl ran across the room and hid her face in Farrell's skirts. The other children began sobbing with her.

"*Christ*, Farrell, ye gave us a turn!" Tommy exhaled, turning to look at her. His own face was the shade of new plaster, making his rust-colored hair all the more striking. "What are ye doing here?" he demanded sharply. "I thought you'd cast your lot with Lord Cardwell, just like your turncoat brother."

"Tommy!" Clare snapped at her husband. Holding baby Timothy on her arm, she broke from her husband's grip and left the circle. She eyed Farrell's torn dress. "Jesus, Mary, and Joseph—what's happened to ye, then?"

Farrell felt her face flood with heat. "Um, Noel Cardwell, he, well . . ."

Aidan turned and gave her a sharp, curious look. He would, she thought, the lady's man of the family. The one who got into fights and drank and gambled.

Liam stepped closer. "Farrell, are ye all right? Did he hurt you?"

"No, I got away before he could more than rip my dress."

Clare nodded, tight-lipped. "So ye came to see that the blackguard is as rotten as a barrel of old apples, did you? Didn't I tell you not to have anything to do with him? Didn't I beg ye to stay here instead of going off to be a servant to the Cardwells?"

Farrell refrained from mentioning that Clare and Tommy had also carped about the extra mouth they had to feed with her living there. "I thought the money would help."

"Aye, well, it took Cardwell, what, just two months to reveal his true intentions? And what did you do?"

"I slapped him and ran home."

Clare and Tommy both groaned. "Oh, God—haven't we enough trouble on our hands?" Tommy asked. "That should turn over the final spade of earth for our graves."

"What? Why?" Farrell's heart began thudding heavily in her chest again. Something was wrong. In her own panic, she hadn't paid much attention to the charged atmosphere in the room, believing she'd brought it with her when she ran in. Now, she nudged Sheelagh out of her way and stepped closer, trying to see past the men's shoulders. "What's happened?" The group parted long enough for Farrell to glimpse something—or someone—on the floor at their feet before they closed ranks.

Clare shut the door. She'd been pretty in her youth but now she looked careworn and older than her years, as though she rarely slept. "There's been an accident."

"Accident?" Someone was dead, someone must be dead. *Dear God, I'm begging you, don't let it be Michael's doing, please—*

Liam took her elbow. "Aye, lass, there's nothing else to call it, and nothing to be done. When

Michael hit his head—hush, weans, so I can be hearing myself—" he said to the crying youngsters. Their tears slowed to sniffles and whimpers.

Farrell pulled free of Liam's grip and pushed her way between Aidan and Tommy. A familiar, well-dressed form lay on the floor, the head covered with a piece of old sacking. She jerked the cloth away to find Michael's lifeless, blue-gray face.

At the sight the children began howling again.

"Michael!" Farrell dropped to her knees beside her brother and touched his chin with a shaking hand. Beneath his head, a small pool of blood spread over the floor like a crimson halo. Anguish stole most of her voice. "H-how did it happen?"

There was a shuffling of feet and clearing of throats, but no answer to her question. Annoyed by their dithering, she looked up at the men. "*How? Don't any of ye know?*"

"Aye, Farrell. I know. And I think you do, too." Aidan O'Rourke, dark-haired and wide-shouldered in a family of reedy redheads, was the only one who would meet her gaze. He hunkered beside her. His upper lip and left brow bore nasty cuts, and a purple bruise swelled his jaw.

Even before he spoke again, Farrell guessed what he was about to say. Images flashed through her mind like the rapidly turning pages of a picture book—of Aidan and Michael, always arguing, circling each other like two he-goats, even as children.

How they had hated each other, senselessly, cease-
lessly. She had never understood why. More than
once she'd heard Aidan wish her brother dead, and
Michael cast the same curse upon Aidan. And now
it had come to pass—one of them was dead. Michael, her brother, all that had been left of her immediate family.

"Don't say it!" she said. "Please, Aidan, don't!"

"But it's the truth, Farrell! He came to *evict* us,
and we've paid our rent all along! He tore the cottage down, with the help of his four hired thugs,"
he replied, as if that justified the taking of Michael's
life. "Ye must try to understand."

"Understand? I know that Michael earned your
hatred, Aidan. But to pay with his life? Did his
death restore your cottage?"

"He ordered our da thrown out into the road—
for God's sake, he put his foot on Da's back and
wouldn't let him get up! And he said things I
wouldn't take from any man. I just—"

Farrell couldn't look at old Sean lying on the
pallet, and she didn't want to hear what Michael
had done. It hurt even more. "So you killed him?"

Aidan fell silent suddenly, as if even he agreed
that nothing her brother had done could justify his
actions. He gazed down at Michael's unnaturally
still face, and the next words were little more than
a whisper. "I didn't kill him. His bootlicks tried to
hold me back—I got these for my trouble." He ges-

tured at his injured face. "But I lost my senses and got away from them. I butted him in the belly, and he fell backward and cracked his head on a cairn. It was an accident, Farrell, I swear before God. I never—"

Pain burst inside her, driving out all caution. Consumed with grief, she drew back and punched Aidan's shoulder with all the strength she could put behind her arm. The sound of it thumped like a rock falling on hard earth, and could be heard over the sobbing of Clare's children and their grandfather's hacking cough. Then silence blanketed the room.

"I don't want your explanations! Is fighting all ye know, Aidan O'Rourke?" she demanded, glaring at him. Her voice broke with anger, and tears made her throat ache. "I would have talked him out of evicting you, had you only come for me."

"You think so?" he asked, his tone sharp and bitter. He stood up and flexed his shoulder, and she quailed, wondering if he would strike her back. "Then it's little ye know about people, lass, if you believe that. I swear on my mother's grave, I didn't mean to hurt your brother. But I wouldn't stand by and do nothing while he threw Da into the road to die, and then put the battering ram to our house because Cardwell ordered it. Michael *enjoyed* what he did to us, Farrell, leaving us with no place to live in the dead of winter. He enjoyed every minute of it. I saw it in his eyes. Him with fancy clothes on his back and good food in his belly." Even now, anger overshadowed the remorse in his eyes. "I couldn't abide it."

It was true, all *true,* her heart wept. Aidan's every word lanced her like knife thrusts but there was no questioning them, because she knew they were true. Michael had evicted a lot of families, some of whom had paid their rent faithfully, all at the behest of the Cardwells. She'd even heard rumors, ugly and vicious, that Michael was not only cheating the tenants, but his employers as well. Money was missing, it had been whispered, and Michael spent freely, as if he were a lord himself. How could she blame Aidan for defending his home and family? What real man could have done less?

She stole a glance at frail, dear Sean, whose breathing was labored with the sickness plaguing his lungs. No remedy she'd tried for his illness had helped much. Pressing her hand to her skirt pocket, she felt the little figure of Brigit, her favorite saint, hard against her hip. It was Sean who had carved it for her. She remembered that he used to whittle small toys for all the children in the *clachan,* including Michael. Yet Michael had evicted Sean anyway.

With a shaking hand, she drew the sacking over his face, knowing as she did the grief welling within her was not for the man who lay there, but for the

child he had once been. There was nothing left of
the baby brother she remembered. Over the years,
he'd grown into a selfish, cruel man who possessed
not a shred of decency.

Farrell felt eyes on her, Tommy's, Clare's, and
even the children's. Shame. It devastated her, making her dread having to meet their gazes. "I'm
sorry," she said, her voice shaking, "so sorry. I
would have stopped him if I could."

"Come on, lass." Aidan put a hand under her
elbow and helped her to her feet. "No one could
have stopped Michael."

"What will become of us?" Clare asked, drawing her other children to her. "We've got him here
on our floor"—she nodded at the prostrate form—
"Farrell under our roof again, and Noel Cardwell
angry with her. The Cardwells will send the authorities, and they'll arrest us all for sure now!
What are we going to do?"

Everyone spoke at once in hushed, emphatic
murmurs, laying blame, lamenting the turn of
events, cursing the English government—all of
which accomplished nothing.

Only Aidan remained quiet, staring at the low
blue flames of the peat fire.

"There's only one thing we can do. We must
leave," he said, keeping his back to the group. "If
we're gone, the rest of you might be safe when the
authorities come nosing around, asking questions

and looking for us. As long as ye can keep payin' your rent, Cardwell might let ye stay. Liam, Da— ye'll have to move in here with Tommy and Clare. But if they can't find us, eventually they'll give up and leave ye alone."

" 'We'? Who is 'we'?" Liam asked.

Aidan turned then and locked his dark blue gaze with Farrell's, where she still stood next to Michael's body. "Farrell and I."

"Farrell! Where can a woman go by herself?" Liam demanded, his expression alive with rare animation.

Aidan lifted a brow at his brother's question. Then he drew a deep breath and faced the family. "She won't be alone. I mean to take her with me." He glanced at her torn dress again. "Noel Cardwell isn't going to let this insult to his manhood and status go unanswered."

Everyone spoke at once, again in an uproar.

"She's your *brother's* intended, Aidan!"

Farrell glowered at Aidan and his bad joke, hoping to freeze him with coldness. "You're not funny atall, I hope ye know."

Aidan stepped toward them, his expression grim. "And neither is the idea of hanging or rotting in prison. But that's what will happen if we stay, and we'll doom the whole family." He gestured at the tiny one-room cottage around them, dark now but for the firelight. "They'll tear this place down, too, if they find us here, and then none of us will have shelter." He fixed Farrell with a hard look. "D'ye want to be responsible for that?"

"No, but . . . saints preserve us, you're serious! I'm not going anywhere with you. I am to marry Liam."

Aidan's exasperation was vivid on his face, made even more so by the cuts and bruises it bore, obvious souvenirs from the afternoon's events. "Aye, in prison with rats for witnesses?"

Farrell's chest tightened and she pressed her clenched fist to her mouth. "No—"

Tommy put a hand up. "Hold a minute now, Farrell. Maybe Aidan has the right idea."

"He might at that," old Sean put in from his pallet, rubbing his bristled chin thoughtfully. "Ye'll have to take Michael away from here, Tommy. Down the road a far distance. Make it look as if he took a spill from his horse so no one suspects foul doings. Praise God we're well thought of in the *clachan*. The neighbors won't breathe a word of what happened."

"No," Aidan interjected. He met Tommy's gaze. "Ye'll take him back to our cottage. Lay him where he fell, with his head against the rocks. And ask the neighbors to tell the authorities exactly what happened." He glanced apologetically at Sean. "I know ye mean well, Da, that ye wish only to spare me the blame. But it's too risky by half. The constabulary might hear of the fight from Michael's thugs. They'll know I had a hand in his death. If you try to protect me, they'll only suspect you of wrongdoing, too."

"But Aidan," Tommy said. "We're talkin' of a murder charge. Think, man! 'Tis no matter that he pushed ye beyond limits or that any man would've done the same. Let us do as Da says and take Michael down the road. Otherwise, they'll charge you with murder and you'll dance at the end of a rope when they catch you."

"That's why they can't catch me," Aidan replied, his blue eyes narrowed with purpose. "I'll be long gone. Far away from here, and easy in my heart, knowing my family won't suffer for the accidental wrong I've done. It's better this way, Tommy, much as I appreciate your loyalty to me. Better for all of you, and since you're the ones who'll be left behind, that's the way it must be."

"Where will ye go, do ye think?" Clare asked, absently smoothing the baby's silky head. "You can't stay in Cork, but maybe in Dublin or another city, you might have some luck findin' work and be able to dodge the authorities."

Aidan's expression grew bleak. "No. We have to leave Ireland. I'm thinking America is the only place—that's where we have to go."

America! Farrell couldn't believe her ears. "And how will ye pay for the passage? I've heard talk that it costs three or four pounds each for fare to New York."

Aidan glanced away, and then returned his gaze to her. "Michael had money in his pockets. A lot of money."

"You *stole* Michael's money?" she gasped, her hand cold at her throat.

"And who should we be givin' it to? Cardwell?" Tommy asked with a lash of sarcasm. "Or maybe we should let him be buried with it? Aidan's right. It will serve us all best if the two of you use the money to leave here and draw the trouble away from us."

"But—" Desperate for a champion, Farrell turned to her cousin. "Clare, do you actually mean to go along with this crackbrained idea?"

Clare's voice was as strained as her own. "I'm sorry, Farrell. Ye know I am. But we've the children to think of. We'll have trouble enough with the police sniffing around our feet about Michael's death, and who will see after the little ones if we're taken? Aidan is right. At least if you go, the blame and guilt by association won't be so likely to rain on us. The Cardwells will get tired of searching for ye eventually and leave us in peace. And our own people won't cut us dead every time they see us."

Sean shifted his bony behind on his pallet. "We can't very well send them off without Father Joseph's blessing, can we?"

They'd all lost their minds, Farrell thought, staring at them. Every single one of them. They needed Father Joseph to bless their leave-taking?

Sean sent his youngest son a sharp look. "Ye'll have to marry her, you know, Aidan—it wouldn't be right elsewise." Everyone nodded and murmured in agreement.

Aidan's answer was a short nod.

"Marry!" The word sprang from Farrell's mouth with the force of a curse. To be wed to Aidan, bound to him in every sense, and powerless against his wild ways and hot temper? And in a strange, faraway land without family to support or defend her? She stole another glance at him—he was a tall man, strong and with well-muscled shoulders and a broad chest. He'd managed to overcome four men who tried to hold him back from Michael. America was said to be the land of plenty—what would he grow into with good food and a better life? She would be defenseless against any demand he made of her.

She caught his gaze and in his eyes she saw a raw, burning possessiveness, as though she were his already—and, stranger yet, always had been. She looked away swiftly.

With her heart beating like a bird's, she turned to Liam. Her betrothed was strong of spirit, he was immutable, like a rock—qualities she so admired and counted upon. She trusted him to do the right thing; he couldn't let this happen. "Liam, in the name of heaven, ye must stop this."

But Liam offered no further protest.

"Will you say *nothing* against this?" she implored, a panicky tenseness tightening her throat.

"Come along, Farrell," he replied, taking her arm and opening the door. He directed her away from the doorway to give them a little privacy. The feeble winter sunlight was about gone, but she could make out his face. Regret etched lines in his gaunt features, making him look years older than his age. His hands closed over her upper arms, the grip of his fingers cold even through her shawl.

"Nothing has turned out the way we'd hoped. You've no future here—not a one of us does." He paused for a long moment, as if searching for words, then continued with a sigh. "Go with Aidan, lass. For all his wild ways, he's a good man—he didn't mean to kill your Michael. Ye'll be safer with him than you would be here. I'm putting you in God's keeping and my brother's. They'll both treat ye well."

Tears burned Farrell's eyes again, and a clattering tremor shimmied through her that had little to do with the cold. She pulled her shawl closer. "But—but Aidan doesn't love me," she murmured, heartbreak making her throat ache again. She pressed her hand to his thin chest. "You must come with us. *You* can marry me, just like we planned.

Maybe we can find land in America and work it together, just like we planned. Liam . . . if you love me, please!"

He shook his head, a faint smile barely visible in the low light. "You trust me, don't you?"

She sniffled and nodded. "Aye."

"Then don't you see it's for the best? Ah, Farrell . . . I can't leave Skibbereen. This is where I belong. I'd be no good to ye anywhere else. I don't do well with change—I can't bend to it. Besides, someone has to see to our da. We can't be leaving him to fend for himself."

"Clare and Tommy can—"

"No. Tommy has more than enough to tend to with his own family. It falls to me to take care of our father, especially now that we have no home of our own."

"But Liam, I might never see you again. Would you send me away like this?" She searched his face, looking for some sign that he would save her from the fate that awaited her, or that he would come with her. She didn't find it.

In his eyes she saw that he cared for her, obviously enough to sacrifice her to his brother.

In fact, no—it had to be a trick of the twilight. She knew that wasn't relief she saw in his face. It couldn't be. He *loved* her. "Liam, please—"

He shook his head again and released his hold on her arms. "I want only the best for you, Farrell, and that's what I'm giving you." As he gazed out over the landscape, his eyes reflected unrealized dreams. He dragged in a shaky breath and sighed. Farrell clutched his sleeve, willing him to meet her gaze. But he kept staring across the fields as if he might find answers there.

"I'm not like Aidan," he whispered hoarsely. "He'll fight for you with his last breath. But me? I haven't got it in me, Farrell." He broke off and finally looked at her. "I love ye, lass, but in God's truth, I don't love you well enough. You understand that, aye?"

Farrell stared at him. She did indeed understand, and therein lay the greatest heartbreak. Her Liam was a gentle, peaceful soul, not given to raising voice or fist. That gentleness had always been what she cherished most about him, what had drawn her to him with all the hope and love she held in her heart. Now it was to be the chasm that forced them apart.

She let her hand drop, feeling as though she'd been given a beautifully wrapped package that turned out to be empty. She knew Liam would never want anything but good for her—that was why she cared for him so. And even now he was protecting her. But disappointment added its weight to the grief and fear already pressing in on her.

Liam pushed his hands into his pockets. "Aidan is the dreamer," he said, as if he'd read her thoughts. "He'll make a success of America, or break his own heart in the tryin'."

Exile.

The reality of it struck Aidan again as he watched his boots send up splashes of mud and water with each step he took. He carried their skimpy belongings—a change of clothes, a razor, a comb, and a few other personal oddments, tied up in a square of old sacking. At least the bundle wasn't heavy, he reflected sourly.

The sky had cleared and a full winter moon, low-slung and pale, shone brilliantly on the landscape. Fatigue and the night played tricks on his eyes. Sometimes he believed he saw riders approaching, only to realize the figures were bare-limbed trees looming in the distance, dark and forbidding, casting long shadows. The wind moaned over hedgerows and ancient rock walls, sounding like the wail of the banshee, and making the hair on his arms stand on end.

Beside him, Farrell trudged along silently, almost brittle in her resentment of him, her face stony, her tension underscored with a nearly palpable wariness.

Those who'd left for America already had probably felt the same as Aidan did now—that they had been exiled from Ireland. Unlike him, though, most had been forced to leave simply to escape death by hunger. Nor was it likely that they had tramped through ankle-deep mud toward the distant harbor of Queenstown near Cork with an angry, unwilling, and resentful bride. A good distance it was, too— Queenstown was about thirty miles ahead.

Michael's death did not weigh lightly on Aidan. Accident or no, enemy or no, the man would still be alive if Aidan hadn't head-butted him like a ram. But Lord Cardwell would have dealt with Michael no more kindly, once he discovered his perfidy, Aidan was thinking. And neither might he have spared Farrell.

He supposed he should say something to comfort her, but he could think of nothing. That he would provide for her, maybe? Or that he'd never be heavy-handed? He had just killed her brother. Somehow he doubted that she would believe his promises, no matter how sincerely he made them. Besides, their circumstances were so dire, he had enough to worry about just keeping his gaze focused on the countryside around them.

Through a rapid, tragic chain of events, Farrell Kirwan had become his wife. Aidan could scarcely believe it. He'd known her since they were children, had watched her grow from a pretty young girl into a beautiful young woman. And he'd looked on with helpless, guilty envy as she'd hung on Liam's few words as though they'd been gold coins.

Aidan's scorched pride and his loyalty to his

brother had kept him from trying to win Farrell for himself. But jealousy had gnawed at his insides whenever he'd seen her gaze upon Liam with almost childlike adoration. What she'd seen in Liam, though, he couldn't guess—his brother had a good heart but he was a creature of habit and as sober-minded as a priest. At age eighteen he'd seemed like an old man.

If Aidan couldn't have Farrell, he'd thought, there were plenty of other girls in the district who found him favorable. Maybe then she would notice him.

But she hadn't.

Perhaps he'd forget his desire for her.

But he didn't.

Despite a lifetime of hardship in poor Skibbereen, Farrell bloomed like a rose in winter, fragile yet unbowed in the snow, with rich cinnamon hair and eyes that were as clear and green as the breakers that flung themselves against County Cork's rock-faced shoreline. Only in his most fevered midsummer dreams had he entertained the hope that she might someday be his. Now, through an unbelievable twist of fate, they were married.

And he knew that she'd rather be any other man's wife but his.

The events of the last fourteen hours were a jumble in Aidan's memory, but he had a lifetime to sort them out and relive them. Michael Kirwan's death, the urgent family council whispering plans in the dark, Father Joseph summoned in the deepest hour of the night for the dual purpose of performing a hasty marriage ceremony and giving last rites to Michael.

Afterward Aidan and Tommy had carried Michael back down to the cottage—no easy task since he'd grown as stiff as an old oak shillelagh—and left him lying where he had died. They left five pounds in his pocket so it wouldn't appear that he'd been robbed. It was Aidan who would be blamed for the death, Aidan who would be hunted down. By God's mercy, perhaps the rest of the O'Rourkes would be left to live in peace.

Sean O'Rourke had produced an ancient pair of boots for his youngest son. Sean had worn them to his own wedding and he'd planned to be buried in them, but thought that Aidan would get better use of them. They were too small for Aidan but at least he wasn't barefoot. Then with hasty farewells and no time to look back, Aidan and his new wife had set out. The only other belongings they had with them were the clothes on their backs, and the kit that Aidan carried.

"Are ye warm enough?" Aidan asked, mainly to break the silence they'd held for hours. He wasn't certain Farrell would answer.

"I'll do."

He tried again. "When we get to Cork, I'll get

us some decent clothes and shoes for the trip. At least we've extra money to do that."

She kept her eyes on the road in front of her. "We should have left a bit with Tommy and Clare to help them along. Now they have Liam and your da to look after as well as their own."

"And how would they be spending it? Everyone knows we're poor as dirt. If Clare bought something from the butcher in Skibbereen, or even a dram of tea at the pub, it would lead the authorities right back to the family and Michael's death. They're no worse off than before, and Liam will get the crop planted."

Farrell trudged along in silence for a moment. Then she said, "I wish I could have done something for them. God knows if they'll be all right."

"Aye, well, getting out of Ireland is the biggest favor we can do them." He kicked at a rock in his path, silently adding, *And taking you with me is the biggest favor I can do for you.*

Convincing Farrell of that was going to be the trick.

CHAPTER TWO

BY mid-afternoon Farrell was starving and exhausted. Her feet were stiff with cold, her stockings wet. Aidan had not said a word for hours, and she wasn't sure if that was good or not, but she couldn't think about it. She was capable of only a single task right now—putting one foot in front of the other.

An hour before dawn, they'd stopped to rest in the shelter of the ruins of a roofless abandoned cottage. Two of its walls, at right angles to each other, provided a corner that was out of the wind, but not the cold. Farrell had slipped into a restless doze but it seemed that only a minute had passed before she felt Aidan's hand on her shoulder to wake her. She didn't think either of them had slept more than a few hours in the last twenty-four.

Despite that, Aidan seemed tireless, like a machine. His rhythmic stride was longer than hers and sometimes she fell behind. Wordlessly, he'd slow to let her catch up. Otherwise he remained a dark, intimidating presence beside her.

The miles stretched out behind them and ahead of them. Above, the clear sky was giving way to clouds again, obscuring the watery winter sun.

They'd encountered no rider or foot traveler since they set out, but she noticed Aidan constantly scanning the road and the far hills, like a wolf sniffing the wind.

Farrell herself looked over her shoulder from time to time, half expecting to see one of the Cardwells or a British soldier gallop up behind them at any moment, lashing his mount and tearing up the soggy turf like one of the Four Horsemen. If trouble came, it wouldn't sneak up on them, that was certain.

She had only a vague idea of how far away Queenstown was. It was somewhere near the city of Cork, she knew, but the distance didn't matter. They had to get there.

Walking away from Skibbereen was the hardest thing she'd ever done. The family—even old Sean and the children—had stood outside Tommy's tiny cottage to bid them farewell.

She tried to take comfort from Father Joseph's parting words, that should the family never see each other again here on earth, they would meet in heaven. Perhaps it was true, but that time was far away and right now she had banishment and this husband to deal with.

Husband . . . husband . . . husband . . .

Every step seemed to echo the word in her mind to remind her that he was more than Aidan O'Rourke, someone she'd known all her years.

More than the boy who'd given and gotten his share of black eyes. Someone else besides the man who could hold the attention of a group with his storytelling.

Yes, Aidan was all of those men. But above all else he was now Farrell's husband, and she could scarcely credit how quickly it had happened.

As she dragged one leaden foot after another, her thoughts were detached and her heart heavy. Her memory of the night's hasty doings—plans whispered in near darkness and accomplished in secrecy—were like still-life drawings, blurred by her heartache and disillusionment. She remembered the priest arriving at the cottage, bringing in the cold night on his cloak. He'd knelt beside Michael in the flickering firelight to anoint him, touching oil to his closed eyes and lips, to his feet and stiffening hands, while he murmured prayers in Latin. It had all seemed unreal, as though she were watching through a window and wasn't a part of the scene.

But stark reality jolted her when she had been called to stand next to Aidan to face Father Joseph. This hurried, secret ceremony was not the wedding she'd hoped for in her feminine heart. She had always envisioned a bright, clean spring day with a gathering of neighbors and family to wish her well. She had even imagined the impossible—a gleaming white wedding gown. No Irish Catholic girl in Skibbereen had ever worn such a gown for her wedding.

They were far too poor for such luxury. But she'd once caught a glimpse of a wealthy landowner's daughter riding by in a coach dressed in a white silk dress, festooned with flounces of tulle. On her head, she'd worn a veil as fine as a spiderweb, and she looked like a fairy princess. Next to her had sat her new husband, and Farrell had stood beside the road, staring in awe at the fabulous spectacle.

Of course, there had been no wedding gown for Farrell. She had changed from the torn uniform into her own dress, the only one she owned. Aidan wasn't even the man she'd expected to marry. Liam should have been beside her. Over the miles, she had come to realize that his talk of fair-weather love had been only a ruse to make her leave so that she'd be safe. He'd sacrificed his own happiness to protect her.

Fate had given her no choice, though, if she would protect those same neighbors and family. And she must because they were just as innocent as she. To shield them, she'd had to take Aidan for her bridegroom, not the sturdily built, sparely worded Liam with his gentle voice, kind smile, and soothing ways.

Liam . . . she loved him. Not with the silly, giddy passion other girls talked of. Her love for Liam O'Rourke was like the man himself—quiet, steady, and as dependable as the morning. Her childhood spent with a lazy drunkard of a father had made her seek a man with Liam's qualities. He was everything that Gael Kirwan had not been, and she'd been drawn to him because of that and his noble spirit.

Farrell had been betrothed to him when she turned twenty and in the past two years he'd exhibited no behavior that made her feel silly or giddy. She didn't even know for sure what other girls meant when they giggled about hot-blooded men with even hotter hands, but it concerned her that they'd often been speaking of Aidan.

She swallowed hard and clenched her hands in her damp skirt, wondering dizzily how she'd landed in this awful fix.

Oh, Aidan knew all about women, of that she was certain. It had been whispered over the years that Father Joseph talked to him more than once about his fast ways with the lasses. Farrell couldn't deny that he was handsome—he turned women's heads wherever he went, even in church.

She cast a sidelong glance at him. He towered over her. Long-legged and broad across the shoulders, he was much more intense than his brother. He had a fine, straight nose and a firm chin, and large eyes that seemed to cut right through a person to look into their heart and soul. Despite the circumstances and the solemnity of the night, a combination of maleness, passion, and vital spirit had pulsed from him in waves that vibrated through her on a primitive level she did not recognize.

But what she remembered most was one question Father Joseph had asked her.

"Farrell Kirwan, do ye promise to love, honor, and obey Aidan O'Rourke as your husband?"

Honor.

Obey.

A husband could force a woman to do these things. He could demand that his meals be served at a certain time, that she defer to him in all matters, even that she submit to him in his bed. And Aidan, iron-willed and fervent, very well might expect all of these and more.

She'd glanced around for Liam, hoping that he would step in at the last moment and stop this ceremony. But he'd merely looked on and nodded at her.

Returning her gaze to Father Joseph, she'd opened her mouth but no sound came. Finally, she'd whispered, "Yes, I promise," her voice muffled by bewilderment.

There had been no point in refusing. After all, she had no one to defend her or speak up for her. Her parents and older brothers had died in the Skibbereen workhouse during the famine, and her one remaining brother now lay dead with his skull cracked open like an egg. Aidan O'Rourke and dire circumstances could force her into marriage.

But Aidan couldn't force her to love him. The human heart did not yield to such pressure.

"Then, Aidan, give your wife the kiss of peace."

As he turned to her, his dark blue eyes had gleamed in the firelight, reminding Farrell of a cat's. His lips had barely brushed hers, but their heat startled her. The same feeling she'd had earlier, that Aidan saw her as his own, now and always, rushed over her again.

He was accustomed to having his way when he could get it, she knew. And he wasn't likely to take no for an answer from anyone without a fight, especially from his wife.

Farrell did not think of herself as a cowardly woman. With hunger and oppression constant threats in good times and bad, a coward could not survive in Ireland.

She took another glance at the lean, powerful man slogging along beside her. When she had run home to escape Noel Cardwell, she'd believed herself to be more afraid than she'd ever been in her life or ever would be again. She knew she might face arrest or some other punishment that he might care to visit upon her. Now she realized there were far worse prisons than the kind with iron bars and that she'd just been condemned to one. Not for just a few months, or even for a few years.

But for life.

· · ·

Noel Cardwell sat in the dark-paneled study at Greensward Manor, rolling a drained brandy glass between his hands. Behind the huge mahogany desk, Lord Arthur Cardwell studied his account book, a thick, leather-bound ledger where he kept track of his tenants' rent payments.

Regardless of the duels he had fought, the women he'd bedded, the horse races he had won, and all the other manly pursuits in which he excelled, in this room, Noel always felt as if he were twelve years old again. Twelve years old and brought here because of some prank or misdeed that his humorless father would not abide. Nothing Noel had ever done had pleased the dictatorial old man; they seemed to be on opposite sides of all issues. Now he did his best to keep from fidgeting in his chair and believed he was making a proper job of it. Not an easy task considering the subject of this meeting, although nearly all conversations with his lordship were enough to drive a man to the brandy decanter.

The endless tick of the mantel clock was the only sound in the room, save the dry, papery drag of the old man's finger down the column of figures before him. God, to actually keep one's own accounts like—like a penny-hoarding merchant or a factor, toiling over long columns and worrying about every single shilling. He suppressed a shudder. A true gentleman hired people to see to such mundane tasks rather than stain his own fingers with ink, scratching away with his pen. That was why Noel had hired Michael Kirwan to do his bidding. It had not been the most sagacious decision, he realized now.

When his father had burdened him with the tedious responsibility of collecting the rents, Noel forced himself to stifle a loud, disgusted sigh. As far as he was concerned, the Irish were nothing but a pack of lazy, drunken, storytelling bog-trotters. Their circumstances troubled his conscience not one whit, nor did he mind the feudalistic system that put money in his pockets for the gaming tables and other pleasant pastimes. Yes, he enjoyed the income, but Christ, he didn't want to be bothered with the grubby collection of it.

Hiring Michael Kirwan as the estate's rent agent had seemed like a brilliant solution. Though younger than their previous rent agent, he was ambitious and surprisingly unencumbered with such impediments as sympathy or loyalty to the rabble that resided on Cardwell land. He knew how the crofters lived and how their minds worked. And he was anxious to acquire the same comforts he'd seen at Greensward Manor. One could almost forget that Kirwan himself came from those same people. Or at least forgive him for it.

But even more importantly, his sister was Farrell Kirwan. Perhaps she, more than any other consideration, had influenced Noel's decision. He rarely paid any attention to the peasants living on the Cardwell acreage. The men were shiftless and brawling, and their women were threadbare old hags by the time they reached their twenties, due to constant child-bearing and carping at their shiftless, brawling men. Farrell was different, though. He'd heard that she was betrothed to one of the O'Rourke brothers, but that posed no obstacle as far as Noel was concerned. He simply wanted her and he was accustomed to get-ting his way. But the flame-haired beauty was as proud and haughty as a queen despite her poverty, and she would not speak two words to him. Even when he'd offered her a kitchen maid's position here in the manor house—a significant step up from the rabbit warren she lived in—she had looked as if she would spit on him, right then and there. She had brushed past him with her chin up and head held high. Her disdainful rejection had only made him more determined to have her.

Noel had hoped that her brother Michael would be able to change her mind. Indeed, Michael had finally convinced Farrell to work at the manor house, and Noel had envisioned that she was at last under his thumb. Still she had resisted his atten-tions, and yesterday had committed the unforgiva-ble offense of actually striking him when he'd tried to kiss her in the library, the ungrateful wench. Oh, yes, bringing the Kirwans on board had seemed like a sterling idea.

Until now.

Now, Farrell Kirwan had insulted him and rent money had gone missing. Noel found himself in a highly disagreeable position. Damn that Michael Kirwan for what he was, a thief and a liar, and ultimately no better than the peasants he'd come from. Damn his sister for being an irresistible jade who'd gotten into his head and his blood. He wished he were in London, far from this place of rock wall mazes and perpetual green gloom, where his breeding, and skills with gaming and horses would be put to much better use.

Despite the clock that marked its passing, time seemed to have stopped. God's eyes, would his father speak or was Noel to be kept here, waiting and wondering how much his lordship knew? He rose to help himself to another brandy.

"*Sit* down."

Noel almost obeyed the command but decided that to do so would be a small battle lost. Instead, he continued casually to the liquor cabinet and re-filled his glass from the crystal decanter. He felt his father's stone-gray eyes boring into his back at this defiance but did not hurry his actions. At last he took his seat again.

At some length, Lord Cardwell slammed shut

his ledger with enough force to make Noel jump. A splash of brandy sloshed over the rim of his glass and landed on his well-tailored trousers.

"Do you know why I gave you the task of collecting the tenants' rents?" his father asked, glaring at the drink in Noel's hand.

Noel shrugged and glanced at Lord Cardwell's ink-stained fingers. "I assumed you were tired of seeing to it yourself."

The older man pressed his lips into a tight, white line that looked more like a scar than a mouth, and a faint blue vein throbbed in his temple. "I did it so you would have a sense of what it means to oversee an estate, because someday all of this"— he gestured at the room and the grounds beyond the windows—"will be your responsibility. I wanted you to realize that the money you spend so freely doesn't fall from the sky like rain." He gestured at the ledger. "Your records are not only incomprehensible, I would say they suggest fraud. You have cheated your own family."

Noel jumped to his feet, quivering with indignation and insult. "I have done no such thing, sir!"

Unruffled, Lord Cardwell continued. "No? Then where is the rent money that should have been noted here? More than one hundred pounds seem to have vanished. What has become of it?"

Gathering his injured dignity, Noel began, "The rent agent must have—"

"Ah, yes, the rent agent. One Michael Kirwan, I believe. Just yesterday I had a warrant issued for his arrest. What a pity I could not have issued a warrant for you as well."

Stung and bearing haughty offense like a shield, Noel said, "I supervised his every move, Father! He reported to me on a regular basis."

"Yes, at the pub in town, as I understand it, where you both drank and gambled and bedded the serving wenches." Lord Cardwell sat back and folded his hands. "I can imagine what kind of report that generated." He went on to recite the extent of Kirwan's activities with regard to keeping the rents and evicting tenants. "I also understand that you hired Kirwan's sister, and that she was seen running from here yesterday with her dress half-torn off after escaping your attentions. Really, Noel, what a clumsy lack of finesse you exhibited. And for all I know, the sister might have been complicit with your rent agent. Have you checked to see if anything is missing? The silver? Valuable artifacts?"

Noel felt his father's withering disapproval now more than ever before. Worse, he realized that his father knew even more than he'd suspected.

"And now Kirwan is dead, killed in a fight by that firebrand Aidan O'Rourke—"

"What? Kirwan is dead?" Noel's dignity slipped again and he felt his jaw drop.

His father looked pleased with the effect of this

news. "Well, perhaps that's one report you didn't receive. He went to the O'Rourkes' yesterday to evict them and knock down their cottage. He scuffled with Aidan and they *say* he hit his head on a rock. He died instantly. One of Kirwan's henchmen blabbered the story around town. The authorities are searching for O'Rourke as we speak."

Noel jumped on this news, hoping to use it to reflect the glare of the problem away from himself. "But that's good! The worthless, murdering guttersnipe."

"Except that I don't believe they'll find him. One of my men says he's been spotted on the road heading to Queenstown."

"Then surely the authorities will track him down as well. We've only to wait for them to bring him back."

Lord Cardwell leaned forward over his desk blotter. "You began this task, Noel. I expect you to finish it."

"Me! And just how am I to 'finish it'?"

"You will bring back O'Rourke yourself."

God, but this was too much. "Surely you can't expect me to ride about the countryside like a constable, searching through shrubbery and under rocks! If you don't believe the authorities will find him, why do you think I will?"

"Because until you return with the man who cheated me out of the satisfaction of seeing Michael

Kirwan clapped in irons, your debts will go unpaid. And quite a stack you have, too." He reached into a side drawer of his desk and produced a sheaf of bills. Leafing through them, he recited, "Tailor, haberdasher, bootmaker, wine merchant—I will tell all of them to find *you* for payment. It should be interesting, don't you think? The hounds chasing the hunter?"

Noel felt the blood drain from his face. "You wouldn't do that."

His father's shoulders drooped slightly. "I've been waiting for you to grow up for years, Noel. I was twenty-three, two years younger than you, when I took over this estate. Your grandfather was deranged and nearly bankrupt when he died and had let this place go to ruin while he followed the same useless pursuits that you do—gaming, women, drinking, and indolence. I've worked hard to bring it back to its present state." His cold, glittering eyes fixed on Noel's. "But I swear to you, before I die I'll burn the manor house to the ground and evict every tenant on the land if I think you'll wreck it again. If you mean to inherit anything from me in the future, you'll do as I say now."

Noel drained his brandy glass, barely restraining the urge to take a bite from the crystal. What a galling situation he found himself in.

His lordship nodded, obviously accepting Noel's silence for acquiescence. "They say O'Rourke is traveling with a red-haired woman. That might slow him down." Noel started. It could be any woman, he told himself. Certainly Ireland had no shortage of redheaded people and O'Rourke's reputation with women was no secret in any quarter. But his father's next words removed all doubt. "The same man who saw O'Rourke believed the woman is Kirwan's sister. So you can bring her back as well."

Kirwan's sister. Why on earth would she be traveling with Aidan when she was supposed to marry his brother? Under any other circumstances, Noel would have refused to do this incredibly menial job, his father's disapproval be damned. But this might be a good way to accomplish two deeds: to win his father's favor, although why that desire continued to plague Noel after all these years remained a mystery even to him, and to finally have Farrell Kirwan exactly where he wanted her—in his bed.

"Very well, then, sir. I shall do as you ask. I'll find Aidan O'Rourke and Farrell Kirwan, and bring them back to Skibbereen."

CHAPTER THREE

FARRELL had asked for no special treatment. But the day was just an hour from dusk, and except for an hour or two, they'd been walking since eventide the night before. She was so footsore and weary, she was about to suggest that they rest for a while when Aidan stopped, his gaze fixed on something up ahead.

"Wait," he said, holding out his arm to stop her. He drew himself up, alert and wary, and his caution telegraphed to Farrell. The subject of his scrutiny was a wagon stopped in the road, pulled by a team of two deep-chested draft horses. The driver stood bent over the huge hoof of one of the beasts.

While she hung back, Aidan approached the man and after a brief conversation, he motioned her forward.

"Farrell, this is Mr. Stephen Riley. He's kindly agreed to give us a ride."

This was welcome news to Farrell. "Thank you, Mr. Riley. We've been walking a long time."

"Pleased to help, missus. Cork's miles ahead yet, and this isn't fit weather for walkin'," Riley observed, gesturing at threatening clouds in the western sky. He was a thin young man, more by natural constitution, it appeared, than from hunger. He patted the big horses' necks and climbed up to the wagon seat. "I think we'll get into town early tonight. I've room in the back of the cart if ye don't mind riding with the butter."

Both Aidan and Farrell stared at the cargo as if it were diamonds; butter had been as rare as gemstones in their lives. The tiny bit that was churned in the *clachan* was sold to help pay rents.

Riley explained that he was taking it to the city to sell for Indian corn for his master's blooded horses. How typical of the English, that their horses were more important than people. She saw Aidan's face color and his dark brows lower, and knew his thoughts were running along the same line. She held her breath, hoping he wouldn't make a sharp comment that would change Riley's mind about giving them a ride.

To her relief, Aidan only thanked the bailiff and assisted her into the wagon. She felt his warm, strong hand through her thin shawl as he took her elbow.

Farrell was glad for the chance to ride, even wedged as she was between the burlap-covered butter crocks. Her thin shoes protected her feet from the bare ground, but they were little help in keeping them warm.

As the wagon rolled forward and the horses

found a steady, comfortable gait, the countryside passed at a somewhat faster pace. Farrell leaned back against a crock, lulled by the rocking motion, and closed her eyes. She tried not to think about fresh, hot bread dripping golden butter and smeared with jam, but it wasn't easy. Only the knowledge that they'd finally eat in Cork kept her from prying open one of the crocks and scooping out handfuls of the churned cream to lick from her fingers.

Despite the turmoil of her thoughts, she felt Aidan watching her. They sat so close in the little farm cart, she didn't dare glance up into his eyes. What would she see there if she did? Perhaps the same indefinable expression she'd seen after their wedding. A look that was assessing, possessing, fathomless. She kept her lids closed, hoping for rest, and seeking escape from his dark blue gaze.

Aidan reached behind him to move a crock that was jabbing his spine, watching Farrell all the while. He couldn't help himself—he'd rarely had such a perfect opportunity to study her, and yet he'd wanted to so often. Fatigue and sorrow were plain in the droop of her narrow shoulders, and in the pale lavender smudges that sat beneath her lower lashes like the gauzy light of a winter sunset. Of course she was too thin; he'd be surprised if she weighed more than seven and a half or eight stone. As she sat huddled in her rough, threadbare shawl, she was the very picture of a refugee.

She was the very picture of Ireland—wounded and grieving and beautiful.

Farrell was the loveliest woman he'd ever laid eyes on, and now she was his *wife,* a fact that he kept repeating in his mind because he could scarcely believe it. A couple of loose russet curls that had escaped their pins fluttered around her face in the winter wind. Her hands looked rough and chapped, and he wished he could fix that. He knew that she'd never lived an easy life. None of them had.

He thought of Noel Cardwell, that filthy-minded bastard, pawing Farrell, his behavior so crude and barbaric that he'd torn her dress, and the hot blood of anger flooded his veins. Thank God she'd gotten away before Cardwell could do more. Now Aidan would be able to protect her and keep her safe from men like that strutting peacock who lived at Greensward Manor.

The wagon hit a rut, jolting the vehicle's contents and passengers. Farrell stirred and her unguarded gaze connected with his for just an instant. In it he saw a heart closed as tight as a fist.

Ah, but God was laughing at him again, he understood bitterly. Aidan had yearned for beautiful Farrell Kirwan longer than he could remember. And now God had bound her to Aidan, but it was no marriage made in heaven. With such distrust and rejection in her eyes, he knew he might never win her regard.

Marriages had been arranged under less favorable circumstances, but right now he couldn't think of one worse. Aidan had killed her brother, taken her from Liam, and was about to carry her off to a strange land and an uncertain life on the other side of the Atlantic Ocean. He shrugged off the thoughts; Aidan had had no problem winning other women's hearts—he'd done so several times. Determination, what his mother had called pigheadedness, Aidan had in abundance. He and Farrell weren't off to the best start, but at least he might be able to make their destination sound more promising.

"When we get to the city I'll see after getting us a room. I'll tell the innkeeper that we're newly wed. That way we might get a bed to ourselves instead of having to share one with a half-dozen other people."

"No!" she blurted, eyes wide, and then amended, "I mean, should we spend money on a luxury like that? We might need it for food or passage . . . ye know."

Yes, he knew. She didn't want to be alone with him. "I think we can spare it, Farrell. Besides, I want to be able to leave you at the inn while I see about what ships are bound for America. If we have a room of our own ye'll be safer while I'm gone."

She toyed with the tail of her shawl. "I suppose."

Aidan wasn't prone to useless chatter, but he was more social than Liam, and the silence between him and Farrell begged to be filled. To his way of thinking, a woman who spoke too little was as bad as one who talked too much. He glanced at Stephen Riley's back; given the man's proximity, he chose his words carefully.

"Last week I heard the Learys have had a letter from their son, Danny. He's in Boston, ye know. He said they have more food than we can imagine— meat, potatoes, bread, milk, whiskey, and more." The faint, sweet scent of the butter around them drifted to his nose, and he gestured at the cargo. "We've never seen so much to eat back here, he said. And his wife, Bridie, she's got three dresses and *two* pairs of shoes. There's good work in America, and wages to be earned. I'm thinking we'll try for Boston or New York."

Farrell's face registered a glimmer of hope. "D'ye think it's true, or is it more of Danny's blarney?" Danny Leary was known to exaggerate from time to time, all in the interest of making a story "a wee bit more entertaining."

"Aye, I believe it. He's not the only one who's written back telling of food and work. Some have even sent a little money for their families." He fingered the frayed edge of his coat sleeve. "I don't think the streets are paved with gold, as some have said. But it's a land of plenty over there."

And Aidan O'Rourke was determined to get a share.

Full night had fallen by the time Stephen Riley dropped Aidan and Farrell at the Rose and Anchor, a dockside pub on the River Lee in Cork City. With a nervous flutter in her chest, Farrell watched the wagon recede into the night. The warm, yeasty smell of ale wafted from the brightly lit pub. Behind them the river gave off a sharp tang, of smells she preferred not to identify, yet curiously, of fresh, water-borne breezes, too.

She glanced back at the water. As it lapped against the quays, the coy moon, half hidden by silver-edged clouds, reflected on its rippling surface like a wavering light on spilled ink.

Aidan's eyes were dark with shadow and caution as he glanced at their surroundings. Although he was a farmer unaccustomed to the perils of a port city, he plainly recognized that they were in a rough section of town.

The side streets were coal-black and sinister, and Farrell felt as if unseen eyes watched them from the alleys. Apparently Aidan sensed it, too. He gripped her elbow in his strong hand and nudged her toward the pub door. "Come on. Let's get something to eat and find lodgings for the night."

Inside, the smoky room was surprisingly lively, filled with fierce-looking seamen from London and

Liverpool and Hamburg. In the corner, a hungry-looking man played a feeble jig on a tin whistle, accompanied by another scarecrow who beat a bodhran. The skin of its drumhead was old and worn to translucency. A few coins lay in a cap at their feet, apparently tossed there by their mostly inattentive audience.

Aidan stood in the doorway surveying the place while the pub's tough patrons eyed them.

"If ye're lookin' for a handout, ye've opened the wrong door!" a short, gray-headed hag barked at them from behind the counter. "This inn serves only payin' customers, 'less ye can earn your supper"—she jerked her chin at the musicians— "which I doubt. And I don't have any kitchen scraps for the likes of *you*." The *bannalanna* was as round as she was high, with tiny, wide-set porcine eyes, and massive, flabby arms that were work-reddened from fingertips to elbows. Her nose was just as red.

The men standing nearby laughed, and Farrell felt Aidan stiffen.

"That's tellin'm, Katie, old lass," one of the sailors said, looking up from his ale pot with a dry expression. He had a long, oiled braid that hung between his shoulder blades. "Never let it be said ye gave a crust of bread to charity."

Indignant, Kate put her red fists on the rolls of flesh that spilled over her hips. "And where would

I be if I started givin' out free meals? Out of business, that's where. The beggars would be all over this place like flies on a dead dog. *Phaw!*"

More laughter ensued, and then the onlookers trailed off to silence, eager to see what would happen next.

Farrell hadn't stopped to think how she and Aidan looked. Certainly they'd never been well off, but she'd grown accustomed to their appearance—everyone in Skibbereen looked the same or worse. Her skirt was carefully mended, but its hem was as tattered as a rag left to blow in the wind. Aidan had a dark stubble of beard on his cut, bruised face, and he looked as worn as his clothes. In all, she supposed they appeared thoroughly disreputable. At least they weren't barefoot, as many were in Ireland.

Aidan took Farrell's hand and pulled her with him to the bar. The insults hummed through him like an electric current, which she felt vibrating in his touch. Dear God, he wouldn't start trouble in here—he couldn't. Not with all these vicious sailors—

The harridan, who stank of garlic and stale wine at this close range, raked Farrell with her wee piggy eyes. The undisguised slight brought a hot flush to Farrell's cheeks and made her worn skirt and her rough shawl all the more conspicuous. Suddenly she shared Aidan's anger and she exchanged a look with him. Tired as she was, she straightened her spine, drawing herself to her full height to stare back at the coarse woman, unflinching.

Aidan leaned across the counter and in a low, even voice said, "Judging by the looks of your other customers, I'd say ye can't always tell whether a man is a beggar just by his face or dress." He pulled a coin from his pocket and put it on the bar between them. "Now I want hot meals for my wife and me, and then we'll be wanting a room. A *private* room, not one that sleeps six to a bed." The quiet, commanding words left no doubt of who would have the last say.

"Humph," Kate grunted, then plucked up the coin. She clamped it between what remained of her big yellow-brown molars, presumably to see if it was genuine, then nodded at the taproom behind them. "Well, get on with ye to a table, then." She bellowed into the kitchen, calling someone named Ann. "I'll have the girl bring yer food. Ye can take room number three upstairs after ye sup." She tossed a large iron key across the bar.

With the matter apparently resolved, conversation around them resumed, and Aidan led Farrell to a corner table. She sank onto a chair, grateful to be sitting on a stationary object that didn't rock, pitch, and rattle her teeth. He dropped into the seat opposite her, his gaze still surveying the people around them.

"I hope you'll move the rest of the coin to a safer place than your coat pocket," she whispered, also glancing around at the pub's clientele.

Aidan gave her a long, wry look with those unsettling sapphire eyes. He whispered, too, but his voice had an intimate quality that she recognized even over the noise in the pub. "Farrell, *I* hope ye don't think I'm a stupid man. And I'd wager that ye'd turn the color of old Kate's nose over there, if I told you where I've hid the other money." He leaned back in his chair and with those blue eyes directed her attention to his crotch, where a noticeable swell stretched the fabric of his trousers. His meaning was plain enough, and she was reminded once more of the power he now held over her. "So I'll just say that ye needn't be worrying about it."

She averted her gaze to the sticky tabletop and her cheeks burned again. In too few minutes, in the time it would take a starving man to devour his food, Aidan would usher her upstairs to room number three and demand his due as her husband. Her right to choose the man she would give herself to had been one of the few things she still owned in the world. Now that was gone, too.

Farrell glanced at his hands where they rested on the table in front of him. They were strong hands, broad across their backs and dotted with old and newer scars from work or fights, she didn't know which. They'd certainly be strong enough to hold her, and he probably would have no regard, no sentiment, for her woman's tender feelings.

Like a child, she hoped that maybe if she lingered over her supper long enough, Aidan would be too weary to do more than sleep when they went upstairs. Yes, it could work, especially if he was like most men—feed them and they went as lazy as swine.

Just then, a scrawny, timid creature, most likely the unfortunate Ann whose name Kate had brayed earlier, brought a tray with two steaming plates of some kind of stew, a couple of old-looking biscuits, and two pints of ale. The moment the food was put in front of Farrell, all of her other concerns, and her plan, were forgotten.

The broth was thin and bland, and the mutton in it had been boiled down to mushy lumps a toothless old man could have gummed with no effort. But after she had walked so many miles, it looked like a king's banquet to her. The aroma alone had the power to bring tears to her eyes.

With no thought for decorum or anything else beyond eating and the most basic will to survive, she fairly jumped on the dish and began spooning the stew into her mouth as fast as she could. She felt Kate's sardonic gaze on her, probably noting her bad table manners. But at that moment, Farrell didn't care how she looked.

The stew was hot and it burned all the way

down her throat, but she ignored the pain. A drop of broth clung to her lip and she lapped at it with her tongue, then took another bite. She swore she could hear each swallow hit the pit of her empty stomach, and as she cleaned the plate, life seemed to flow back into her veins. Then, barely stopping for breath, she turned her attention to the biscuits, ripping one in half like a barbarian at an orgy to sop up the last of the broth.

"Lass, ye'd best eat slower," Aidan advised, watching her with a serious expression. "No one will steal your food from you, and it might come right back up if you gobble it that way."

With the bread already in her mouth, Farrell realized how unladylike she must appear. What did it matter, though? She had no reason to impress Aidan O'Rourke as if he were a suitor. He was only her husband—

Husband.

Honor.

Obey.

She stopped chewing and swallowed the dry lump. "Excuse me," she murmured, embarrassed.

"I know you're hungry," he said quietly. "We've all had our share of hungry times. There's no shame in it." A sudden grin crossed his face. "Of course, it's no grand blessing, either." He put down his own spoon and took a long drink of ale. If only he wouldn't look at her that way, she thought, proprietary, determined. "After we're done here, we'll rest. You'll need your strength for the days ahead."

Not wanting to acknowledge what he might mean, Farrell took a cautious sip of her own ale and asked, "Do you think anyone yet knows that we've gone?" She lowered her voice. "I mean, people who might be interested?"

He shrugged as he swallowed. "It's hard to say, but I wouldn't think we should dawdle here longer than need be." His own plate and cup empty, he pushed back his chair. "Are ye finished, then?"

Heaven help her, yes, she was. There was nothing left on the table to consume, and no excuse she could think of to keep from going upstairs. Nodding, she rose from her chair with foot-dragging reluctance.

Aidan piloted her to the stairs on the far end of the room. As they reached the first landing, he moved his hand to the small of her back and its heat startled her. She glanced over her shoulder, almost hoping for rescue from someone in the pub. She didn't want to be here, she didn't want to be married to Aidan O'Rourke. For a frantic moment she considered shouting out that he had kidnapped her after killing her brother, and that she wasn't his wife at all. But what good would it do? she chided herself. The men in the pub didn't appear to be chivalrous defenders of females in distress. She had no money, and with the authorities probably searching for them both, she had nowhere else to go.

Aidan followed her up the steps, and Farrell felt as if she were going to her own hanging, prodded along by a handsome executioner.

On the second floor, Aidan took a lantern from a hook at the top of the stairs and unlocked the door with a numeral 3 carved on it. He stood aside to let Farrell pass. The flame threw tall shadows on the rough walls of the small cupboard that contained a narrow bed and a tiny table with a chamber set on it. After lighting the candle stub that stood on a chipped saucer next to the bowl and pitcher, Aidan returned the lantern to the hall. The room held a musty, closed-up smell, as if the bedding had been used many times and not changed, and it was so cramped Aidan couldn't close the door behind him without touching her.

Farrell perched on the edge of the bed and eyed him warily.

Aidan stood in front of her and watched her just as intently, as if trying to see into her thoughts. Her heart began to thud in her chest under the scrutiny, but she made an effort to conceal her fear, and lifted her chin.

"Ye don't want to be here with me, aye?" he asked finally.

The question took her aback. The answer seemed so obvious, she couldn't imagine why he asked. "No, I don't."

A more clever woman might have lied, perhaps to escape her new husband's wrath, but Farrell couldn't make herself tell him something that wasn't true. "I wish I was back in Skibbereen with people who love—" She stopped. Fearing for her own family's safety, her cousin Clare had been anxious to be rid of Farrell, and Liam— She was sure that Liam had sent her off for her own good, but still . . . "I just wish I was home," she finished simply.

"That's what ye'd wish for? To be home?" Aidan threw the small bundle of their belongings on the bed and sat on the far end of the lumpy straw tick. "But neither of us has a home to go to, not anymore. The battering ram turned mine into a pile of old stone and thatch." He needn't have reminded her—the image was as sharp as broken glass in Farrell's mind. "And you're an orphan, with your family dead in the workhouse years ago."

Orphan. A grown woman of twenty-two years couldn't really be considered an orphan. But Aidan's words struck her as cruelly true, and she was filled with a bereft loneliness so profound she could hardly bear it. Too many things had happened in the last two days, horrible, earth-shattering events that tore at her heart and left her feeling defenseless. Tears stung her eyes. She would *not* begin crying again, she told herself. Swiftly she turned her head so that he wouldn't see.

"Yes, I guess I am," she replied, her face still averted.

"But then, ye know I suppose I am, too, in a way."

She felt his weight shift on the tick and she stole a glance at him. He sat with his elbows on his knees and he stared at the floor between his feet. "What makes you think that? You have your da and two brothers."

He shrugged. "Well, yes, but I've left them behind and I'll probably never see them again. And I can't say that I'll meet someone from home in America. It's a grand place, a huge land, full of strangers and near-naked, wild savages who paint their faces and wear animal skins. Indians, they're called"—he smiled, more to himself—"though I'm thinking they sound a bit like the ancient Celts."

If he meant to give her courage about what lay ahead, he failed. "Aren't ye scared to leave Ireland, then?" she asked in a small voice.

"Not scared, but I wish to God I didn't have to."

Utter exhaustion gave her frankness. "*I'm* scared."

Aidan turned his head and looked at her. She knew she was probably as pale as milk. He sat up and reached out to capture her chin between a rough thumb and forefinger, turning her face to his. "Ah, t'will be all right." Apparently it didn't occur to him that he was part of what she feared. "Your mother and Father Joseph saw to it that we all learned to read and to write a decent hand—we'll need that more than ever in America, I'm thinking."

She nodded, and couldn't help but smile. She remembered the valley's children crowded into the Kirwan cottage while her mother had schooled them. They hadn't learned much beyond writing, reading, and ciphering. But learning at home was far preferable to attending one of the British-established National Schools, where it seemed the primary goal was to teach Irish students not to be Irish. "Do ye remember the day Moira Healy came home and recited that horrid verse?

> *"I thank the goodness and the grace*
> *That on my birth have smiled*
> *And made me in these Christian days*
> *A happy English child."*

Aidan chuckled. "I thought her da would burst a blood vessel, his face was so red. Ye could hear him roaring oaths up and down the valley. He made the wee lass wash her mouth out with lashings of whiskey—he said it was the only thing that might kill the filthy words on her tongue."

"Aye, and didn't she hate it! Poor Moira. It was after that, Mam offered to teach us herself," Farrell reminisced. Her smile faded then, and she dropped her gaze to her lap. She had known Moira Healy all of her life, had seen her face alight with a sweet smile that always reached her mist-gray eyes. Farrell knew she'd never see her again. "I will miss her something terrible. I didn't even get to tell her good-bye." Loss, loss, and more loss—was it to be Farrell's legacy?

"At least we're not alone," Aidan put in. "We know each other, you and I." That wasn't much comfort to her, either. "Everything will be all right," he repeated. "Ye'll see, *céadsearc*." *Sweetheart.* The endearment rolled off his tongue so easily, he must have used it lots of times.

Startling her, he moved closer and took her face between his hands. His eyes roved over her features. "God, do ye know how fair ye are, lass?"

"F-fair?" She thought her mother might have told her once in her life, but it sounded altogether different coming from Aidan. Liam had mentioned her appearance, comparing her to a spring day. But this was different.

Aidan's haggard good looks swam in her tears.

"Aye, as pretty as a rose, all velvety and sweet-smelling." Farrell wasn't a vain woman, but something about the sound of Aidan's voice, rich and low, almost made her believe him. She smelled the smoke from downstairs in his hair, and a scent of his own that made her remember again the giggling comments girls had made about him.

Then she recognized the intense purpose in his eyes as he lowered his lips to hers. They were gentle—no doubt he guarded the cut on his upper lip—but searing, and she had the sudden fear that he would devour her if he could.

His mouth moved over hers, possessing and insistent, and unbidden, in her mind rose the image of Michael's putty-colored features, stilled forever by the very man whose hands cupped her face. Anger welled up in her again, fortified by a hot meal and his presumption. She made a noise of protest in her throat and arched her back to get away. Working both hands up between them, she pushed against the solid wall of his chest with all her strength.

"No!" She glared at him. "How dare you? Do ye expect to whisper a few sweet words and think I'll forget everything that has happened? That I'll welcome you with open arms? Michael's barely cold. This marriage wasn't my idea, you'll remember. The rest of you decided for me. I wanted to marry your brother. I *love* Liam and ye've taken me from him."

Gripping her shoulders, he drew back and considered her again, a frown linking his dark brows. "Whether or not you like it, you're married to me. And while you have reason to be angry with me, you're my wife, Farrell Kirwan O'Rourke. Before God and a houseful of witnesses ye agreed to that. And ye promised to *obey!*"

Yes, she had agreed to be his wife, stunned and herded along by events moving too swiftly for her to grasp. Yes, in a daze she had promised to obey, but it went against her basic nature to follow like a docile sheep.

She pulled against his grip, but it was fast and firm. "I suppose you can force me to your will," she uttered between clenched teeth, "but I'll not give you the satisfaction of anything more, ever."

"I've never had to force a woman in my life, and I won't be starting now!" he snapped, clearly insulted. He released her and stood.

"Why did ye marry me, then? You could have left me in Skibbereen or anywhere along the road."

Farrell thought he would have been pacing like a caged beast if the room were big enough. "Leave you in Skibbereen to bring disaster down on everyone's heads?"

"You didn't have to make me your wife just to save me from Cardwell. After all, *I* am innocent. I didn't do anything wrong." She saw by his expression that her barb hit its target.

He leaned down to her suddenly, anger and some other emotion in his dark blue eyes making her recoil. "Ye slapped the young heir, *your better*, don't forget, and no matter the reason you can be sure he wouldn't let that pass." It then occurred to her that it would be foolish to get on Aidan's bad side, with his temper and his strength. "We're bound, and that's the end of it. I promise ye—"

He left the sentence hanging ominously, and with that he reached out and opened the door. He might have slammed it shut behind him, but he didn't. It closed with a soft click and Farrell scrubbed her mouth with the back of her shaking hand.

The racket from the pub's customers and the tuneless music were muffled up here, although now and then she heard a louder thump or a raised voice that further unnerved her.

Scared to death that Aidan would come back, she worried even more that he wouldn't.

CHAPTER FOUR

AIDAN sat on the quay in front of the pub and sighed, creating a cloud of vapor in front of his face. The river lapped at the wall, a pleasant sound compared to the din coming from Kate's establishment. Overhead, the stars, one for every soul in heaven, his mother had told him, looked like distant points of cold blue fire flickering in the utterly black sky. If his mother had been right, a lot of those stars belonged to Irish souls who'd waged countless battles over hundreds of years or died for their faith.

He jammed his hands into his coat pockets, mindful of their fragile, tissue-thin fabric. Gritty-eyed from complete, marrow-deep exhaustion, he still had enough energy to curse himself backward and forward, and to throw in a choice word for Farrell, as well. Why had he married her? she wanted to know.

Why, indeed? he wondered. What sane man would willingly bind himself to a woman who blamed him for her brother's death, and loved another?

Because he'd wanted her. Unreasonably, unswervingly, from the first moment he realized that the barefoot, dirty-faced child he'd known as Farrell Kirwan had suddenly become a woman. At least her transformation had seemed sudden. No woman since—and there had been more than a few, as Father Joseph had admonished him about—could make him forget Farrell.

He'd already told himself it could take a long time to win her over. Given the way she looked at him, it was impossible to forget. He would have to approach her in small, unthreatening ways that would gain her trust, if not her respect. That might come eventually, but not any day soon, he knew.

And yet . . . and yet when he'd sat down next to her in the close little room and looked at her face, cleanly made and softly rounded, he'd been unable to stop himself from touching her. He'd wanted to feel with his fingertips the fineness of her skin, the smooth warmth of her cheeks. And his eyes had not deceived him in that. She felt as sweetly pretty as she appeared.

Aidan had known beautiful women in his time; he hadn't traveled much but he was convinced that no female on earth was more striking than a well-favored Irish lass. And Farrell put all others to shame.

He'd watched her from a distance for years, and tried every way he could think of to impress her. He could outdance, outdrink, and outfight just about any other young man in their village nestled in the valley. And, given the right amount of poteen and a proper audience, he could also sing fairly well and tell a good story. The women rarely failed to notice—except for Farrell. In fact, the harder he'd tried to impress her with his abilities, the more maddeningly aloof she became, and the more his pride suffered until his anger turned inward as well as outward.

Sure, and a body might think she was simply a cold woman, pretty on the outside, and on the inside as brittle as a leafless tree in winter. But it wasn't true. She had a soft heart for a sad story, and for every stray dog, mewing cat, and crying child in Skibbereen. Didn't he have the proof of that in her stubborn defense of her brother Michael? Never had a more shiftless, faithless scoundrel been born, yet Farrell had always seen the good in him and blinded herself to the bad. Such a streak of loyalty was a sterling trait in a woman, one that Aidan greatly admired—and wished for in a wife. He had only to think of a way to win Farrell's heart to make the wish a reality.

In his mind he had an image of her that he carried to his dreams some nights. It had been the first time he noticed her as a budding young woman. He had been looking for the O'Rourkes' errant pig—the silly beast tended to wander off and root in others' gardens if not watched. In his search, he'd had to pass the Kirwans' tiny plot of land.

Farrell had stood in her da's field that Saint Patrick's day, planting potatoes. That wasn't remarkable; everyone planted on March seventeenth. It was tradition. Since old Seamus Kirwan had been the most unreliable of men, the task of caring for the family fell to Farrell and her older brothers. The scent of moist, turned soil had hinted at spring and perfumed the air that day.

Just as he'd looked at her, she glanced up and their eyes met. She'd looked like a faerie grown to full size, with ripening curves and a smile that could stop the progress of the sun across the sky. Cool mists had drifted down from the green hills and settled lightly upon her dark copper hair, making it curl into ringlets. Then suddenly the sun had broken through the clouds to sparkle on each crystal drop, and she'd looked as though she wore a magic cowl of fire and diamonds. Even now, five years later, Aidan felt the same shiver fly down his spine, and the same stirrings in his groin and his heart as he had then.

Since that day, no other woman had fascinated him or frustrated him to the extent that Farrell Kirwan did.

But she was in love with Liam, the ungrateful wench. And she was furious that Aidan and circumstances had taken her from him.

Aidan felt his shoulders slump. In truth, Michael Kirwan was responsible for much of their immediate trouble. But only the lowest coward with no conscience held a grudge against a dead man, especially when he'd had a hand in that man's end.

His gloomy thoughts were interrupted when a pair of sailors burst out of the pub, obviously so full of drink and off-key song that even Kate would tolerate them no longer.

"Be gone wi' ye!" she barked from the doorway like a fat, angry terrier. "And don't be comin' back till ye've learned some manners, which I won't wait for. *Phaw!*" She caught sight of Aidan and gave him an even, assessing stare before turning to go back into the pub. He could only hope that she wasn't the type of person who would happily tell all she knew to an investigating constable or dragoon about the country couple staying in room number 3 above her barroom.

He glanced at the stars again. Let Michael Kirwan answer to God, he thought as he rose from the cold wall. As for himself, he had more pressing concerns—to save his own neck and that of his wife.

Unable to move, Farrell stirred from a deep sleep to a state of half-consciousness. She didn't know what had roused her until she glimpsed the familiar shape of Aidan, looming over her in the darkness. He smelled faintly of porter and wood smoke. She'd fallen asleep in her clothes after the candle had burned out. Fearful that he had come back to exercise his husbandly rights, she waited with her breath trapped in her chest.

"Good night, Farrell," he whispered. She heard him settle on the floor, which offered precious little space between bed and wall for his broad shoulders. His boot scraped the mopboard as he shifted to get comfortable. The chill of the room touched Farrell's cheeks. She tried not to think of how cold Aidan might get during the night without the hint of a blanket or cover. He'd killed her brother, after all, and wasn't deserving of her concern.

The thought circled in her sleep-fogged mind, truer than true. Even so, it wasn't in her nature to stand fast in such hard judgment. Reluctantly—and begrudgingly—she bunched one of the thin blankets in her hands and tossed it down to him, assuring herself that she'd do the same for a stray dog.

"Thank you," he said softly.

Determined not to respond, she rolled onto her side with her back to him, released her breath, and let sleep overtake her once more.

"Where are ye going in America, exactly?"

Early the next morning in a relatively quiet corner of the pub, Farrell and Aidan sat across the table from a derelict-looking ship's master, one James McCorry. He wore a stained blue wool coat with tarnished brass buttons, and his craggy, weather-beaten face bore a couple of scars that appeared to be souvenirs of knife cuts. Heaven only knew if his vessel was as dilapidated. A few careful questions Aidan had asked of Kate's patrons had directed him to the captain.

The man took a long drink of his ale and wiped his mouth on his crusty sleeve. "This time we're bound for New Orleans."

Farrell possessed no great knowledge of American geography, but she didn't think that city was mentioned as a destination by many Irish immigrants going to the United States. They went to places like New York and Boston, Philadelphia and Baltimore. Obviously, Aidan didn't think much of the location, either.

"That's a wee bit farther than we hoped to go."

"Aye, it's five thousand miles from here. New York is but three."

"Ye'd not be going to New York or Boston?"

"No, but at this time of year, the weather will be better when we dock in the southern climes than it would be up north. The other ship in port, the *Exeter,* is going to New York. She sails in three days."

Aidan pushed away his empty tankard and prepared to stand. "I thank ye, Mr. McCorry. My wife and I will see about passage on the other—" He broke off so suddenly, Farrell stared up at him. But he wasn't looking at the captain or at her. His stance was rigid, his gaze was fixed on a pair of soldiers who had just come in. Armed with muskets, they made their way to the bar and began asking Kate questions Farrell couldn't make out at this distance. Aidan sat again.

"D'ye sail soon?"

"In a fine hurry, are ye then?" McCorry asked, letting his eyes drift to the soldiers, then back to Farrell, where they lingered just long enough to make her uncomfortable. "We leave on the noon tide. I've already got my cargo—there's a great lot of unhappy Irishmen wantin' to go to America. But I've room for two more. I provide water and one pound of food every day we're under sail, providing the wind favors us. If ye want more, you'd best bring it. Ye must bring yer own bedding and dishes, too. It's nothin' fancy but it'll get you where you want to go."

"Sounds fair," Aidan replied. Farrell was less sanguine about traveling with James McCorry, but a glaring reminder of why they needed to make hasty departure stood at the bar in the form of the two soldiers.

McCorry held out his hand. "Five pounds passage for each of ye."

"Ye'll get your fare when we come aboard," Aidan said.

"T'would be a pity if I had to sell your berth to someone else," McCorry sighed with feigned regret, and cast another glance at the military men. He smiled, revealing rotting teeth, and the knife scars pulled his face into a frightening grimace. "I can hold it if ye pay me now."

Aidan's expression remained carefully blank, but it was as if Farrell could hear his thoughts while he considered their options. Ten pounds was a fortune to people who lived off the land. Farrell didn't think she'd ever seen that much money at one time in her life, and it would be a lot to lose if McCorry turned out to be nothing but a pirate.

Aidan folded his hands in front of him on the table and gave the captain an even stare. "A pity it would be but there are other ships, and we'll find passage with one of them if needs be. And ye don't look to be the kind of man who would pass up the chance to make ten pounds, even if it comes later in the day." He lifted one brow. "So, Mr. McCorry, would ye be kind enough to tell me the name of your vessel so we'll know which one to look for?"

The captain let out a roar of laughter. "Aye, boyo, ye're no bumpkin, after all. Come to the *Mary Fiona* as soon as ye like. We sail just after noon."

The two shook hands then, and McCorry rose from his chair and made his way to the pub door. As he passed the soldiers, he threw them a loud greeting. "Top of the day to ye, boys."

"Can we trust him?" Farrell asked as she watched McCorry's departure.

"No, but it's a bit less worrisome with our ten pounds still in my—uh, pocket." He gave her a sudden, wicked smile that she was annoyed to find quite disarming. Oh, and didn't the sight of it probably make all the girls melt away like hot butter? she thought dryly. Well, it didn't fool her, though she made a pointed effort to ignore the little jolt that shimmied through her. "And I'll ask about to make sure the good captain isn't after telling us a tale about other ships bound for New York."

While Kate had disappeared into the kitchen, the soldiers still stood at the bar, and now they were casually scanning the pub patrons. At this time of day, there weren't many to look over, and it wouldn't be long before they discovered Aidan and Farrell.

"Do you think they're searching for us?" Farrell whispered, her stomach fluttering nervously. Aidan sat next to her on a short bench with his hard thigh pressed against hers. She felt the tension in his muscles through her thin skirt, and half expected him to leap up at any second, grab her arm, and make a run for the entrance.

Their exit was to be more subtle, though. "Best that we not find out. Come, wife," he answered quietly. "We will be leaving now. Don't hurry, but don't lag, either."

Aidan stood and extended his hand. Farrell closed her fingers around his and drew comfort from his warm, firm grip. He led her across the room and toward the door, slipping past the soldiers with the nonchalance of a man escorting his wife. Just as he had his hand on the knob, Kate reappeared and brayed, "That's 'em now! The man and the woman I was tellin' ye about."

Aidan swore vehemently under his breath, cursing the pub owner with a profanity that Farrell had heard only once in her life, and with his fingers still tightly interlaced with Farrell's he jerked open the door and pulled her along with him into a heavy rain.

Terror arced through her like lightning, and Aidan's iron grip on her arm was so tight, her fingers tingled.

"Halt!" one of soldiers called from the pub doorway behind them. But Aidan didn't stop until they reached a narrow, garbage-filled alley on the next block. Plunging between the buildings, he pushed her into a tall, shallow depression in one of the brick walls and flattened himself over her, breathing hard.

Farrell could scarcely breathe at all. Her face was pressed hard against his chest, and his shirt buttons dug into her cheek. Heartbeats, strong and fast, mingled with her own galloping pulse, making it impossible to separate hers from his. The male scent of him, laced with a tang of high tension, filled her head. From the street she heard the sound of running footsteps as they passed the alley, but Aidan didn't move for several moments. To Farrell, who was beginning to grow light-headed from lack of air, the moments seemed like hours.

Finally Aidan pulled away and her knees buckled, pitching her forward into his arms.

"God, lass, are ye all right?" Aidan whispered, alarmed by her paleness. How easily Farrell fit in his embrace, he realized—her forehead nestled against his jaw. But there was so little to her, all fine bones and softness. She felt much different from the sturdy maids he'd known. And much better. Her hair against his cheek was silky and warm.

She straightened away from him and nodded, gulping in deep breaths. "Aye. J-just let me get my wind."

"That was too close, the bleedin' bastards," he muttered, glancing over his shoulder toward the street.

"Are—are they gone? Those soldiers?"

"Yes, but they may still be creeping about out there somewhere. We were only lucky that they didn't think to look in here." His mind racing with strategy, he turned back to her and took her by the shoulders. "Have ye got your feet under you again? We can't go to the pub and collect our belongings. We'll have to buy a few things from one of the shops here and get to the *Mary Fiona* as soon as possible. If we're caught, we'll be doomed."

"I know." He recognized the fear in her eyes; after all, he'd sometimes seen it when she looked at him. He didn't want to frighten her but there was no way to put a pretty face on their circumstances. They were dire. Nevertheless, he admired her for not whining as some females might about the personal things she was leaving behind. Farrell had had little to call her own in her young life. He knew she'd brought along her most precious treasures— her mother's rosary, a small whalebone hairpin, a linen handkerchief. Not important things, and of little value, but her treasures all the same. Yet she uttered not a word of reproach, simply accepting what she knew he couldn't change. When they reached America, he would buy her new and better things. She deserved no less for her bravery.

"All right, then," he said and edged toward the alley opening. Rain fell in windblown sheets and the street was nearly deserted as people sought shelter in doorways and shops. Across the road, the gray river so closely matched the slate-colored sky it was difficult to tell where one left off and the other began. But the soldiers were nowhere to be seen. "Keep a sharp lookout and follow me."

When Farrell and Aidan arrived at the *Mary Fiona,* they were both laden with bedding, some used clothes they'd bought, supplies, and a few odds and ends, all of which were getting soaked in the downpour. Darting between buildings and the quay had been harrowing; Farrell expected to see soldiers lurking around every corner. Once, she even thought she'd seen Noel Cardwell, that villain, mounted on a fine black gelding. Fear had squeezed her heart in a cruel grip—if he caught them, she knew he would drag her back to Skibbereen and do unspeakable things to her. But it seemed impossible; Noel would not have ridden on horseback all these miles and in this weather. He would have traveled in nothing less than a coach and four. In any event, the man had not noticed them. Luck had been with them, and they made it to the ship without being seen.

Aidan's discreet inquiries around town to verify McCorry's information had proven the man to be telling the truth. There were no other ships in port sailing to New York or any other city on America's east coast. Hamburg, South America, *China,* for the love of God. But nowhere Aidan and Farrell needed to go.

So they were bound for New Orleans. They'd find a way to travel north once they arrived, he told her.

The *Mary Fiona* was a small, rather tired-looking three-masted barque, and when Farrell first set eyes on the ship her heart fell to her feet. She didn't know much about sailing, but still, how would such a little vessel navigate the Atlantic, an ocean said to be icy and storm-ridden at this time of year?

Coming aboard, Farrell had sat on a coil of rope, so as not to be seen by passers-by. While Aidan spoke with James McCorry, she'd started to feel a bit more hopeful. The ship might be no longer than five or six large farm wagons set end to end, and less than half that in width, but it offered passage, and what other choice did they have? The answer to that question was impressed upon her even more strongly when she picked up a bit of Aidan's conversation with the ship's master.

"Aye, laddie, those boys from the pub were already here lookin' for ye. There even came a dandy in fine clothes with a silk kerchief pressed to his nose, askin' about a red-haired woman and man such as yerself." Dear God, Farrell thought, it *had* been Noel whom she'd seen. McCorry squinted at him. "The soldiers said ye killed a man. The dandy claims yer missus worked in his manor house and stole the family silver."

Aidan turned to look at Farrell, and her jaw dropped when she heard that barefaced lie. "They lie," he said simply.

McCorry continued. "Well, be that as it may, I told 'em all ye couldn't meet my price for passage. But they might come back. I suggest you and your wife stay belowdecks till we cast off."

Taking McCorry's advice to heart, they had

carted their new purchases below and found accommodations built with rough planks of timber, nailed or otherwise wedged into place. The two-foot-wide bunks were stacked three rows high on either side of the dark, stuffy hold, and a narrow aisle ran down the middle. Those already on board—single men and ragtag families with crying babies and wan children of varying ages—all jostled to carve out a place for themselves.

How could her life have changed so dramatically so quickly? Just over three days ago, she'd been at home in Skibbereen, expecting to marry another man. Now she was on a creaking ship, ready to cast off for a land thousands of miles away, with that other man's wild brother.

They spent the afternoon traveling down the River Lee, and now as the ocean came into view, Farrell and Aidan stood on deck watching the green, misty hills of their homeland slip past in the dusk. Wild and lonely and tragic, it held rivers and lakes, cliffs and hollows and castle ruins, and magic and stories that went back to the beginning of the world.

It was the place where her family was buried.

It was the place that owned her heart.

Her throat grew tight with tears and sorrow. In the west, a bright band of sunset melted the clouds and lighted the horizon. And in the west lay America.

Although the rain had stopped, a brisk wind chilled her, but she only pulled her shawl closer. She didn't want to go below and miss the last sight of Ireland she might ever have. Apparently, neither did the other sixty or so people making this trip with her and Aidan. They clung to the railings, their faces full of wistfulness and optimism. Some of the women dabbed at their eyes with their apron hems as they comforted their frightened children. The men looked as though they'd all aged ten years in a single afternoon.

Aidan looped his arm around Farrell's shoulders, and at this moment of farewell she found comfort in his touch. "We'll see her again, *céadsearc*. Someday." He spoke with the rusted voice of a man whose thoughts were far away and in days long past, in the rain-washed glens and dark, magical woods where the fey people were said to dwell. "But we'll find none like her till then, not even if we search the whole world."

She glanced up at him, but his gaze was fixed on the beautiful landscape with its tiny inlets and harbors. Angry, hot-blooded Aidan O'Rourke, the man she feared, didn't look as dangerous at that moment. In fact, she saw tears standing in his eyes.

Plainly embarrassed to be caught with his emotions showing, he released her and dashed his shirt-sleeve across his eyes. Then he reached into his pocket. "I got this while ye were choosing the blankets." He withdrew a plain, thin silver band and held it out on his open palm. "Since we're wedded, I thought you should have a ring. Tommy gave Clare my mother's wedding ring when he married her. This one isn't as grand—it has no carving on it or writing inside. But, well, I thought ye might like to have it."

Surprised, she reached out a tentative hand. "I guess I hadn't thought of a ring. Everything has been so—so—"

"Desperate."

She sighed. "Aye. Desperate."

"Still, I know how much little things like this mean to a woman."

She tipped a glance at him. "Yes, I'm sure ye do." He looked sincere, but she couldn't let herself accept that. She remembered the neighborhood gossip last summer when he'd taken wildflowers to Bridget McDermot every day for three weeks. Everyone—including Bridget, no doubt—had expected to hear news of a proposal. But it hadn't come, and Aidan moved on to Moira Flannery. Moira had received no flowers that they knew of, but she and Aidan had been seen walking in the moonlight often enough. For a while, anyway. And his prior history with women was no different. Still, that had all happened in the past, and there was no point in being ungracious, especially now.

"Thank you, Aidan," she said simply. Taking the ring from his palm, she slipped it on her finger and held out her hand for his inspection. "It fits just fine."

That earned her a faint, satisfied smile, as if she had accomplished some spectacular feat. And for an instant, she saw that look again in his eyes, possessive, without beginning or end, beyond place or time.

"That's good. I only guessed at the size." He glanced up. "Farrell," he said softly, and nodded toward the receding island of their birth. "Look your last."

Farrell turned to let her eyes drink their fill. Ireland shone in the brilliant sunset, distant and green and luminous, like the gemstone it was often compared to. Overhead, gulls squawked in the rigging as the sails filled and they left the last of the cove waters to set out upon the ocean.

Somehow, someday, she would return to the land of her birth. Somehow. But right now she had control over nothing but her heart and her own mind. She could let grief and fear consume her, or she could choose to survive. For Farrell, there was really just one choice. She would go to America and she would survive.

"*Go mbeannaí Dia duit,*" Aidan murmured to the tiny emerald on the eastern horizon.

"Go mbeannaí Dia duit," she echoed faintly, her wet gaze fixed on the tiny speck of land as she crossed herself with a trembling hand.

May God bless you.

CHAPTER FIVE

"A *murderer*, ye say! And a thief! Didn't I just know it!" The owner of the Rose and Anchor, who called herself Kate, wore a shocked expression and slammed a meaty fist on the bar. "I thought the pair had the odd look about 'em. But them so weary and tattered and all, I couldn't turn 'em away. I sold them stew and let them a room. What else could a God-fearing woman do but show a little Christian charity?"

This question raised hoots of derisive laughter from nearby patrons.

"God-fearin'!"

"Christian! That's a ripe one, Katie, girl."

"I could use some o' that charity meself, Kate."

"Shut yer filthy gobs, the rotten lot of ye! *Phaw!*" she bawled at them, her braying voice gurgling with phlegm. Then she favored Noel Cardwell with a helpless, ingratiating smile and said, "I'm just a poor widow woman and I have me business to run. I can't be too choosy when . . ."

While she prattled on, Noel eyed the massive, ochre-toothed hag of an innkeeper and wished for perhaps the hundredth time that he'd never let his

father maneuver him into making this miserable
trip. And he silently cursed Aidan O'Rourke for
stealing his woman—for he saw Farrell as his pos-
session now, much as he viewed his horse and his
lands. He also cursed O'Rourke for being the baseborn dross that he was, forcing Noel to track him
down in the most unsavory of places. He knew that
Farrell hadn't stolen anything from Greensward
Manor, but the claim gave more weight to his story.
The pub was filled with rough-looking barrel scrap-
ings of humanity, all watching him like ravenous
curs waiting for a crumb to drop. By one of the
steamed-over windows, a wretched specimen sawed
out some tuneless noise on a fiddle, adding to the
general din. The stinks that assaulted Noel's nose—
boiling pig's feet, dirty human feet, unwashed bodies, smoke, overloaded privies, and God only knew
what else—made him wish for his handkerchief-
mask again. But that wouldn't do in this place. As
it was, he could feel the assessing gazes of those
curs upon him, examining his dress, trying to gauge
how much money he might be carrying and whether
he was an easy mark.

"Where have they gone to now, these two with
the odd look?"

Kate's expression turned regretful. "I hate to be
the bearer of bad news to a such fine gentleman as
yerself, but I believe they found passage on a ship
that left on the early afternoon tide, about five hours

gone now. Some soldiers were in here earlier lookin' for them as well, but I think the scurvy pair got away."

"Where was the ship bound?" Noel asked, feeling as if he were trying to pull teeth from a chicken.

Kate put a thick, reddened finger to her chin in a revolting but sincere imitation of a coy gentlewoman. "Well, now, I can't seem to remember what I overheard. After all, they didn't tell me . . ."

Pulling a half-crown from his pocket, he held it up to her. He was nearly as repelled as amused by the greedy gleam that came into her small, pale eyes. She made a swipe at it but he held fast and closed his fingers around it.

"Are you sure you don't know?"

"They went out on the *Mary Fiona,* bound for New Orleans."

Damn that James McCorry, Noel thought savagely. The bastard had lied to him. Ignoring the grubby countertop, he leaned an elbow on the bar and briefly rubbed his forehead. God, this was far worse than he'd imagined. "New Orleans—*America?*"

"Yes, indeed."

"And it docks nowhere else before heading out to sea? Liverpool, perhaps?"

Kate's nearly hairless brows snapped together and, for a moment, the ridiculous, feigned expression of a demure lady cracked. "Jesus bleedin'

Christ, do I look like a bloody port schedule?" He showed her the coin again, and she resumed her mannerly pretense. "I mean, no, sir, not so far as I know."

He pushed the half-crown across the bar and she snatched it up so quickly, the motion was a blur. Sighing, he straightened and lifted his elbow from the sticky bar. He knew the *Exeter* was in port. His father was the majority shareholder of the ship. It was just more bad luck that O'Rourke hadn't decided to buy passage on her. If he had, this would all be over by now.

"Ye'll be needin' lodging and board for the night, I would imagine, sir," Kate ventured, still posturing. "I've a nice room upstairs and a leg of mutton turnin' on the spit in the kitchen—" She turned toward the kitchen doorway. "Ann! Cut a piece off that mutton and put it on a plate! A *clean* plate, mind!"

"Thank you, no. I've already taken other lodgings," Noel replied, flipping open his cloak to reveal a wicked-looking pistol tucked into his waistband, just in case some of the denizens of this filthy place had ideas about following him. "But I appreciate your help."

"Anytime, sir, anytime," were Kate's croupy words. "It was my pleasure." This last, apparently, was more than the men in the bar could bear with straight faces. As Noel escaped to the dark street, the wave of muffled snickers gave way to full-throated hoots and catcalls that only added to the fury mounting within him. From within, Kate rebuked her customers with a string of colorful obscenities.

The cold night air, though laced with the odors of river and fish, was clean and blessedly crisp compared to the interior of the Rose and Anchor. Mounting his horse, a fine black his father had grudgingly given him for the trip, he made his way to a bridge that crossed the river, watchful for unseen threats that might lurk in the shadows, ready to pounce on a well-dressed, prosperous-looking man. He saw no one but an occasional doxy, sidling along the narrow street. They called to him but he ignored them and rode on.

America. That bastard O'Rourke had sailed for America and had taken Farrell with him. He had become the focus of Noel's wrath. He'd stolen Noel's intended mistress, the woman who had literally wriggled from his grasp and humiliated him.

If not for O'Rourke, he could have smoothed over his father's outrage. After a time, the whole fuss would have died down and his life would have resumed its comfortable routine. Instead he was faced with the twin catastrophes of Michael Kirwan's thievery and the escape of the man's killer.

As Noel spotted the tall masts of the *Exeter*, a burgeoning resolve grew along with his anger. He would find Aidan O'Rourke and Farrell Kirwan, even if it meant sailing to America himself.

"I'm sorry, Mr. Cardwell, but I've got cargo going to New York, and people there expecting it. I can't be taking the *Exeter* on a pleasure jaunt to New Orleans." Ship's master Oliver Royce faced Noel over the worktable in his low-ceilinged quarters. The cabin was tidy and clean, and decorated with souvenirs from all over the world. Fragrant smoke from the pipe clamped between Royce's teeth scented the air. The table was covered with a number of navigational charts and instruments. Royce unrolled a map of America's eastern coastline and gestured with his pipe stem at the distance between his intended destination and Noel's. "You can see it's a hell of a trek out of the way. His lordship wouldn't appreciate such a delay."

It had been easy to board the vessel once Noel identified himself to the watchman. The Cardwell name did open doors, he was pleased to note. But he resented the fact that Arthur Cardwell's name carried far more weight with the master than did his own. Noel realized he might need to be a bit more persuasive to achieve his goal.

He smiled blandly at the reference to his father. "This is not a 'pleasure jaunt,' Royce. It was Lord Cardwell who dispatched me on this errand."

Despite a full, neatly trimmed beard, Royce was

obviously a young man, perhaps even younger than Noel himself. In contrast with James McCorry's derelict appearance and manner, Royce was sober and earnest-looking, with a dignified loyalty to his employer that irked Noel. "Well, I believe another ship, the *Fortunate Maid,* will be docking in Cork within the next week. She sails to New Orleans from here and you could be on your way."

Noel put both hands on the table and leaned forward slightly. "As I already explained, I'm searching for a man who has committed murder. He has a good day's head start. I must find him, and every hour counts. I can't wait a week for another vessel. I assure you, I can make it worth your while." The ship's master eyed him but didn't respond. "Do you have a family? A wife, children perhaps?"

His face brightened. "Aye, sir. Nell and my three lads."

"You must miss them when you're gone. And of course they miss you. Maybe Mrs. Royce would like some small comforts for herself and the young ones. Something to make their lives easier in your absence?"

The man smiled, more to himself. "Oh, she's got it into her head that she'd like one of those fancy new machines that sews stitches. I made the mistake of telling her that I saw one in New York."

Noel straightened and held his hands open

wide. "There you are, then. You can take me to the very place I need to go, and then go on to New York and bring your wife the gift she craves with the bonus I'll pay you. Shall we say half again as much as you would earn this voyage?"

The master appeared to think it over, then shook his head. "No, sir, I can't be doing it. His lordship wouldn't like it at all."

Noel clenched his jaw. He might seem incorruptible, but if Noel's experience at the gaming tables had taught him anything, it was that every man had a price. Or point of desperation.

On the poop deck outside, brisk footfalls sounded, then faded beyond the closed door.

"You might consider this option, then," Noel went on in a quiet, matter-of-fact tone. "I can put you off this ship right now and you will find yourself in want of a position. It would be a grave error on your part to underestimate my influence, or to assume that you know what my father wants. And if I put out a few words to the right ears, the only work you'll find will be on a leaky whaler bound for Greenland. It's dirty work, I hear. Dangerous, as well." The *Exeter,* a sleek, well-tended, well-trimmed ship, drifted gently against her moorings, as if in protest.

Oliver Royce's dark brows met briefly. "I don't take kindly to threats, Mr. Cardwell."

"*I* don't take kindly to being refused. Nor does

my father." Noel leaned a hip against the table. "If you no longer wish to captain this ship, I'll have another master aboard and piloting me to New Orleans within twenty-four hours. Now what's it to be, Royce? Will your wife get a nice gift from this voyage, or merely learn that her husband is out of work?"

A tense, nearly palpable pause hung between them.

"We'll sail tomorrow night on the evening tide." The man's teeth clamped so tightly to his pipe, Noel heard his jaw pop. "For New Orleans."

Noel nodded. "Excellent. Now if you would be so good as to have someone show me to my quarters, I'll settle in."

On deck, Farrell's eyes snapped open at the sound of gurgling screams, distant and yet so filled with terror, she was positive she had dreamed them. Yet she felt warm and comfortable for the first time since leaving home. So surely, she must have been dreaming.

But she hadn't been.

"Man overboard! A man overboard!

She realized that she was warm because she lay nestled against Aidan's side with her head pillowed on his chest and his arm looped around her waist, a fact that made itself plain when he came awake with a start, as well. Hastily, she moved away and sat up. Her skirt had wound itself around her legs and she freed them, then pulled her shawl closer to her shoulders.

"What're they saying, then?" Aidan asked, instantly alert. He was only a dark silhouette in the feeble light of the ship's few lamps.

She tried to see beyond his shape where crewmen scurried. "God above, I think someone has fallen into the sea."

"Jesus." Instinctively, he crossed himself, then pushed his dark hair off his brow and stood. He held out his hand to help Farrell to her feet, and they went to the railing. But there was only a scrap of moon, and the stars were overlaid by a gauzy film of clouds. They didn't provide enough light to see much. Another gurgling cry sounded, faint and indistinct.

"Can ye see anything?" she asked, her fist at her chest. "Can you see the poor soul?" How much more fragile life seemed when cast into an immense expanse of black water.

Closer to the bow, life buoys and a crate splashed into the water. Aidan still held her hand in his, a strong, warm hand that, oddly, gave her comfort, and instinctively she squeezed it, her fear momentarily overriding her desire to keep her distance from him. Around them, the other passengers asleep on deck woke up, confused, asking questions, speculating.

"Lord save us, someone's gone into the ocean."

"A passenger?"

"I don't know. Maybe it's that poor old Paddy Hannigan. He's been so seasick, he's spent most of these past six days hanging over the railing and—"

"Bring her up into the wind!" came an order shouted from the first mate, Mr. Quisenberry. He stood on the quarterdeck, barking commands over the frightened murmuring of other passengers. "Haul up the mainsail! Brace aback the after yards!"

All the nautical talk sounded like a foreign language to Farrell, but replies of *aye-aye* were followed by the slap of feet running across the deck and ship's hands scrambling up the rigging.

With some adjustment of the sails, the ship began to slow her headway. Two crewmen clambered into a boat and were lowered to the ocean to pull the hapless victim aboard. Lantern light from the little rescue craft bobbed on the waves like a fairy's magical glow over the peat bogs back home. A crewman held the lamp at arm's length as they searched the swells.

The men in the boat circled the ship several times and backtracked over its wake while passengers watched anxiously from the rail. Farrell never took her eyes off the little light. But after a half hour, Mr. Quisenberry called the boat back in.

"More than twenty minutes in that icy water would freeze the divil himself."

Captain McCorry had turned out at the first alarm, but Quisenberry was handling the matter. After a bit of investigating, it was determined that the ship's cook, a kindly bulldog of a man from Liverpool known simply as Doctor, had gotten drunk and fallen from the fantail. He'd been generally well-liked, always ready with a joke or a smile.

"Oh, no," Farrell mourned, still clinging to Aidan's hand. "Not Doctor. Please, God keep him." For the moment, she was grateful that Aidan, solid and steadfast, stood with her, someone from whom to draw strength and courage.

McCorry, who didn't hold with the crew drinking at sea, declared that he would have keelhauled the man himself if he hadn't drowned. "Aye, well, it's one less mouth to feed. Let that be a lesson to any seaman who might be entertainin' the notion of having a wee nip. The fishes'll be havin' him for tea." He added tersely, "I'm back to my bunk, and I don't mean to be disturbed again this night."

Quisenberry said nothing but when McCorry left the quarterdeck, his tight expression spoke for him.

Those passengers who'd witnessed the proceedings huddled together by the gunwale amidships and grumbled among themselves about the captain's attitude. He treated them as human cargo and this was just another example of his lack of feeling.

"Will ye listen to that?" Farrell whispered to Aidan. "Could he not say a word for the poor man's soul? You'd think he's the Holy Trinity rolled into one to hear him talk so!" She clapped her hand to her mouth, aghast at her own blasphemy.

Aidan lifted a brow. "I imagine you'll feel the need to be sayin' a few Our Fathers for that bit. But, aye, ye're right about McCorry." His face hardened in the low light, and the shadows around his eyes seemed to grow darker. "He's no better than the landlords back home, working people like animals, without a single care for what happens to them. May they all rot in hell for their cruel ways."

An awkward silence fell between them. They had both made a point of avoiding the subject of Michael's death since they left Skibbereen, but now it rose between them like a ghost.

Farrell realized then that she was clutching his hand like a frightened child. When she tried to disengage her fingers, he tightened his grip. Her heart froze in her chest as their gazes locked. She was his wife, after all. If he was of a mind to touch her, he had the right. She could object but would it do any good?

At last, he shrugged and loosened his hold. "The first mate seems to be a decent enough man, at least."

While Alfred Quisenberry did indeed seem to be a gentleman, as did Charles Morton, the second mate, the ship's master was as crude and rough as he'd first appeared during their meeting in the Rose and Anchor. He'd promised nothing fancy, and it was a promise he'd kept.

They'd been at sea for six days, and so far had not seen another ship. The first night out, there had been music and dancing in steerage. Some of the men played jigs on pipes and fiddles, and another had produced a keg of good, stout porter. An air of hope and anticipation had radiated from the passengers. Yes, they were leaving Ireland, dear as she was, but they were bound for a new land, a new start, where it was said that every man had a chance to make something of himself.

The merriment hadn't lasted long. Seasickness had claimed nearly everyone, including Farrell. Aidan, on the other hand, had not been troubled at all by what one passenger called "mal de mer." In fact, he'd been quite unruffled by the ordeal, but he'd been surprisingly attentive to her. Fortunately, she'd managed to get her sea legs after a day or two. Others were not so lucky, and many of them, already weakened by hunger and poor health, could do nothing but lie on their hard, narrow bunks and suffer.

After almost a week at sea, the foul odors of illness, spilled slop buckets, and close-packed bod-

ies made life unbearable in steerage. If they closed
the hatches, the air became so thick and fetid, no
one could breathe. But when left open in bad
weather, rain and seawater washed across the deck
and down into the hold, contributing to the wretch-
edness. The crew manned pumps but that only kept
the quarters from flooding.

So Farrell, Aidan, and the other passengers who
were able, remained on the crowded deck rather
than descend into the miserable conditions below.
Unless rain prevented it, they slept outside, too.

"Come on, lass. Let's try to get more rest before
the sun rises over us. There's naught to do for that
poor wretch now."

Farrell followed Aidan back to their blankets on
deck with a heavy heart. When she lay down, she
was careful to leave a foot of space between them.

And tried to forget how nice it had felt to rest
against him.

"Tell me, Mrs. O'Rourke, could ye be givin' me a
piece of bread for me wife? I know that the captain
says as how we're not allowed more than our ration,
but it's the seasickness she's had for days now. The
bread seems to help." Ryan Dougherty spoke to
Farrell in a low voice.

Farrell stood at the ship's stove in the galley,
passing out today's menu, boiled potatoes, from the
galley doorway. Barely two weeks at sea and she'd

found herself working as ship's cook for a shilling and sixpence. "The chamomile didn't help, then?" She had made a tea for the ailing Mrs. Dougherty from supplies she found in the medicine chest, which was also kept in the galley.

Dougherty's face was typical of so many she'd left behind in Ireland. He could have been any age between thirty and sixty, but weather, worry, and hard times had seamed his features like a walnut shell. "Och, aye, some it did. But bread is all she can keep down."

She nodded, glanced at the passengers lined up behind Dougherty, and searched for any crew members that might be loitering about. McCorry was strict about how much food was allotted each passenger. The captain and his mates, however, enjoyed chicken and salted beef and pork along with their potatoes and bread, and an occasional orange or lime to guard against scurvy. She tucked a piece of bread under the potatoes on the plate Dougherty had given her and handed it back to him. "Keep this to yourself," she whispered. "I'll come down to see how she's faring later on."

"D'ye think your man might be having a word with Captain *Stoneheart* to let the ailing have a little extra? O'Rourke seems to get on with him a bit, though how I don't know. Saint Patrick himself couldn't reason with that serpent's get."

Her man. Farrell tightened her grip on the big

cooking spoon. How odd that Aidan, whom she'd known only for fighting and flirting, had become the intermediary between the crew and the passengers. "I'll ask him, Mr. Dougherty."

He nodded his thanks and Farrell went on spooning up potatoes to the hungry. The menu on board offered no more than the one back home. Some days they had oatmeal, some days rice, which was barely enough to keep body and soul together. Most passengers had brought no other provisions with them and were forced to make do with what she dished out.

After the cook drowned, McCorry had put a cabin boy to the task, but although the fare was exceedingly plain and simple to prepare, the youth managed to destroy every meal he touched. Since he also cooked for McCorry and the mates, the captain's patience had quickly run thin. When the boy had nearly burned down the galley, he was sent back to his other duties. McCorry had no other hands to spare, so he recruited among the passengers for a cook, offering a shilling and sixpence, to be paid at the end of the voyage. Aidan suggested the job to Farrell, and when she agreed, he'd approached McCorry, insisting upon receiving the money in advance. Surprisingly, the master consented.

"With a blackguard like him, it's best to have the coin in hand—ye might say," Aidan had told

her with a sudden grin, after putting the money in
the same hiding place as the rest of their cash.
Dougherty was right, Aidan *had* managed to win
McCorry's grudging respect.

Farrell, who came from a land where the fey
people lurked in mists and shadows, had expected
to feel the dead cook's presence in his galley, and
perhaps his objection to hers. But as she'd exam-
ined and handled the utensils and pots and stores,
no ghost came calling or complaining. Perhaps
Doctor had gone on peacefully to the next world.
At least he didn't seem to mind that she tread on
the one he'd left behind.

And she was glad for the work. The galley was
warm and out of the slashing rain and wind. Cooking kept her busy and helped pass the time, which
was filled with mind-numbing boredom and occasional queasiness from sickening ocean swells.

What she couldn't forget were worries about the
people back home, and the questions rolled through
her mind like an ever-turning wheel. Were the families safe? she wondered. Had Lord Cardwell given
up his persecution when he realized that she and
Aidan were gone? Had Noel returned to Greensward Manor after traveling to Cork?

Did Liam miss her? Had he come to regret
sending her away, or not coming with her?

Although she would be able to write to the family when they reached America, there would be no

way to hear from them or learn their fate for many months, perhaps even years.

Worst of all, when she wasn't fretting over them, her thoughts turned to Aidan. She told herself it was only natural that he came to mind, considering the circumstances of their bond and her frequent contact with him. After all, there was no place to escape to, really. She had only to gaze over the passengers on deck and there he'd be, braw and a bit taller than anyone else, a wee more wide through the shoulders, with a straighter back and—

Disgusted with herself, she flopped potatoes onto a tin plate passed to her by a wan, pregnant young woman named Deirdre Connagher. Those without proper dishes had brought along whatever they had at hand, since the *Mary Fiona* provided no eating utensils. She'd seen all manner of items pressed into service, including a barrel lid, a bodhran, even handkerchiefs.

Aidan's dark-haired good looks rose in her mind again, and she tried in vain to push them away. Wasn't he the reason they were here on this whittled-out cork, bobbing along to an unknown land? Providing, God save them, that they weren't swept overboard, or the ship wasn't smashed to smithereens by a storm or one of the sea monsters she'd heard the sailors talking about. Because of Aidan O'Rourke, she might never see her home again.

"Might ye spare a wee bit of flavoring for those spuds, dearie?" a ruddy-faced woman asked, intruding upon her indignant thoughts.

Farrell pushed a steam-damp curl from her forehead and reached for a bag of salt on the shelf above her head. Then, her arm extended, she halted. Her exile from Ireland was not really Aidan's fault. Events had piled up, one upon the other, to lead her to this place and time. She was as much responsible for her situation as Aidan. Honesty forced her to admit it. Michael had damned himself with his wrongdoings, and she had turned a blind eye to those deeds. She would have been in a vast amount of trouble without Aidan's help.

But she didn't have to dance a jig about it.

Closing her hand around the salt, she took it and sprinkled a bit over the potatoes. If she had to be out here, it was good to have an occupation and a purpose, and both Mary and Jesus knew they could use the extra money.

And here in the galley, she could keep her distance from *her man.*

Just before sunset, Aidan sat at the little table in Charles Morton's cabin, facing him over a fan of cards. He held a pair of sevens and three other useless cards. Morton stared at him, and he bore the scrutiny with an expression as blank as a blind man's. At least he was fairly certain that he did.

What an interesting game, this poker that the second mate had taught him. Morton said he'd learned it in America in dockside pubs. "Saloons" they were called there. The game was played in many places, but enjoyed great popularity in southern port cities where wealthy men had both the time and means to wager. Aidan was no stranger to gambling, but this was new to him.

Charles Morton was a young man, probably younger than Aidan. He wore his light hair cropped short and sported the same full beard Aidan had noted on the other seamen. He bore his position with more dignity than did his captain, but without the seasoned self-possession of Quisenberry. As with Quisenberry, his general appearance was much better than that of his captain's, and as far as Aidan could tell he worked harder than any other officer on board. He'd seen the man do large jobs and small, go aloft, dispense tools and spare sails, and tend to all manner of tasks. He even doled out provisions to Farrell for her cooking.

Earlier she'd asked him to talk to McCorry about increasing her stores, but he knew that Morton was the one to see.

At last Morton threw his cards on the table, apparently unable to tell whether his opponent was bluffing, and unwilling to take the chance that he wasn't. "Well, I'm out. You've picked up the game very well."

"Will ye play again?" Aidan asked, pulling the coins and cards toward himself. Some were British currency, others were American.

Morton leaned back in his chair and smiled at his student. "You've gotten all the money from my pockets, Mr. O'Rourke—that's my limit. And I won't see pay again until we reach New Orleans. I've nothing left to bet, save my grandfather's gold watch." He fingered the chain attached to the time-piece.

"Nay, man, I won't be takin' that. I hope you're not offering it, and shame to you if you are. 'Twould be wrong to risk something so dear on the turn of a card." Remembering the silent, ragged skeletons queued up outside the soup kitchens in Skibbereen during the famine, he added, "Unless you're starving."

Outside, three bells sounded which, Aidan had learned, meant that it was five-thirty. Night would be upon them soon and he knew that Morton was due back on duty. He had yet to put forth Farrell's request.

He gathered the cards together, idly tamping their edges on the tabletop. "My wife asks if it might be possible to give her a little more food for the *frainies,* the puny children and weak souls on board, the ones who could not bring their own rations."

Morton sighed. "McCorry would hang my hide from the yardarm."

"Ye're a workin' man. I've seen you laboring on all kinds of jobs. You know what it's like to be hungry, I'd warrant."

"The problem is that if I give you extra now, we'll run short of provisions before we make port." He met Aidan's gaze briefly. "We usually do anyway. There's barely enough—barely, mind—for a voyage that he thinks will last a certain number of weeks. But he's not very good at planning—the trips always outlast the food."

"It doesn't sound like a mistake to my ears. We were promised there'd be meals for every day we're aboard."

Morton shifted uncomfortably in his chair. "Could you persuade those with more to contribute a bit?"

Aidan lowered his brows for a moment, then shrugged. "Aye, I'll ask. It's as we've always done—protected our own from those who would starve us."

Color rose in the younger man's face and Aidan knew he'd unintentionally struck a nerve. Morton might have seen the world, though perhaps not into the dark hearts of evil men. But it wasn't his fault he worked for a knave. Aidan released him from a riveting stare.

"Would ye win some of this back before you stand watch again?" he asked, gesturing at the money before him.

The second mate chuckled, obviously relieved for the change of subject, and shook his head. "I tell you, I've got nothing left to wager."

Aidan glanced around the tiny cabin, with its neat bunk, round window, wall mirror, and lamp. It might not be grand to some, he supposed, but compared to the hold, it seemed most luxurious. To be able to sleep with his wife, out of the weather and away from the living hell that steerage had become, was a great incentive, indeed.

Aidan smiled, too. "Ah, but I think you do."

CHAPTER SIX

FARRELL was busy plucking two chickens for the officers' dinner when she heard her name. She didn't need eyes to know who was at the galley door. But when she looked up, her heart lightened to see Aidan standing there, grinning as if he knew the answer to one of the brain-wrenching riddles his father used to pose beside the peat fire. He'd charm the birds straight from the trees with his handsomeness, she thought with some irony. That he affected her the same way worried her.

"And what would you be looking so pleased about?" she asked, dragging her forearm across her brow. The cookstove put out a lot of heat and the close confines of the galley were stuffy. Chicken feathers swirled like snow and stuck to her hair and apron front. Then she perked up a bit. If he was that happy—"Were you able to get more *whack* for the sickly folk below?"

"No," he said, and his smile faded. He ducked through the doorway and stepped into the little space. His head cleared the overhead by only two or three inches. He brought with him the scent of fresh salt air, and traces of porter and someone's pipe tobacco. Looking at the half-plucked chicken in her blood-smeared hands, he nodded at it. "They aren't doing without, are they?" he asked, meaning the officers. "I wasn't able to convince Morton to give you more rations." He related the second mate's explanation. "It's sorry I am, *céadsearc*. He wouldn't budge. So I told him we'd take care of our own, just as we always have."

Her hands fell still. "But how? There is so little to go round."

"Aye, well, we can give a bit, and I'll convince those with more to provide."

She looked at the chickens again. "Maybe when I cut these up for stew, the men might not notice if a leg or wing is missing."

He shoveled a hand through his dark hair. "Aye, and how will you decide who'll get the leg or wing, while the rest watch? Nay, lass, that won't do."

"I could make broth," she proposed. Then she sighed at the futility of it. Someone would be sure to notice an extra kettle on the stove, and even then, there probably wouldn't be enough to go around. "I suppose you're right." Turning a sharp eye on him, she asked, "So that was why you were grinning like Mary's donkey at the doorway? To deliver this news?"

The smile reappeared. "What if I told you that we won't be sleeping on deck tonight?"

Her shoulders drooped with disappointment.

"Oh, no! Is it raining again?" She craned her neck, trying to see around him through the open door. What could a body expect in the North Atlantic in late winter besides rain?

"Yes it's raining, but that's not what I'm talking about."

But all she heard was the state of the weather. The prospect of spending the night in steerage filled her mind. "Dear God, I can't sleep in that hold, it's so brutal down there. I know the poor souls don't mean to be sick, but—"

Aidan took her shoulders and turned her toward him, mindful of the mess in her hands. "Whisht now, little red one. Will ye be throttling that chicken all over again?"

She looked down and realized she was squeezing the limp fowl's neck. She loosened her grip and looked up into Aidan's dark-blue gaze.

He released one of her shoulders and reached into his coat pocket to produce a tarnished brass key on a short, braided leather thong. He looked quite pleased with himself.

"What's that?"

"This, Mrs. O'Rourke, is the key to our room for tonight."

Her brows rose. "Our *what*? Are ye having me on, Aidan?"

"No. While I was visiting with Mr. Morton, we played a few hands of cards. Ye know, just to be friendlylike. When I won all of his pocket money, I suggested that he might wager his cabin." He shrugged. "He lost."

"No!" Farrell was impressed despite her mild disapproval of his gambling.

"Aye, and look at this." He reached into his pocket again and brought out a handful of money. Her eyes widened at the sight. "There's nearly a pound here." He put a coin in her apron pocket. "I owe ye a shilling and six. Here's thruppence on account."

"Ye shouldn't be gambling and I don't know that I want money gained that way."

"The man wanted to play cards. Who was I to say no?"

"But what about Mr. Morton? Where will he sleep?"

He waved a hand. "He said he'll bunk with the lads in the forecastle." He told her about the hand of cards that had won them this bounty. He'd wagered her sixpence, somehow turning it into extra money and a cabin for them. On top of that, he had left the second mate in fine spirits and feeling as if he'd done Aidan a good turn.

So Farrell would be sharing that room with her husband tonight, a prospect she viewed with disquiet. Sleeping on deck, or even in the hell that was steerage, had prevented any intimacy between them. He'd not so much as kissed her cheek since they'd set sail, and that had been fine with her. Tonight that would change. Those sturdy, capable hands that had smashed faces in fights and soothed the neighborhood children's scraped knees, his lips, that big body—he'd be right next to her with more privacy than they'd had since that dreadful night at the Rose and Anchor when he'd tried to claim his husbandly rights. A tingling shiver raced over her scalp and down her back.

She looked at the key he held and felt as if it were as dangerous as a serpent. God in heaven, she thought, how did Aidan do it? How did he manage to convince others to do his bidding? He had the gift of blarney, that was sure, with a wee bit of diplomacy thrown in for good measure. Where he'd learned the latter, she couldn't imagine because she'd never seen much evidence of it back home. He also had a gift for card-playing and gambling in general.

"Well, I have to finish this business"—she gestured at the chicken—"and then tend to Deirdre Connagher and Mrs. Dougherty below." Although a ship's captain often acted as physician at sea, all McCorry knew of doctoring, when he could be bothered, was amputation and purging. At least that was what she'd overheard from Mr. Quisenberry. Trying to follow in the footsteps of Saint Brigit, Farrell had assumed the job of seeing after the passengers, and they were happy to have one of their own dosing them. She couldn't do much for them, but she did her best with the medicine chest at her disposal.

"Must ye see to them tonight?" Aidan asked.

"Saint Brigit would have me do no less."

Of all the saints on the calendar, Brigit was Farrell's favorite. True, Father Joseph taught them that Brigit had become a nun after Saint Patrick baptized her. But Farrell's elderly aunt Kathleen had told her that Brigit had been a loving and powerful Celtic goddess long before that, and the early people had worshiped her as the mother of the earth, goddess of healing, the crafts, fire, poetry, and farming. In Kildare, a sacred, eternal fire had been kept burning in her honor, attended only by women. Later, when the Church realized that the Irish would not abandon Brigit, they canonized her and built a convent on the site of her shrine. At least that was what Kathleen had told her.

When Farrell had asked Father Joseph about her aunt's story, he'd sternly dismissed it as "pagan blather," and ordered her to say a Hail Mary for her impious questions about one of God's chosen handmaidens. He'd also instructed her to pray an entire rosary for her aunt's soul. But secretly Farrell liked Kathleen's story best, one about the strong, loving mother of earth and poetry and fire. It fit so well with her own sense of connection to the land and healing. In her pocket she always carried the little carved figure of the goddess-nun as her talisman.

There was at least one pregnant woman aboard, Deirdre, who would most likely give birth before they reached America, and although she had no real knowledge of midwifery, Farrell checked on her daily because she was so gaunt and pale. Her sense of helplessness was eased a bit by the attention she was able to give the woman, and in knowing that other women below were watching after her, as well.

"I suppose ye'll do what ye see fit," Aidan replied.

"I'll bring your meal after that." She swallowed and clutched the lifeless chicken in her hands. "T-to Morton's cabin?"

He gave her a knowing smile. "Aye. I'll leave a handkerchief tied to the door so you'll know which it is. I'll be waiting for ye."

Once she'd served the chicken stew, Farrell hurried over the damp deck and down to the hold to see Deirdre Connagher and Mrs. Dougherty. Expecting to be stopped by other passengers, though, she also carried with her things from the medicine chest that she thought she might need—brewed chamomile, quinine, turpentine, laudanum, lemon syrup for cough (the lemons she'd snatched from the crew's supply), a special treat for Deirdre, and two bottles of patent medicine. These she'd put in a handle basket covered with a cloth.

Coming down the ladder, she heard the buzz of murmured conversation, crying children, and a few voices raised in angry tones. After the sun went down, widely spaced lamps swaying from the overhead timbers provided the only light. With its yellow-white gleam, the lamplight gave every face a slightly bilious appearance. The stench wasn't so strong this evening, but bad enough.

People sat in their little bunks, which were not much more than shelves built against the hull of the ship—six feet long but only two feet wide. Others perched on overturned kegs, boxes, or creepies, three-legged stools brought from faraway firesides. Here and there, lines had been strung on which to dry clothes and babies' nappies, adding to the stifling humidity.

She made her way to the space assigned to Mrs. Dougherty. She was sitting up with her feet dangling from the second-row bunk. Her hair hung in limp, gray plaits on her shoulders, its color nearly matching her face. Her clothes were as drab and travel-worn as the others'. Farrell's own clothing had been so big for her it barely stayed on her body until she'd taken a needle and thread to it. The stitching wasn't fancy, only functional.

"How are you, then, Mrs. Dougherty?" she asked, putting her basket on the floor next to her.

"Sure I'm in a terrible state. I swear, Mrs. O'Rourke, this must be purgatory we've all come to."

"Did you eat the bread I sent with your husband?"

"Aye, and I thank you for it. But now my head aches something fierce, so it does." She squinted as though even the low yellow light made her headache worse.

Farrell nodded. "I might have something for that." She reached into the basket and produced the bottle of lavender water. "Do ye have a handkerchief or a strip of cloth?"

The woman passed her a piece of what looked like an old petticoat. It had probably been beautiful once, but now it would serve as a compress. She dribbled some of the fragrant water onto the cloth. "Put this on your forehead and try to rest for a while."

Mrs. Dougherty lay down on her thin bedding, and heaved a long sigh. "God bless you, lass. I pray God will make this journey short—I'm just about worn to a nubbin."

"And I'll send a prayer to Saint Brigit to speed you back to health." Farrell patted her hand and began to pack up her lavender water.

Ryan Dougherty, who had been in a conversation with some other men, came to see what remedy Farrell had provided his wife. Satisfied, he asked, "Do ye know if Aidan has put in a word with the captain for us, missus?"

"I know he talked to Mr. Morton, the second

mate. He's the keeper of the stores. It was no good. He couldn't shift him." She lowered her voice. "But Aidan said he has another plan, so let's not give up hope yet." She didn't want to reveal just what he had in mind. Persuasion seemed to be one of Aidan's specialties and she decided to leave it to him to convince others to share their food with families like the Doughertys.

Intent on seeing Deirdre Connagher, Farrell was stopped along the way to bind a toddler's cut knee, dispense lemon syrup for a man's deep-chest cough, and prepare a turpentine chest flannel for his wife's stubborn cold.

At last she reached Deirdre's bunk and what she found was not encouraging. She lay on her side, her eyes closed. With a sense of panic, Farrell put her hand under the woman's nose to feel for her breath. At the touch, Deirdre opened tired, dark-circled eyes. Her paleness was accentuated by dull, raven-black hair that she wore in a single, long braid.

"Oh, Farrell . . . ye've come."

Farrell reached for her hand and was frightened by its chill. She didn't know why, but she felt special empathy for this poor soul who was seventeen years old, pregnant, a new widow, and alone. Her husband had died just before they were to board the *Mary Fiona* in Queenstown. With nowhere else to go and determined to leave Ireland, she got on the ship to join her brother and his wife in America.

"Yes, I'm here," she answered, making a brave effort to smile into the small, thin face. "How are you feeling?"

"Och, I'm so tired. And the babe has been kicking me in the back since this morning. It seems to be getting worse as night comes on."

Farrell put her basket on the bunk and opened it. "I've brought ye a little something," she whispered. She hated not being able to give everyone what they needed and having to sneak about with morsels of food. She lifted out a crockery cup of chicken broth that she'd appropriated from the officers' meal. It was covered with a square of waxed cloth, tied in place with a length of twine, which she removed. "It's not much but it might give you a wee bit of strength. Drink this."

Deirdre lifted herself to her elbow and took the cup from Farrell's hands. After taking a sip, she lowered herself again, putting the cup next to her. "Thank you."

"While it's hot," Farrell urged, wishing she had something else to offer. But nothing in her basket could really help. Looking at the girl, she felt a sudden clutch of dread squeeze her heart like a fist. She reached into her pocket and touched her wooden carving of Brigit.

"Yes, while it's hot," Deirdre parroted in a thin voice. "As soon as I rest a minute." Her heavy eyes closed and she was lost again to the dim world between wakefulness and sleep.

Or life and death, Farrell thought with an anxious shudder. As she made her way back to the ladder, she asked a few of the stronger women to keep watch over Deirdre.

Farrell herself still had a man to feed in a private room.

Aidan washed and shaved, then washed again as best he could in the room that was now his and Farrell's for a night. They were allowed six pints of water per day for drinking, cooking, and washing, and it didn't go very far. His clothes didn't fit very well, and neither did Farrell's. Hers were too big and his ran to the small side, but they'd been in a hurry when they'd bought them in the second-hand shop in Cork City. He ducked to view himself in the little mirror hanging on the wall. He spotted a tuft of unruly hair and he licked his palm to smooth it down. Waiting for Farrell, he felt as nervous and awkward as a boy bringing flowers to his first colleen. And kept him waiting, she did. He heard the ship's bell ring the hour of eight. She would come, wouldn't she? he wondered.

Her face and form rose in his mind's eye. Her skin was as pale as new cream and bore not one freckle, despite her coloring. At least none that he could see. She had a pretty, rounded chin and a slim, fine-cut nose. Her clear green eyes were fringed with long, dark brown lashes that made him think of an artist's sable brush he'd once seen in a Skibbereen shop window. Her copper hair, well, it was as thick and heavy as a Percheron's tail, and he longed to run his hands through it, to learn if it was as silky.

And, unlike some of the other girls he'd known, there were strength and courage in her that matched the attributes of the goddess she so admired. Brigit would be proud of Farrell, he believed.

He hoped that his wife would come to care for him, though their marriage would never be a grand passion, considering the way it began. He suspected that in her heart, she imagined herself married to Liam. Nor was she the type of woman to submit to his will without question. Farrell had too much pride and independence for that. But if he could win her regard, at least it might be a start.

A tap at the door jerked him from his musings. He crossed the tiny room and flung open the oak panel. There she stood in a shawl and clean blue dress that almost fit her, balancing two plates. It was still raining; droplets clung to her hair, dim crystals in the lamplight.

"What've ye got here?" he asked, taking the burden from her hands. He put the plates down on the small, round table where most recently he'd played cards. She stepped into the cabin and he reached behind her to close the door.

"It's not proper mash, but I used potatoes and

mixed in some of our oatmeal and a wee bit of chicken broth," she replied, taking off her shawl and shaking the rainwater from it. He could smell the aroma of the food, but he also detected the scent of ocean and some sweet fragrance, like flowers swishing from the folds of her skirts. From her pocket, she produced two pewter spoons.

"What's that sweet smell? Like wildflowers?"

"Oh, when I was in the hold, I treated Mrs. Dougherty for a headache. I used a bit of lavender water for a compress to her forehead. I suppose I got a bit of it on me." She looked around the cabin and he could see the relief in her face.

"A nice improvement, aye?"

She nodded, trailing her hand over the back of a chair, her woman's eyes taking in the tidy, luxurious warmth of the place. "Aye, it is."

"Here, lass, sit down. Ye've been working hard." He'd fetched two of Morton's glasses from a small rack mounted to the wall and poured lashings of poteen into each from the small stoneware flask in his coat pocket. He'd been saving the strong liquor for a special occasion, and if this wasn't a special night, he couldn't think of one better.

"Where did you get that?" she asked, nodding at the flask.

He smiled. "Ye didn't think I'd take a trip of thousands of miles without bringing a bit of Da's poteen, did you? I've been perishing for a taste, but saving it since there's so little here." He handed her the cork to sniff and though her cinnamon brows rose at the strong smell, she smiled, too. It was well known in their district that no one made better whiskey than Sean O'Rourke, although in the last few years, his failing health had reduced production quite a bit. Everyone expected either Tommy or Liam to take up the task of distilling the illegal spirits and carry on the family tradition.

He lifted his glass and she followed. "May the good saints protect ye, and the devil neglect ye!"

She laughed at the toast and took a cautious sip. "Ohhh!" she gasped. "God, it's like fire in a bottle!"

"Aye, it is," he agreed companionably. "But it's got rounded corners on it so it'll go down smooth-like."

After she took another taste, she gave him an arch look and a cough. "Smooth, ye say."

"Angel's tears, Farrell. That's what Da always called the poteen."

"I'd hate to see the eyes these tears came from," she retorted, amused. "They'd be bloodred."

She looked lovely in the pale golden light of the lamp. Her smile was full and unfeigned, reaching her green eyes. God, dimples she had, too. How had he missed those?

"Aye, well, some of Da's customers had blood-red eyes, as well."

Farrell dug her spoon into the mash. "Mmm,

this tastes *much* better with the chicken broth."
They both ate ravenously, enjoying the first bit of
nourishment they'd had with real substance since
coming on board.

When Aidan pushed away his plate, Farrell
said, "I wonder how they all are at home. I think
about them every day, Clare and Tommy, your da,
Liam . . ."

His brother's name hung between them like a
tangible thing. He swallowed the rest of his whiskey. "Do you miss him so much, then?" he asked
in a low voice.

"He was my intended. Of course I miss him.
We were to marry, come, well, spring, or perhaps
after the harvest."

He gave her a pointed look. "Or by Christmas,
or maybe Saint Patrick's Day next year or the year
after. Liam *never* would have married you, I don't
think. Not even if all the trouble hadn't happened.
He'll stay at home and remain a bachelor, and an
old one, if God wills that he should live long
enough."

Farrell stared at him. "What are ye talking
about? Of course he would have married me. We
were promised to each other."

He shook his head and put down his glass.
"Nay. He's my brother, aye? I lived with him all
my life. He's a good man, a kind one. But he's as
serious as a priest and knows only two things, farm-

ing and how to worry. It's not in him to nurture a dream or plan for the future. He doesn't have what it takes to commit to a woman, to give his body and soul to her, and he knows it."

"He did—he must have! Why else did he ask me to be his wife?"

Putting his elbow on the table, he leaned forward. "I'll ask you one better—why did it take him so long to do it? Da finally told him he'd better make up his mind about ye, yea or nay, or let ye go to a more deserving man. Liam let Da talk him into offering for you."

Farrell took another swallow of "angel's tears" and kept her gaze riveted on Aidan's face. Over the whiskey fumes, the male scent of him, of soap and saltwater, mingled with the comforting aroma of food. Warmth flooded her limbs but not her heart. "My, my, but ye know how to flatter a girl and make her feel special, don't you?" she asked with some asperity.

"I'm only telling you the truth of it. The night we left, when you went outside with him, what did he say to you?"

"He said—he told me—" Liam's words came rushing back to her, and there wasn't much good in them.

I love ye, lass, but in God's truth, I don't love ye well enough.

She'd told herself then that he said those things

only to make her leave for her own good. She could not bear to think anything else, such as Aidan implied—that her love for him truly had not been returned. That love still burned in her heart. It couldn't be extinguished as easily as a candle flame. After all, her affection for Liam had grown over a period of years. But it gave her no joy now, as love should. It felt like a fist in her chest that squeezed hard enough to hurt.

She couldn't admit any of this to Aidan. It would only rub salt in the wound that was her heartache. She looked at her lap and murmured what she could. "He said that I should go with you. That he was putting me in your keeping and God's, and both would treat me well."

He poured himself another drink from the stoneware flask. "He was right, Farrell."

"I never featured myself married to you," she said, still stung by his tactless revelation of the truth. The whiskey also freed her tongue. "Ye aren't the type of man I wanted—wild as you are and with a scandalous reputation to boot, always turning women's heads with a look and breaking men's heads with your fists." She paused. "After all those years with my own da, with his drunken ways and cruel words, and the b-beatings, I preferred Liam's quiet ways and placid nature. I wanted to be his wife. I didn't want a man like my own father."

Aidan stared at her. "Do you think I'm like

Gael Kirwan? Do you really feature me lifting a hand to you?"

Farrell dropped her gaze. His eyes burned like two dark stars, and she heard both indignation and astonishment in his questions. "Maybe not now, not yet . . . but someday, when—if . . ." She couldn't finish the sentence.

He didn't respond, but after a moment he sighed. Then he reached across the table for her hand. She withdrew hers, so he gripped his whiskey glass and took a healthy swallow. "Farrell, I swear you'll have a good life, a better life, in America. With me."

She said nothing more, but pushed back her chair and began gathering the dirty dishes to avoid the possessive look she saw in his eyes again, the one that seemed to say that she had always been meant for him. He rose as well, and his hand on her arm stayed her.

His touch was warm and vital, almost frightening in its vibrance.

"Sit a moment."

"No, I've still work that needs—"

"Sit." He took the plates and put them back on the table.

The timbre of his voice altered slightly; it was deeper, richer, almost angry. She chanced a look at him and he filled her field of vision. All she saw were a strong mouth and dark blue eyes that seemed alighted with a fire that burned deep within him. He was so different from his brother. Not long ago she'd believed the differences were only bad. Now, knowing him a little better, she wasn't so sure, and it was hard to accept.

He advanced on her, tall and menacing, and she edged away until the backs of her thighs hit the side of the narrow bunk. The poteen had made her a bit unsteady and she sat down hard on the thin mattress.

"What're ye after, Aidan O'Rourke?"

"I mean to answer your earlier question. Yes, I *do* know how to make a woman feel special. And it hasn't a damned thing to do with being quiet or placid." He stood over her and pulled her to her feet again so that only an inch or two separated them. To her amazement he lifted her hand to his lips and kissed it lingeringly. Fire and ice ran up her arm to her shoulder. From her hand he moved to her chin and strung a line of soft, hot kisses along her jawline. When he reached her earlobe, he took it gently between his teeth and ran his tongue along its edge.

Farrell shivered with the sensations he evoked in her. No one, certainly not even Liam, had ever kissed her this way. She fought the urge to reach up and thread her fingers through his hair. If merely kissing her jaw and ear made her feel so, what would his lips feel like upon her own? As if reading her mind, he took her mouth with his, demanding and fierce, yet tender. Her legs seemed to be nothing more than boiled greens, limp and weak.

Aidan cradled the back of her head with one hand. The other he planted on her waist, pulling her close to his work-toughened body. Had that soft moan come from her? Shouldn't she object to his behavior? she wondered, caught in a muzzy fog of his touch, her escalating pulse, and the delicious excitement of his kiss.

He hovered just above her mouth. "I'll tell ye what placid is good for," he muttered, the angry note still there. "Nothing. It won't keep you warm at night, or put a babe in your belly, or fight to keep you safe." His lips, pleasantly whiskey-flavored, covered hers again, and his hand reached for the pins in her hair.

A ghost of Liam's voice came back to her then, faint and whispery, as if from a dream.

He'll fight for you with his last breath.

Then the thought was gone again as he loosened her hair and plunged his fingers into it. A hot thrill went through her like a bolt of lightning. Her arms went around his neck as if they had a will of their own, and she found herself kissing him back. He sat down on the bunk and pulled her with him. She landed on his lap, and his arms went around her while he kissed her again with a fiery urgency. When his tongue sought hers, she responded. Her own voice in her head hissed that surely this wasn't decent and insisted that she'd lost her mind. But reclining in Aidan's lap and with him snaking a warm hand over the front of her dress, she ignored the warning. No, this wasn't placid. This was dizzying and exciting and—

Suddenly, there was a heavy pounding at the door. "Mrs. O'Rourke!"

Farrell froze.

More pounding. "Mrs. O'Rourke, are you in there?"

She recognized Charles Morton's voice. Aidan lifted his head from her mouth and uttered a vivid profanity. She looked at where she was sitting and realized what she'd been doing, and was mortified. How could she have given in to his caresses so easily? She felt foolish and, worse, disloyal to Liam.

Farrell leapt from Aidan's lap and went to answer the summons.

She smoothed her skirt and opened the door a crack. "Mr. Morton?"

"I'm sorry to bother you, ma'am." His gaze drifted from her unbound hair downward. Farrell looked at her bodice and found the source of the man's interest. Four buttons were open. Blood rushed to her cheeks, scalding them. She shot a venomous glare at Aidan, then clutched the fabric together with one hand. Immediately, Morton returned his attention to her face, and he seemed to be blushing, as well.

"It's no bother. What can I—we do for you?"

"Um, well—they're wanting you below, ma'am. I was asked to fetch you to visit someone. Mrs. Connagher, I believe her name is."

"Oh!" An icy sluice of worry flew down Farrell's spine. "She's very bad, then?"

"I don't know. I think so. I was told that she's asking for you and to bring you right away."

Farrell felt Aidan's approach and knew he stood right behind her. She glanced at him. "I must be going. If she asked to see me, I have to go to her."

He nodded. "Go with Mr. Morton. I'll follow in a minute."

She grabbed her shawl and hurried after Morton. Behind her, she heard Aidan utter another curse that would earn him extra time in purgatory, to be sure.

"And so we commend these two souls into God's keepin' and mercy, and hope they find peace in the next world." James McCorry, bristle-faced and unkempt, had been roused at this early hour to say a few hurried words over the subjects of his entreaty as they lay on a plank on the ship's deck. Those passengers who could, crowded around Deirdre Connagher and her dead child in the rain, crossing themselves and murmuring prayers. Farrell stood nearby, her throat aching from the choked-back sobs and knot of grief lodged there, and her hand closed upon her carved figure of Brigit. She felt the heat of Aidan's solid form behind her shoulder and she drew comfort from it.

Farrell had not been able to do anything for Deirdre, and though none of the other women in attendance could help, either, she bore a stinging guilt. The child had been stillborn and Farrell held Deirdre's hand until she drew her last breath a few hours later.

"A broken heart killed her, sure," one woman had whispered last night as they had stared at the lifeless pair in the gloomy confines between decks. "First her husband lost back home, then the babe. She couldn't go on." She'd crossed herself and sighed. "They're together now with the angels." A ripple of murmured agreement flowed through the group.

Farrell had helped the other women stitch the grief-felled mother and her infant into some burlap sacks they'd sewn together. The men had retreated to the other end of the hold; preparing the dead was women's work. The guilt had come to lodge in her heart then. While she had been dizzy with poteen and letting Aidan have his way with her—and actually *enjoying* it—poor Deirdre had been suffering in the dank hold, trying to birth a baby that could not live.

Now, with a nod from McCorry, Aidan and several other men stepped forward to hoist the plank to the gunwale. Mother and child, bound together in their burlap winding-sheet, slipped over the side into the cold, indifferent arms of the Atlantic. Farrell bowed her head as tears slid down her cheeks. Not one among them was a newcomer to death and loss, but she could not get accustomed to it. She'd not even seen Michael properly buried. She felt it keenly that the matter was dispensed with so easily.

This poor young woman and her baby, with only strangers to mark their passing—no one would ever know what had become of them. It brought home to her Aidan's comment that night at the Rose and Anchor: she was an orphan and he was as good as one. She swiped the back of her hand over her tears, but her own determination to survive was shaken by this burial at sea.

The mourners began to drift away, dispirited and solemn. The steady, cold rain had been falling for hours, and now the wind had picked up. Farrell's shawl was soaked through.

She looked at the vast expanse of gray-green water beyond the rail, searching in vain for some hint of land, but saw nothing but the same monotonous view of ocean, rising and falling, rising and falling. Even the seabirds had forsaken them several days earlier, as the ship ventured deeper into the open sea. Overhead, the rigging creaked and groaned in the wind.

During the hardest years of her life, Farrell had wondered occasionally what it would be like to sail the seas and visit distant lands. She hadn't wanted to leave Ireland forever. Mostly, she'd just wanted to see if there was a place where existence wasn't as dire. Now, as she stood on the rolling, pitching deck of the *Mary Fiona,* Farrell felt that it was not much more than a barrel overflowing with humanity and all of the related miseries that came with an ocean voyage. If there was a better life somewhere, she couldn't picture it. As far as she was concerned, there was nothing left on earth but this ship and the ocean.

In Skibbereen, they'd heard fragmented and alarming tales of "coffin ships," the vessels that had carried starving, evicted Irishmen from their famine-stricken home to America during the height of the potato plague. Disease and starvation had run rampant aboard many of them. Some ships were lost in storms, others landed with most of their passengers gone, having been buried at sea. Might that happen to them? After all, they'd lost three people so far. Would they be picked off, one by one? The fear and uncertainty nearly drove her to her knees right there on the deck to pray for God's protection.

"Ye ought to get out of the rain. There's a fair spot against the galley wall."

She heard Aidan's voice beside her, low, rich, familiar. But she couldn't take her eyes off the roll-

ing swells. She gripped the railing, cold and salt-
sticky beneath her hands. "We've come on a fool's
errand, Aidan. God Himself couldn't find someone
out here." Her words sounded bitter, even to her
own ears.

"What are ye going on about?"

She turned and lifted her gaze to his familiar
face. "At least when someone dies on land, there's
a priest to pray over the poor thing, a grave to visit,
a place to put wildflowers. But here . . . there's no
one. Deirdre was dropped into the ocean and no one
can come to mourn over her. Ever. D'ye know what
I mean?"

He paused before answering. His own dark hair
hung in damp tendrils and his thin, ill-fitting coat
clung to his shoulders from the wet. "Aye, I know."
She saw understanding in his eyes, as if he'd
thought of it, as well. "I think the girl would have
died anywhere. She was sickly and as thin as whey.
But I'll tell ye, we're not on a fool's errand. This
is a trial, to be sure, one that we'll survive. America
will be grand and we won't live in poverty anymore. We'll have plenty to eat and a place to live
that doesn't flood in the winter or bake like a cow
flop in the summer."

This tenderness and understanding was not
something she expected from the Aidan O'Rourke
she knew in Ireland. Without thinking, she reached
up to push a wet lock of hair from his forehead,

then snatched her shaking hand away, startled by how easily the gesture had come to her.

"Do you really think it can be so, Aidan?"

"I'll see to it, and make no mistake." He took her elbow. "Come along, little red one. It's a tea day." Twice per week they were allowed tea, sugar, and molasses. "Go to the galley and make yourself a cup."

"Mrs. O'Rourke!" Mr. Morton was bellowing at her over the sound of the rain and wind from his place on the quarterdeck. "There's a storm brewin.' If you're going to do any cooking, you'd best see to it. The fire will have to be put out shortly."

She nodded at him, then looked at the group gathering outside the galley. They reminded her of so many baby birds, waiting for their mother's return with food. "Aye. As soon as I cook the morning meal."

Aidan shook the rain from his hair and coat, and remained at the railing, standing beside the spot so recently occupied by Deirdre Connagher and her child. Farrell had not been the only one affected by the woman's death. Although he had not known her, Aidan felt it just as keenly, but for very different reasons. Yes, it was tragic that she'd been put over the side, buried at sea with no marker for her grave. But people died every day, often long before their time. If the famine hadn't proved that, nothing else would. He was still plagued by night-mares about some of the gruesome scenes that had taken place in Skibbereen on a regular basis, and not so many years past.

No, Deirdre's death had brought home to him another realization: the vulnerability of a pregnant woman.

Aidan had railed and cursed at his missed op-portunity to bed his wife last night. He burned for her with a desire that he'd never felt for any other woman, and he'd had her right there in his arms, warm, responsive, firm, and yielding to his touch. For the moment, her anger with him had been put aside, and she'd lost that high-nosed look she some-times gave him. Then Morton had come knocking.

After they'd gone below, the second mate had reclaimed his cabin, only too happy to escape the gamey quarters of the forecastle. Chances were slim that he'd be willing to bet it again in a card game.

But if they had not been interrupted, and Aidan had consummated their marriage, suppose a child had resulted? he wondered, staring at the vast emp-tiness of water. He had plans, grand plans, for their future. They would travel from New Orleans to New York and begin a new life. But he didn't know the exact distance between the two cities, how they would get there, or how long it would take. He wanted to give Farrell a safe, secure place to bear his children. He glanced at the empty deck next to his feet again, remembering the burlap-wrapped bodies. If he lost her because of his own selfishness, his own impatience, well, it would be the worst sin on his soul. Worse than causing Michael Kirwan's death. Worse than anything.

He looked up at Farrell, standing in the galley doorway and handing out this morning's breakfast to the ragged, silent passengers. Despite her own sorrow and the gloom of the day pressing down upon them, she was as fair as a June dawn in County Cork. He knew this promise he made to himself would chafe in the days and nights to come.

But for Farrell, it was a promise he swore he would keep.

CHAPTER SEVEN

"HAVE ye ever seen the like of it?" Aidan asked as he stripped off his thin coat. He stood wedged beside Farrell at the railing, jockeying for a place among all the other passengers who'd crowded up to have a look. His eyes were full of an almost childlike wonder.

"No. Not even in my dreams," she answered, but she was a bit apprehensive.

Coming up the wide Mississippi River, the *Mary Fiona* passed grand homes sheltered by trees that bore gently waving gray curtains of some vegetation. The weather was unlike any Farrell had ever experienced. Simply breathing seemed to require effort—the air was as moist and heavy as a wool blanket just pulled from a hot kettle, and perfumed with the cloying scents of various plants and exotic flowers in full bloom. Some plants were giants, boasting leaves the size of umbrellas, and grew in great, intertwined snarls that stretched languidly skyward.

This wasn't simply another country. This place was so strange and bizarre that if Farrell had been told that she'd journeyed over the Atlantic to the land of Tir na nOg, she would have believed it. That mythical place held a treasure of gold and silver and jewels, of wine and honey. The trees bore fruit, blossoms, and green leaves, all at the same time, year round.

Though the sun was not overly hot, perspiration dampened her body, making her clothes cling in sticky patches. The coolness of the Mississippi and the wind that pushed them upriver were little help in this steamy climate. The other passengers on deck began shedding caps and tugging at their collars.

After more than two months at sea, Farrell had had a desperate craving to reach America. Although they had lost no other crewmen or passengers, the chore of cooking, of being confined to a ship that seemed to grow smaller with each passing day, and the monotony of the voyage had her nearly screaming for journey's end.

Water rations had been cut two weeks earlier, seawater had to serve for bathing, which was almost worse than no bathing at all, and though everyone had eventually pooled their rations, they were nearly out of food. Landfall was not only anticipated, it had become necessary to survival.

Now, here was America, and it was not what she had imagined. Well, she didn't know exactly *what* she'd expected, but this wasn't it.

Toward late afternoon, New Orleans came into

view in the distance, and Mr. Quisenberry gave orders to the crew to make ready for docking. The buildings grew bigger along the wharf and Farrell saw other ships and swarming activity. People, cargo, mules, horses, wagons—they all hustled to and fro. As the lines were cast and tied, she heard a babble of languages and strange accents. Some of the words *sounded* like English but she couldn't be certain. But whether in English or some other tongue, the cursing was unmistakable.

And what odors. There were the smells of wood smoke, tar, and old fish, of cooking, sweat, and overflowing chamber pots. The river gave off its own scent, and Farrell supposed that neither she nor Aidan were very clean, either. God, for a bath with fresh water and even the crudest soap, she thought.

As they docked in New Orleans, the gangway was opened and they disembarked. Some knelt and kissed the grimy dock planks and crossed themselves in thanksgiving. Others wept openly, grateful to have lived through the voyage and reached their destination. At least the journey was over. They were here at last, even if the weather was suffocating. Carrying her own bundle, Farrell tottered drunkenly against Aidan, surprised to find her legs as unsteady as a new foal's. Around her, others were having the same difficulty.

"Let's get out of the crush," Aidan said, taking her arm. Almost as unsteady, he led her to the wall of a warehouse to stand amid big, stacked bales of tightly packed white tufts.

"All those weeks on that bloody ship have taken my balance! People will think we're as drunk as pigs that've been at the mash."

He laughed at her outburst and leaned against the wall next to her. "Aye, we've got to get our land legs back. But it's good to have our feet on firm ground again."

"It is." She looked at the bales. "What would this be, then?" she asked, touching a hand to the soft fleece.

He bent his dark head to study it a moment, then reached out to feel it. "I think it's cotton."

"Cotton!" She'd never known what it looked like in its natural state. "It puts me in mind of clean lamb's wool."

"It's probably bound for the mills in England. Mr. Morton told me a lot of cotton comes from this part of America." He gave her a quick head-to-hem glance. "Have ye got your pins back under you?"

"I think so."

"Good. Morton also told me about an inn where we can get a room."

Farrell picked up her bundle again when a shocking sight caught her eye. Two groups of very dark-skinned people, men in one and women in the other, were chained to each other and being prodded along by men with riding crops and sticks. The

snotty tone made Aidan long to grab the man's greasy forelock and smash his head on the counter. He forced the impulse into a small box in his mind and closed the lid on it. Someday soon, he vowed to himself, no man would dare to look down his nose at Aidan O'Rourke or his wife. Certainly not some froggy who was dressed little better than they were.

He replied, "Aye, laddie. I'd like meals for my wife and me, and a bath brought to our room." He pushed a gold half-eagle across the counter. "This should cover everything." Five dollars was far too much to squander on luxury, but Aidan thought they deserved it after what they had been through. From the corner of his eye, Aidan caught Farrell's expression of surprised delight, and decided it was money well spent. He smiled and picked up the key to their room, leaving the clerk to goggle at the coin.

After a climb to the second floor, Farrell's sea legs felt as thick and shaky as a brick of head-cheese. Aidan unlocked the door and ushered her into a room that held a big iron bed, a chiffonier, a small desk, a washstand, and an upholstered chair and footstool, all far past their prime. The late afternoon sun was dimmed by shutters on the windows that cast stripes of bright light across the pine floor.

He crossed the floor to open the shutters and

looked out. "Hotel *Grand* View, eh?" he commented, his hands braced on either side of the window frame. "It looks like an alley down there to me, and it smells like a privy in this heat. Must be the chickens someone is keeping." The sound of enthusiastic clucking drifted upward through the window, along with noises from the street and neighboring businesses.

She dropped the bundle of her belongings on the floor and sat on the bed. "Ohhhh," she uttered, unable to stifle a sound of pleasure. "A real bed to sleep in. Even in Clare's house I slept on a pallet with the children. This will be like heaven after—"

She glanced up suddenly at Aidan, who had turned to look at her. His gaze upon her felt like two hot coals burning through her chest.

There it was again, that look in his eyes, unsettling, possessive, hungry. She wished she'd been able to demand a separate room, but she couldn't defend the cost. Besides, she didn't believe that her husband would agree to such an arrangement, although he had made no other advances after the night in Morton's cabin. She was glad of that, she told herself. Yes, glad. Her heart still belonged to Liam, even if he hadn't loved her as she'd have wanted. She thought of him every day and she didn't know when that would end. Or if it ever would.

Of course, Aidan had had no real private moment with her on the ship, although she knew that some couples had contrived to find hiding places in the cargo hold to be alone. Thank heavens he hadn't suggested something like that. Yet, a contrary part of her wondered why he hadn't. There had been nothing—not one more kiss, not a peck on the cheek. He hadn't even tried to hold her hand. After that one display of passion, she might have expected . . . Perhaps he'd found her lacking or displeasing that night, compared to the other women he'd known. The possibility vexed her in a way she didn't care to analyze.

With another glimpse at his eyes, gleaming blue and feral, she jumped up from the bed as if it were on fire. Sitting there might suggest an invitation that she hadn't meant to extend.

"You'll take the bed," he said gruffly. "I'll sleep in the chair."

The tension in the room was as thick as the humidity. "N-no, t'would not be fair. I shouldn't have the bed every night. You must share it with me—I mean, we can take our turns." She could imagine him watching her in the darkness from that chair. But more shameful still, she had a guilty curiosity about what it would feel like to have him lie beside her in the night.

"I've slept in worse places," he insisted. "The chair will be fine for me."

"No, maybe we can cast lots—"

A brewing disagreement that had little to do with fair play and everything to do with a man and a woman, disguised with excruciating courtesy, was interrupted by a knock at the door. Aidan reached it in two long strides. In the hallway stood three African serving women wearing white aprons over their plain dresses and colorful turbanlike scarves on their heads. They all bobbed quick curtsies upon seeing him. Between them they carried a round wooden tub and pushed a cart bearing a tray of redolent food, all of which they brought in without a word. The tub was put in a corner behind a dressing screen.

In a moment another serving girl followed, carrying two heavy buckets of steaming water which she poured into the little tub. She made another trip downstairs to refill the buckets. When she'd emptied these, she said to Farrell, "This water right off the stove, mistress. You let it cool some, else you look like a boiled crawdad."

Farrell didn't know what a crawdad was, but she supposed that it must be red.

"Yes, thank you," she said, peeking behind the screen at the tub. She dipped her hands in the hot water and washed them with a bar of soap tucked inside a folded towel that sat on the floor. As soon as she ate, she would finally have a chance to wash from head to foot, including her hair, which was stiff with salt spray.

Just as the women left the room, she emerged from behind the screen with red but clean hands. She and Aidan prepared to eat the first really nourishing food they'd had in months.

"Well, now, what would we be having here?" Aidan asked, pulling up the footstool to the cart. Farrell brought the chair from the desk. He lifted napkins and looked into covered dishes, inhaling all of the aromas. "Some kind of rice with other bits mixed in, I think, bread, butter, wine—"

Just as he was about to fall upon the meal, Farrell interjected. "Shame on ye, Aidan. Don't you think it would be fitting to give thanks for getting here in one piece and for the food?"

Aidan gave her a sheepish smile, feeling a trifle guilty. "Aye, of course." Women, he'd recognized long ago, were probably all that kept men from living a mean, crude existence in caves, and going about unshaven and unshriven.

"Bail na gcúig arán agus an dá iasc," she began in a low, clear voice, *"A roinn Dia ar an gcúig mhíle duine, Rath ón Rí a rinne an roinn, Go dtige ar ár gcuid is as ár gcomhroinn."* The blessing of the five loaves and two fishes that God shared with the five thousand, the bounty of the King who made the sharing, come upon our food and all who share it.

She spooned the spicy-smelling rice dish onto their plates while he poured the wine.

"What d'ye think this is?" she asked, piercing a crescent-shaped pink morsel with her fork. She nibbled on it and smiled. "Mmm, it's very good. Would you like a taste?" she asked, holding out the fork so that he could pluck the remainder from it.

Instead, he leaned forward and took it directly into his mouth, craving the taste of both her and the unknown delicacy. "Aye," he said, holding her gaze, "delicious."

A tiny smile, as fleeting as a fairy in the mist, crossed her face before she turned her attention back to her plate.

"I'd have no trouble getting used to this," he said as he slathered butter on a chunk of soft white bread. "Servants to cook and wait on us—I'd like that fine."

She paused with a large, pink shrimp speared on her fork. "Ye can't mean to say you'd want to own slaves!"

He frowned. "God, no! I wouldn't want that on my conscience. It's just not right. No one can own another person." He took a swallow of wine. "But a body can *hire* servants and pay them. Like—well, like Lord Cardwell."

Farrell stared at him. "Like Lord Cardwell! Mother of God, that's no better than owning slaves. Aidan, have you taken leave of your senses altogether?"

He wondered the same. Why in hell had that

name come to mind? "I meant it only as an example. After all, he was the only one in our part of the county who had enough money for such a luxury. I didn't mean like Lord Cardwell himself."

Her green eyes flashed fire. "Do ye know what life was like at Greensward Manor for the servants? Noel Cardwell was always grabbing at me, a pat on the rump, a tweak on the chin. Twice he tried to coax me into his bedchamber before that day I ran away. With hard work and a smile, he said, I would gain privilege and move up the servants' ranks. Oh, I knew his drift, well enough. A smile. Bah! I guess I found out what he meant by that."

No, Aidan hadn't known the details of that day at the manor house. A rumble of anger stirred in him like a sleeping wolf disturbed. "Did ye tell Liam about it on your visits home?"

She looked away. "No. I mean yes, but . . ."

"But it didn't trouble him?"

"It did," she insisted, and made a great fuss over polishing her teaspoon with her napkin. "But he didn't think it was worth getting into a state over. He didn't think Noel would actually—" She stopped, obviously realizing what a bad light she cast on Liam.

"I don't suppose he could get into a state over anything. Did ye tell anyone else about it?"

"Michael knew." Now she took to serving him more food from the dishes on the tray. "He said we'd all benefit from, well, from the association."

Aidan felt his blood begin to simmer in his veins. He drummed the side of his thumb on the edge of the cart. "Oh, he did, aye? Did no one defend your honor?" His own brother had shrugged off Cardwell's degenerate proposition and *her* brother had encouraged it.

She looked up at him. "My honor doesn't need defending. I'm not a timid milkmaid, ye know."

"No, you aren't. But now you know how black some men's hearts can be."

"We've left that all behind in Ireland, haven't we? The Cardwells and then Michael is—well, he no one's problem any longer." There was no accusation in the statement. Instead, Aidan heard resignation and regret.

They finished their meal without much more conversation. Aidan pushed the footstool back into place and said, "I'm going to find out if there's a place to get a bath around here."

She stood and stacked the dishes on the tray. "Oh, but there are just the two of us. The water will hold."

He knelt beside the small bundle of his belongings and found the clean clothes he'd saved for their arrival in America. "That's all right, lass. You'll want your privacy, and I just want to soak my old bones." What he *didn't* want was to sit on the other side of that dressing screen, listening to her splash water over her pale, slender limbs while he imagined the damp warmth of her body as she soaped and rinsed. Just thinking about it sent an aching desire shooting through him to settle in his groin.

When he caught her gaze, he thought he saw a glimmer of something in those clear eyes that mirrored his own craving. But no, that wasn't possible. He was just being daft. Farrell barely tolerated him as it was. On top of that, she was an untried lass who would be shy and innocent of the ways of men and women together.

In any case, it didn't matter. He'd made a promise to himself and he intended to keep it. He would not bed Farrell until they reached the place that would be their home. It might be modest in the beginning, but soon they'd have a wonderful house, just as he'd promised *her*.

"Will ye put the cart in the hallway on your way out?" she asked.

He gave her a smile and a little salute. "Keep the door locked until I get back, aye? And don't answer it if someone knocks. I'll come back as soon as I can."

She nodded as he pushed the cart out of the room. He heard it close behind him, and the lock click into place.

That was good, he thought, turning away with a gusty sigh. Knowing that she would be stripped to the skin and lounging in a hot bath would most certainly make him forget his manners and his good intentions if he remained.

This was the closest to heaven that Farrell had ever been. Long after she'd scrubbed off the dirt and washed her hair—and wasn't it a joy to feel clear water sluicing through the strands?—she lingered in the tub.

At Clare's house, bathing had always been a hurried event, with the whole family using the same water because toting and boiling it was so much work. A person had to get in and get out as quickly as possible.

But this—she let the water cascade from her cupped hand—this bath was just for her. From beyond the open windows, faint music floated up to her, and the last of the evening sun, golden and mellow, gave everything a warm glow.

The clean, white cake of soap she'd been given was embossed with some kind of writing, French she thought, and it smelled wonderfully sweet. She didn't know that soap like this existed, she was so accustomed to the harsh, homemade lye soap they'd always used. Sometimes they'd even had to barter for it because they didn't often have pork or beef fat to render. The lye soap took off the dirt, but it could take off a layer of skin, as well. This made her feel sinfully *pampered*.

It was a completely new sensation.

A little guilt crept into her heart that Aidan had left to go find his own bath, but not so much that she couldn't enjoy this. It was probably just as well that he'd gone. She would have felt very inhibited and self-conscious, knowing that he waited on the other side of the painted screen, and she would have been compelled to hurry through her washing, as she had at Clare's.

But more than that, tonight he'd caught her looking at him, considering him in a way that confused her. She didn't love him. She still loved Liam, foolish or not. But there was something so very male about Aidan O'Rourke that she simply could not ignore. Other women had fallen prey to his charms, but not her. At least not until recently. Even now, she felt a restless awakening within her that made her long for his return and wish that he could join her in the tub. It was an immodest thought, one that popped into her head without warning or invitation. Lord, he might have that effect on other women, but she hadn't expected to feel it herself.

At last, when the room had purpled with shadows and twilight, and her fingers were as wrinkled as a dried-out potato, she rose from the cold bathwater and dried herself with the towel. After she wrung the water from her hair, it hung in long damp plaits down her back.

Then she realized that her nightgown was tied in the square of old sacking that served as her bag, and she'd left it beside the bed. She peeked around the edge of the dressing screen, as if expecting to find someone there. Of course that was silly. She was still alone. Wrapping the towel around her torso, she lighted the two lamps in the room. Then she walked to the bedside and bent to riffle through her things. It wasn't as if she owned so many possessions, but she had to take everything out to find the blessed thing. The towel worked its way loose and fell in a puddle around her feet. At last, she spied the nightgown's long sleeve and pulled on it.

At that moment a key turned in the lock and the door opened. She looked up to see Aidan standing in the doorway. For a moment they were frozen in the tableau: she poised beside the bed, and he still gripping the doorknob. At last she let out a squeak and made frantic grabs for both the towel and the nightgown, but couldn't seem to catch either. He stood there, an expression of almost comical surprise on his face, staring at her as if she were a leg of lamb at Easter dinner and he had not yet broken his fast.

"For the love of Saint Patrick, turn around!" she snapped.

Jolted into action, he leapt back into the hall and shut the door.

Farrell pulled the nightgown over her head, and a thin thing it was, too. On the ship, she'd always slept in her clothes, so modesty hadn't been much of a problem. Now she grabbed her shawl to throw around herself. The night was far too warm for it, especially with the furious blush scalding her face and head, but she had nothing else to put on.

"All right," she called, cinching the shawl tight. "You can come in now."

Aidan poked just his profile through a narrow crack in the door as if expecting a shoe to be thrown at him. "Ye're sure."

"Yes, yes, come in." He edged his way in and closed the door behind him. She stood rooted to the spot beside the bed, feeling as awkward as she ever had in her life.

She had trouble looking him in the face, but when she did, she saw that he was blushing, too, scarlet all the way to his hairline. He was washed and shaved, his hair still damp.

"I'm sorry I didn't knock. At least ye didn't scream. I don't know how we would have been explaining that."

She faced him with her arms crossed over her chest and her chin out. "Aye, well, I guess you'll think to knock next time."

"I'm glad ye didn't have a pistol. I'd now be searching the corridor for my brains or my manhood." He gave her a wry grin. "Although you might be thinking both reside in the same place."

Her arms dropped to her sides. He was impossible! she thought, unable to stifle a hoot of laughter. He laughed with her, and for the moment, the tension was broken.

"Ah, it's good to hear you laugh, Farrell, lass." He walked around the bed to take her upper arms in his big hands. "It's like music, ye know?"

"Is that more of your blarney, Aidan?" she asked, trying to ignore his clean, soapy smell, mixed with a bit of bay rum and the scent of him that she'd come to know so well.

He gave her another smile, a soft one, and said, "Nay, girl. It's the truth."

Whether it was or not, it was nice to hear.

And wasn't this the finest form of torture God had ever visited upon one of His mortals? Aidan wondered in the warm darkness. Here he sat in a chair with his feet propped on a stool, dressed only in his underwear and listening to the night sounds of New Orleans—a distant piano, soft laughter from the street, a carriage rolling past. Meanwhile, his wife— a wife in name only—lay in a bed not more than three steps from him, and he dared not touch her. God was truly having a fine joke at his expense because he'd been allowed to see this wife, a woman he'd craved for years, wearing nothing but her long russet hair. Those creamy arms and legs, full, rounded breasts with rose-pink nipples, and a dark copper triangle at the apex of her thighs—He pounded a closed fist on the arm of the chair, once, partly from frustration, and partly to distract his thoughts. The promise he'd made to himself the morning of Deirdre Connagher's burial at sea had come back to test his resolve as soon as he and Farrell first set foot in this room.

Maybe it would be all right if they made love. Women didn't get pregnant every time they lay with their husbands, he tried to reason. Then ruefully he had to admit that Irish women seemed to. The street lamps below provided enough light for him to make out her soft silhouette in the bed. He wished he had the right to share it with her. But beyond his promise, he knew that if he was ever to win her regard, it must happen in slow steps. Farrell was not a woman who would take to being bullied, and that wasn't his way to treat women in any case.

At the public bath he'd visited earlier, he was asked if he'd be requiring more than just the bathing facilities. Had he been a single man, he would have taken advantage of that offer. Even now he wondered briefly why he'd chosen to remain faithful to this marriage when he knew that Farrell was, in her heart, married to his brother.

He shifted in the chair, trying to find a more comfortable position so that he might forget the hard, heavy ache low in his belly. Finally, he got up and searched quietly through his kit and located the flask of his da's poteen. If he couldn't satisfy his hunger for Farrell, maybe he could put it to sleep with a dose of whiskey. He uncorked the bottle, took a large swallow, and welcomed the merciful fire of the "angel's tears" as it slid down his throat. Tomorrow, he vowed, tomorrow he would learn about getting them to New York or Boston, somewhere permanent where they could put down roots.

Eventually, his tight muscles began to loosen and he dozed, drifting in and out of a hazy landscape of half-dreams, where a woodland goddess with a flowing gown and two yards of red hair succored the land with grace and goodness.

Chapter Eight

The next morning, Aidan woke in the chair as sore and stiff-muscled as an old man. The day already seemed hot, and then he realized that Farrell's shawl covered him from waist to mid-calf.

She was up and dressed, and sat at the little writing desk, scratching a pen across a sheet of paper. Obviously, she had covered him, not wanting to look at a man in his drawers. He watched her for a moment as her hand moved busily across the surface. Now and then she paused to dip the pen in the inkwell.

"What are you writing there?"

She glanced up at him, a bit startled. "I'm sending a letter to the family back home to tell them we've come safe this far." She paused to look at the lines she'd written. "I wish there was a way to learn what has happened to them. With us moving around like Romanies, it will be months and months before we know."

"We did the best thing we could for them." Absently, he smoothed the nap of the worn upholstered chair arm with the palm of his hand. "We did the *only* thing we could. All we can do is hope that they're well, and have faith that they are." Hope was what had sustained Aidan through the dark times and even now kept him looking forward instead of back. But he was more inclined to action than to trust in wishing. Still, it was all he could think of to tell Farrell, and it was all either of them could do now.

She tapped the end of the pen against her chin. "I suppose you're right. But I'll feel much better when I'm someplace where I can have a letter from them."

"Then I'd best be up and about. We'll find a place to get breakfast, then I'll start asking around about passage north." He threw off the shawl and Farrell returned her attention to her letter, carefully keeping her eyes on the paper. Her cheeks had bloomed with a very becoming pink, and he smiled as he passed her turned back.

He knew from living in the cramped quarters of an Irish cottage there was very little that remained private. She was no stranger to men or anyone else in various stages of undress. But he found her embarrassed innocence endearing. Arousing, in fact.

God, he'd better not entertain notions like that this early in the day. Last night had been difficult enough, and there was no sense in starting his morning with thoughts that would only torture his mind and body.

The serving women had come for the tub

shortly after his return last night, and now the washstand stood behind the dressing screen. After he
washed and dressed, they found a little restaurant,
La Maison Blanc, that served them tea, sausages,
and something called beignets, sweet, fried pastries
that tasted wonderful.

Afterward, Farrell returned to the hotel room to
finish her letter and Aidan began his search for
transport north. It had long been his experience that
a good place to gather information was in a pub.
He walked down the street to a barroom with a
name that made him grin—Lass of Killarney.

He stood in the doorway, waiting for his eyes to
adjust to the dim interior. It smelled vaguely like the
pubs back home, full of cigar and pipe smoke, the
rich, warm odor of ale and the sharper tang of whiskey. Flowing through the open back door at the end
of the bar came the acrid stink of piss from the out-
door jakes. Except for the large painting of the naked
lassie hanging behind the bar, which no pub in his
experience could have afforded, it was fairly familiar.

The patrons were slightly less disreputable-
looking than the ones at the Rose and Anchor in
Queenstown, so he crossed the floor to the bar.

"Sure, and after she had her way she wanted to
have another go, and me dead from her efforts.
Dead, I swear to ye, Jack. She brought me back.
She could do things to a man that would make his

eyes roll back in his head. My heart stopped entirely at least twice, it did!" The storyteller, a big, broad-shouldered man with carroty hair, sucked down the entire contents of his ale mug in one gulp, then dragged his forearm across his mouth. He shook his head regretfully. "I do miss that old girl. She was even more entertainin' than her daughter."

"Ah, Flanagan, if I wouldn't go broke, I'd give you free ale just to hear your stories," Jack, the barkeep said, laughing. "Your heart stopped. Har-har!"

"So it did! Maybe it was three times, at that!"

In a land where even English sounded like a foreign language, Aidan's ears immediately picked up the welcome sound of a homegrown voice.

"And what will yours be?" Jack asked him, still smiling over the other man's story.

"I'll have what he's having," he replied and nodded at the burly Irishman.

Flanagan looked at Aidan. "I take it ye're not from these parts."

"Nor you—I can understand your speech."

The other man gave a hearty bark of laughter. "Aye, I know what ye mean. I'm Colm Flanagan, most recently from Philadelphia."

"Aidan O'Rourke. I've just come from County Cork with my wife." He put out his hand, which Flanagan wrung in his own beefy paw.

"County Cork, is it now? Well, keep your valuables safe because there be Yankee tricksters in every port, eager to take severe advantage of the newly come."

Aidan nodded. Charles Morton had told him the selfsame thing. "As I've heard."

"I'm from Strokestown in County Roscommon meself, but I haven't seen it these eight years past."

"Ah, ye'd have left during the famine, then." Aidan took a big sip of the ale put in front of him.

"Aye. Eighteen-forty-seven was a terrible year, you might remember. My family were tenants of Major Denis Mahon."

Fascinated, Aidan leaned forward a bit. "We heard he was a tyrant, banishing his tenants on those coffin ships. Worse than Cromwell, it was said, and that he got what he deserved when he was shot dead in his own carriage."

Flanagan shrugged philosophically. "He was in a position I wouldn't wish on the devil himself. The estate was thirty thousand pounds in debt when it came to him, and the rents were three years in arrears. Then the potato *miadh* struck and the famine followed. He offered passage to Canada to any tenant who would give up his wee patch of land. So my brothers and I, we said all right. The major chartered two ships and both of them lost a lot of passengers to typhus by the time we reached Quebec. My brothers were among them. But I lived. Maybe I wouldn't have if Mahon hadn't given me the chance to leave." He sounded glad to have gone.

"Don't ye miss Ireland?"

The big man gave him a half-smile that Aidan knew well; he'd seen it, at one time or another, on nearly every Irish face he'd ever known. It reflected heartsore regret and the reality of life. "That I do, boyo, every one of my days, just like I miss my sainted mam. But I know I'll not see either of them again in this life."

Aidan was silent for a moment, realizing that Colm Flanagan spoke for him as well, and for God knew how many other Irishmen. He drained his ale.

"So ye came to Philadelphia and then New Orleans, and you've been here all these years?" Aidan signaled the barkeep to bring two more pints.

"Oh, Jaysus, no. I've been to New York, Boston, Providence, Newport—all up and down the East Coast. I dug ditches, I worked on docks and in factories and on the railroads. But the work— harder than anything at home, mind—was never steady. And ye take your life in your hands in most cases. The bosses aren't too choosy about putting their workers in dangerous jobs. There are always others eager to take a dead man's place. I've seen men worked to death, killed in accidents and by sickness. I gave up on those cities and came down here, but I've got a plan for something better. Something different altogether." He lifted the mug brought by the barkeep and nodded at Aidan. "Thank you. In the name of Erin."

Aidan lifted his mug as well. "Name of Erin," he intoned and took a long swallow of ale. "Is there no solid work up north?"

"Aye, lad, there's work, but the pay is bad, the hours longer than ye can imagine, and now we've a new enemy in America." Flanagan looked around the barroom, and his voice dropped to a near whisper. "The Know-Nothings."

"Eh? No what?"

"It's a political party. They're called Know-Nothings because they operate in secret against immigrants, and most especially Catholics. Hate us, they surely do. They got the name since when they're asked about their evil doings, they claim to know nothing. They've murdered Irishmen and destroyed churches. Nobody stops them."

Aidan stared at him.

"Not what ye'd heard back home, aye?" Flanagan's chuckle was grim. "You probably got letters from America, or knew someone who did, who said this is the land of milk and honey, or maybe tea and whiskey. Food galore, enough to make a man fat, gorgeous houses, and two-three sets of clothes."

It was Danny Leary's letter almost to the word, the one Aidan had told Farrell about the night before they sailed. No, Flanagan's account wasn't what he'd heard. He could only shake his head. "Are they starving in America, too?"

"No, no, all those things are here—*miles* of

good crops, herds of cattle, flocks of sheep and chickens—this *is* a place of plenty. But Irishmen might only see it all going to someone else. The poor souls get here, most of them can't read or write, some of them can speak only Irish, they don't know how to do anything but work the land. The priests and politicians here urge them to settle on farms, but none can afford that. So they end up sweeping floors in places like this—" He gestured around the barroom. "Or turning their lungs black in the coal mines, or digging canals. Sometimes they do work that plantation owners won't risk their slaves to do. Our women, if they're lucky enough, and if ye can call it luck, go to work in rich men's homes as servants or cooks. Otherwise they toil in the textile mills, breathing in lint, and God keep them from burning to death if the places catch fire. There's nothing wrong with hard work, but a man ought to be paid for what he does, and not have to risk his life in the doing. It's a disgrace, so it is."

By this time, Aidan had begun to regret that he'd met Colm Flanagan. He felt as if someone had plunged a knife into his heart and twisted the haft. If what the man said was true, his life and Farrell's would be no better than it had been in Ireland. It sounded as if no one was willing to prevent the abominations he described, and because this was America, it made the situation that much worse. Aidan wondered what he was going to do, after he'd made Farrell all those grand promises. Surely, given the man's talent for yarn-spinning, he must be exaggerating.

Flanagan must have seen the disillusionment in Aidan's face. "Aye, things aren't what we expected—life isn't so rosy and the streets aren't gold paved. But there are opportunities." He leaned close again, as if he were about to reveal a treasured secret. "For myself, I'm going to try my luck with a new enterprise I've learned of in the Oregon Territory near the Pacific Ocean. A man with enough money to make the trip and the grit to carve a life out of the wilderness could prosper."

He went on to tell Aidan the fantastic story that a man could settle on one hundred sixty acres and claim it as his own. All he had to do was build a house and work the place for a couple of years. And if he had a wife, she could acquire the same size parcel in her own name.

"And no one there will tell ye that you can't work because you're Irish or because you're Catholic or any of that blather. It's wide open land, free for the taking."

"*Free?*" Aidan repeated. "Nothing is free in this life. Someone always has their hand out to be paid."

"That's the grand part of this, lad. The American government is eager to expand the country and settle the West. They passed an act to give away

land through the end of this year." Flanagan drained
his ale mug. "So if you've a mind to go, you'd best
get on with it." He glanced at the wall clock and
grimaced. "Christ, I've got to get down to the docks
and see if I can pick up a job for a day or two."
He straightened away from the bar and put out his
hand to Aidan again. "It's been a pleasure, Aidan
O'Rourke. Good luck to ye, and if you decide to
go to Oregon, maybe we'll meet again."

Aidan watched him leave, then paid his bill.
What Flanagan had told him about the Oregon Territory sounded too good to be true. He intended to
find out if it was.

"You want to travel two thousand miles west? Past
the bounds of civilization and into the domain of
naked savages, God help us! You've been gone all
day and now ye come back here, smelling like the
floor of a pub to tell me this? And how will we be
getting there, Mr. O'Rourke?"

Farrell stood with her hands on her hips and
faced him across the width of the rug in their hotel
room. She knew she probably sounded like a scold,
but Aidan's news was so astonishing, so *alarming,*
she couldn't help herself. Every scheme he had
dreamed up beginning with that night in Clare's
cottage was more crackbrained than the next. Their
weeks at sea, the misery, the discomfort, the danger
that they had endured came washing over her. Here

they had just landed and he was talking about going farther still. "And what happened to the plan of going to New York or Boston or—or somewhere closer, if I may ask?"

Patiently, Aidan went on to repeat the story of his chance meeting with Colm Flanagan. "After that I nosed around a bit—yes, in pubs—asking questions to confirm everything he'd told me. Most of it was true, including the bad things. We don't want to go to a place where we're treated like dirt again, and kill ourselves working just to barely survive. There's land out west, miles and miles of it, that no one owns." He scratched at an insect bite on his jaw. This semitropical climate was like Eden to the beasts. "And from what I could learn, people have been going to Oregon in droves, following a path they call the Oregon Trail. It might be hard at the beginning but we'd settle in soon enough. We'll grow acres of crops and work the land—it'll be heaven."

"But Holy Mother, it's too far away entirely!"

He held out his hands in an expression of exasperation. "Too far away—from what, I ask ye? From New Orleans? This town isn't home to us. From New York, a place we've never even seen and have no attachment to?"

His question forced her to admit her true fear. She lowered her chin and stared at the worn pattern on the rug. When she answered, her voice was as small as a girl's. "It's too far away from Ireland."

A moment of silence passed and she looked up at him. She saw the echo of her regret in his eyes, that they would never see their homeland again.

At last he replied, "Ah, little red one, Ireland is always with us. Here"—he pointed to his temple— "and here," and he put his hand over his heart. "It will never matter how many miles we travel. So it's settled, then. We'll go to the Oregon Territory."

His pronouncement infuriated her. She wasn't asked if she wanted to go or how she felt about the decision. He simply told her they were going. The very same kind of decree had sent her across the Atlantic. Her brows met over the bridge of her nose.

"I didn't want to come to America in the first place, but ye kept telling me we'll have a better life, and I began to believe you. Well, we're here now and it still isn't good enough for you. I'm sick of traveling. I just want to light someplace, and I don't see why we have to go all the way to the *damned* Pacific Ocean to do it! What will be next? China? I won't go, I'm telling you. I won't."

He took a step back, as if she'd slapped him. Her arms were rigid at her sides and her hands closed into fists. The sudden silence in the room was broken only by the raspy sound of their breathing. The vehemence of Farrell's outburst surprised even her. She was not a retiring creature, but neither was she given to losing her temper.

She let her hands relax, but every other muscle was locked with worry and anger. "Do you even care about what I want? Can ye not understand how it feels to be ordered about like a dog?" she asked, more quietly.

"I do understand, and I don't mean to give you orders." He came close again and she could smell the scent of clean sweat, and the faintest whiff of wood smoke and porter. "But I also remember what it feels like to starve, and so do you. Think, girl, just think." He gripped her arms in his big hands, his face alight with the passion of a man aching for freedom. "Wild game and fish without end, wide-open land, never plowed once, they say, begging to be planted and *free for the taking*. The O'Rourkes will finally own land again. Farrell, lass, how can we not go?"

Her shoulders sagged under his touch but she did not respond.

"Will ye think on it, at least?" he implored. His expression was so appealing, so full of hope, she couldn't refuse him outright. Liam had once told her that Aidan's chief failing was not his rebelliousness or his passion. It was hope. Hope, Liam had said, and Aidan's certainty that he could make his dreams come true would bring him the most trouble and break his heart. That a man ought to accept his lot in life and make the best of it had been Liam's opinion.

"Aye, I'll think on it," she replied glumly, and felt as if she were agreeing to think about spending a year in jail.

"Farrell, will ye get up and come to see Mrs. Kinealy, then? She's askin' for you."

It was her mother's voice Farrell heard, so clear and bright, not weak from hunger and sickness. Although she couldn't see her, Farrell knew she was a young woman again, and she herself was but twelve years old.

"I'm coming, Mam," she called and ran to the front door of their cottage to see her mother and greet the neighbor. Friendly Mrs. Kinealy, she was the poorest of the poor, and everyone loved her. Through the open front door, though, all Farrell could see was a gray dusk, as if the world had taken its last breath. The trees were tall, leafless skeletons, rattling their limbs in the cold wind like dry bones picked clean. Everything was gray and white—all color had drained away.

"Farrell, are ye coming?"

She hurried down the road, past the empty cottages, past the destroyed, diseased potato gardens, toward the sound of her mother's voice, but she couldn't see her. "Where are you, Mam?"

"Just here, lass, here with Mrs. Kinealy. Come along, now, we're waiting for you."

She rounded a fallen tree and saw her mother. She was dressed in rags and she was as gray as the landscape. "Say good morning to Mrs. Kinealy, will ye?"

There, beside her mother, stood a dog that looked just as skeletal as the trees. In its slavering jaws was a woman's head, hanging from its teeth by her hair. The head's eyes opened and looked at Farrell.

"Mrs. Kinealy!"

"God love ye, lass. I've come to a bad end, I have. We all starved, me, your mother, your father and brothers. All of us. Don't let it happen to you. Don't you come to a bad end, you and your man."

Farrell tried to run but her feet would not move. The foul-smelling, plague-infested soil seemed to be sucking her down. She tried to scream, but could make no sound. She tried to look away, but her eyes would not do anything but stare at the dead woman's talking head, gray and collapsed and shriveled.

Farrell sat bolt upright in bed and heard a shrill cry that came from her own mouth.

"Farrell! Whisht, wee *céadsearc*! Ye're dreaming!" Aidan scrambled onto the bed beside her, fumbling for a match and trying to comfort her at the same time. "It's only a dream." He struck the match and held it to the candle on the table beside the bed. Light poured over them and she recognized the hotel room. This wasn't Skibbereen. It was New Orleans, in America.

"Oh, God, Aidan!" She buried her face against his chest, grateful for its solid strength. His arms enclosed her and she cried, terrified and heartbroken.

"It was real, so *real*!" she gasped between sobs.

"No, lass, it wasn't. It was only a bad dream sent by the fey people to trouble you, that's all."

She pulled away and looked up at him. "No! It was Mrs. Kinealy! And she talked to me, right there, hanging from the dog's mouth."

His eyes widened, and he drew her back into his embrace. "Jesus Christ," he muttered, resting his cheek against her head.

Mary Kinealy had died during the worst days of the famine that had ravaged the countryside. People were dying every week in their cottages. Often, days passed before they were found. Mary had been one of those unfortunates, but a worse fate awaited her. After she was buried in a hastily scraped-out grave, a dog that had as yet escaped capture for someone's stew pot had dug her up. Farrell had seen it running through the *clachan* dragging

Mary's head by her hair, and she chased after it, her empty stomach churning with bile as the dog growled at her around the gruesome prize it held in its teeth. She'd screamed for Liam to help and it had taken a half-dozen men to corner the dog, wild and vicious with hunger. At last Aidan managed to come up from behind and fell the beast with a rock, then reclaim poor Mrs. Kinealy's head for burial. Everyone who could come out to see the commotion was screaming and wailing, especially the children.

The nightmare had plagued her often, especially during the blackest days of the famine. She always associated the memory with one thing—hunger. Now it had a new twist. Now Mary warned her to save herself and Aidan too.

They sat entwined and quiet for a few moments, and Farrell realized how natural and comforting it felt to lie in his arms.

"What did Mary tell ye?" he asked at last.

Her sobs had slowed to intermittent, watery hitches of breath. She knew they were both Irish enough to believe in signs and messages from beyond the grave.

"She said she came to a b-bad end and that I shouldn't l-let it happen to us."

"Us?"

"Aye, you and me."

"What meaning do ye take from that?" He dried

her face with the hem of the thin sheet.

Farrell sighed and glanced past his shoulder at the candle flame. What else could Mary have meant? "I think we're supposed to go to Oregon."

Aidan tipped up her chin and she saw that glimmer of hope again. "Are ye sure?"

"Yes, I'm sure. God help us, I don't want to go, that's for certain. But neither do I want us to suffer more than we did in Ireland."

He grinned. "Farrell, ye're a hell of a woman, ye know. There's a lot of Saint Brigit in you. Smart, courageous—" He lowered his mouth to hers. The kiss was spontaneous and tender, but electricity arced between them. She drew back to look at him and she realized that he was dressed in only his drawers. That broad, strong chest she had cried her tears upon was bare except for the dark hair growing in a T, from nipple to nipple and down the center of his belly. He lay down beside her, taking her into his arms to kiss her again, more deeply. His tongue grazed hers, warm and slick, and he nibbled at her lower lip. One hand slid around from her back to her ribs to cover her breast. His touch was like fire and ice, surging through her in shimmering waves of hot and cold. Every nerve was alive under her skin. How he did that to her she didn't know, but his kisses always melted her reluctance, as if a fleeting insanity overtook her, blocking out her objection that he was not the one she loved. He worked open the buttons of her night-gown and brushed the fold between her breast and her ribs. Gooseflesh erupted all over her body.

Through the thin sheet and her thinner night-gown, she felt his hipbone press against her thigh. Then she realized that it wasn't his hip at all, hot and insistent and rubbing against her leg. This frank evidence of his manhood made Farrell's blood course through her body like a flood, and her memories of Liam faded to a dim ghost.

Then a groan sounded in his throat and he pulled back. He looked at her and in his face she saw not only desire but an odd, frustrated regret that she didn't understand at all.

"Go to sleep, little red one," he said, his voice thick and tight. "I'll be here if Mary Kinealy comes back." He left her side and returned to his chair, leaving Farrell aroused, confused, and lonely.

Chapter Nine

ALTHOUGH Farrell had agreed to go to Oregon, how Aidan and she would get there, and how they would pay for the trip, were still unanswered questions.

"All we need is the money," he said the next morning over rashers and biscuits at La Maison Blanc. He might as well have said, "All we need is the moon and maybe some stars, too." He had enough to pay for a few more days in the hotel, a little food, and nothing else. Money—it had always been his problem and he was thoroughly fed up with it. He vowed to himself that when they got to Oregon, he'd make the most of the opportunity and wring success from fate.

"How much do we need?" Farrell asked, buttering a flaky biscuit. She looked tired, he thought. He didn't believe either of them had slept well since leaving Ireland. Shipboard conditions had not contributed to restfulness, and now, even though they had a hotel room, the tension and uncertainty between them was no help at all.

"I'm not sure. I've asked around—people who go by wagon on the Oregon Trail need about one thousand American dollars for a wagon, a team of oxen, and a supply list that's longer than the number of saints on the calendar."

"How much is that, a thousand dollars?"

He poked at a strip of bacon on his plate. "About two hundred pounds."

She stared at him. "Two hundred pounds! Where in heaven or hell will we get that kind of money?" she whispered urgently.

He could hardly credit the amount himself. He didn't think he'd ever seen more than a few pounds in his whole life, and doubted that Farrell had, either. "There's another way. We can go by stagecoach. It's much faster and not as dear."

"That's *good,* isn't it?" She took a bite of the biscuit.

"Aye, but we won't have anything when we get to Oregon. That's the problem. People live in their wagons until they can get their cottages built. Oh, here they call them cabins."

He explained the advantages and liabilities while Farrell savored her tea. Going by wagon was a hard trip.

"Hah! Harder than that ocean voyage?"

"Probably, though it's difficult to credit. I'm told that the women end up walking beside the wagons because the ride is so rough, they get sick and bruised from bouncing around. And the wagons move so slowly, they have no trouble keeping up.

There are rivers to cross, sometimes the wagons have to be hauled up cliffsides because there's no road. It takes about five or six months to get there."

Farrell made a sour face and pushed away her teacup on the small tabletop. "Are ye sure we can't go to New York or Wilmington? Holy Mother, maybe we should stay right here!"

"That's not what Mary Kinealy told ye."

She sat back in her chair and looked at her lap, her cheeks filled with roses again. "No, it wasn't."

"That's why I was thinking the stagecoach might be the better of the two. We have no personal possessions to transport, as many people do who are going West, and it would cost less, about two hundred dollars apiece. We'd have to take a boat up the Mississippi to St. Louis and get the coach there. Then it would take about four or five weeks to reach Oregon."

"But we don't have four hundred dollars, either."

He smiled. "I think I can remedy that."

Aidan delivered Farrell back to the door of their hotel room. "Where are you off to?"

"I've got to find the money for our fares."

"And where would you be looking for that?"

"At the end of a leprechaun's rainbow," he replied, tweaking her chin.

She gave him a look. "Leprechaun, of course.

Ye're headed off to play cards again, aren't you? Your brothers never gambled. Clare wouldn't have put up with it from Tommy, and it wasn't Liam's way. It's as bad as thievery."

He opened the door and ushered her into the room. "Farrell, it's not. I don't know how to do anything but farm. Even if I found work here, breaking my back on the docks, or hauling ale barrels in a pub, it would take years to earn that kind of money. We don't have years. We have just a few months to get to Oregon to take advantage of that land offer."

"Ye could lose everything we have."

"Maybe. But I won't. I'll win and we'll be on our way. At any rate, you're not married to Tommy." He gave her a sharp look. "Or to Liam. You're *my* wife, aye?" His words and their tone left no room for doubt.

She nodded stiffly. "Go, then." As if she could stop him, she thought.

"I'll be back in a few hours." He stepped into the hallway and closed the door behind him.

Farrell went to the bed and flopped in a huff that made the springs screech like a banshee. She reached into her pocket for her familiar talisman, her carved figure of Brigit. Her rosary had been left behind in Queenstown and she hadn't heard a proper mass since her last Sunday in Skibbereen. It seemed wrong to pray for a man to succeed at gambling, but beyond asking for the health and safety of her people back home, there was little else she could do.

Turning, she dropped to the floor to kneel beside the bed. At first, it wasn't formal prayers she sent heavenward, but the same one, over and over. "God, please look after the family, and please give Aidan a chance. I know he'll manage if he just has the chance." Raised as she'd been to revere tradition, though, the murmured pleas soon seemed inadequate, and she resorted to praying the rosary, counting her fingers for the beads she didn't have. She knew the Mysteries by heart, and it was easy enough to pretend she held her mother's rosary in her hands.

She remained beside the bed on her knees, her hands folded on the mattress. She knew Aidan was right—the opportunity in the Oregon Territory was too good to pass up. She saw his logic and understood his fervor. It would be a bold undertaking, but in her heart she felt that if anyone could make a success of this venture, it was Aidan. And though she might not love him, she was strong enough to follow him to the edge of the earth.

What choice did she have?

But in fact, did she really want anything else? Rising to her feet, she went to the window and looked out at the street below. There was no denying that she had begun to feel an attraction to him, and her heart was at war with the fact. True, he wasn't the quiet, pensive man she'd believed she'd have in Liam, and a feeling of disloyalty rose in her when she thought about the brother she'd left behind. But Aidan was a doer. He didn't wait for fate to deliver his lot. He went out and tried to bend fate to his will.

And then there was that other part of him. She felt her cheeks burn even now, and her heartbeat quickened as she recalled his hands and lips on her last night, and how she, like softened candle wax under his touch, had warmed and molded herself to him. This was the man that the girls had whispered about, the hot-blooded man with hotter hands, the one whom Father Joseph had chided for his wanton ways. She had come so close to giving herself to him, it frightened her. Yet he'd pulled away from her again. Too shy to ask questions, she had no idea what had stopped him.

Morning drifted into afternoon, and Farrell ate the lunch that she'd ordered with her breakfast. The café proprietor had sliced roast beef and put it between two crusty pieces of bread dressed with a tart and creamy French sauce she called *mayonnaise*. Then she'd wrapped up the whole business in a napkin.

The hours drifted past and still Aidan didn't return.

Silly, fickle woman, she told herself. She had

resented his inescapable presence on the *Mary Fiona*. Now she disliked being separated from him almost as much.

Almost, but not quite.

Aidan sat at a large round table in the Lass of Killarney. Seated with him were three other men, all waiting for the dealer to give them new cards. In the center of the table was amassed a small fortune of silver and gold coins. It held every cent Aidan owned and had won, save the gold dollar in front of him and a half-eagle in his pocket. The combined odors of cigar smoke, ale, whiskey, unwashed laborers drinking their pints, and a greasy stew gurgling on the stove behind the bar wafted around him and lingered in the corners like the smell of something newly dead. Meanwhile, the nude in the painting that hung behind the bar—the Lass of Killarney, herself, it was said—viewed the proceedings with a fixed, bashful smile.

Aidan had been here all day, as various players sat in and dropped out. Early on, his cash had dwindled to a dangerous low, the result of bad hand after bad hand. But two hours ago, things had begun to turn around. Now, as the evening sun waned, the battle—and he saw it as such—had come down to himself and these other contenders. He faced a plantation overseer, in town on business for his employer, a stonemason who built crypts in St. Louis

Cemetery, and the current dealer, a stevedore from the docks. Whiskey flowed freely. Some of his opponents held their liquor better than others. One or two had made reckless wagers that would enrich the winner. For his part, Aidan counted himself lucky that he'd inherited a steady head.

His stomach was in a knot as tight as any fist he'd ever made. It wasn't easy, but he made every effort to maintain a nonchalant countenance. A prize of almost six hundred dollars was riding on the next turn of the card. A lot of the game had to do with luck, he knew. But skill and judgment were involved as well, in watching men's faces, in picking up the clues of a bluff. It was nerve-wracking and he wouldn't want to earn a living this way, but if he could win his dream, it all would have been worth it. If he lost . . . Well, he couldn't think about that now. He didn't dare.

He picked up his new cards and watched the top left corners of the cards as he opened them like a peacock's tail. Ten, nine, a six, and a pair of treys. He drew a very careful breath. It was a lamentable hand, a nearly worthless hand, and his heart thumped so hard, it fair pummeled his ribs. There was but one thing to do.

When the call for bets went around again, all but the stonemason and he were still in the game. The man stared at Aidan over his cards. It was an intense gaze, meant either to shake him or make him reveal something about his hand. Aidan's expression did not change. "I'm in for another dollar," the stonemason said at last, and a coin clinked onto the pile.

"I'll match that dollar of yours," Aidan replied, giving what he hoped was a good show of unconcern. "And raise it five more." With a silent prayer to Saint Jude, for if ever there was a desperate situation this was it, he added his last six dollars to the center of the table.

An endless, tense moment followed while his opponent tried again to size him up, and failed.

"Bah! Have it all then, you goddamned greedy bastard!" he growled at last, throwing in his cards.

Shivers of relief and gratitude sluiced through Aidan as he pulled the winnings toward him. Visions of vast, fertile acres flashed through his brain, and beside him, sharing it all, was a redheaded spitfire of a woman.

But general grumbling arose among the most recent losers who'd stayed to watch the outcome, and he could easily imagine the situation turning altogether ugly.

He was a stranger, an outsider here among many people who knew each other. Men at the bar and at other tables fell silent and turned their attention to him, plainly waiting to see what would happen next.

Realizing he might not even get out the door,

much less back to the safety of the hotel, Aidan called to the barkeep, "Jack! Jack, a bottle of your best whiskey to each of these fine gentlemen, with my compliments." After tucking the money away, he rose and turned to them. "My thanks to ye for a grand evening, and for being such entirely grand lads yourselves."

The gesture had the desired effect, and the grousing diminished to grudging but sincere murmurs of thanks.

Jack arrived at the table with five bottles of whiskey, including one for Aidan, and five glasses. Aidan slipped him his payment, and after the bottles were uncorked and drinks poured he said, "Sure and a toast to you fine boys. May ye be in heaven half an hour before the divil knows you're dead."

Good-natured chuckles rolled over the group, and they downed their drinks in one gulp. The liquor, heavy and full-bodied, tasted almost as good to Aidan as Sean O'Rourke's poteen.

"When my wife finds out I lost me pay again, she'll hang me hide on the front door," the stevedore observed with a grim face.

"If you drink enough of this, you won't remember a thing about it," the stonemason replied. This time the laughter was more hearty, and Aidan breathed a quiet sigh of relief. He might get out of here alive yet. Only the plantation overseer remained unsmiling and unimpressed.

"Ye're all right, O'Rourke, for a newcomer. Which county do ye hail from?" the stevedore asked.

"From Skibbereen in County Cork."

"And is a murdering mick from Skibbereen man enough to buy a drink for his better?" a voice called from a corner table.

A silence as profound as a grave's fell upon the Lass of Killarney, and all heads turned toward the man who had posed the insult.

Slowly, Aidan turned as well, just as Noel Cardwell rose from his chair. He could scarcely believe his eyes, so remote had seemed the possibility of ever seeing his old landlord again. But there he was, resplendent in his fine clothes and looking so out of place in this workingman's pub, Aidan wondered how he had dared to venture inside. It had to have been either stupidity or unshakable arrogance that brought him here. And maybe they were one and the same. The place was filled with Irish and other men who had fled to America to escape tyrannical governments or masters.

"My *better*?" Aidan repeated, his voice as cold and clear as an Atlantic-borne wind.

The low grumbling began again and this time, angry looks were cast at Noel, who bore little resemblance to the languid, spoiled landlord's son Aidan had known in Ireland.

"I don't drink with any man who thinks he's

better than everyone else. And I surely won't pay for such an intolerable dishonor," Aidan said. Apparently, he wasn't the only one here to whom the thought had occurred.

Noel drew himself up to his full height, which still put the top of his head at Aidan's eye level, and strolled to the table. "I've come to take you back to answer for the murder you committed."

"It was no murder, ye lyin' scum. It was an accident and you know it. Even my wife has forgiven me for the death of her brother." For a moment, Noel's haughty mask slipped and he saw behind it a howling lust at the mention of Farrell. Jesus God, he thought, she was in danger as well. A raging desire boiled up inside Aidan, the same one that had made him take on Michael Kirwan and his hired ruffians, a desire that urged him to plant his fist squarely in the middle of Cardwell's smug face.

Around him, the grumbling grew into a hum of angry voices. Only the sullen plantation overseer demurred. "You don't know how things work down here, do you?" he said to Aidan. "When the master speaks, you jump."

From the corner of his eye, Aidan saw the bartender quickly moving glasses and bottles from the back bar to cupboards below. Aidan hadn't really wanted anything to do with a man who made his living ordering slaves about, but if he could take

the bastard's money and put it to better use, he'd
do it.

"I have no master, at least not on this earth, and
never will again in this life."

"By God, if you worked for me, I'd have you
whipped for your impertinence," the overseer said,
full of Aidan's whiskey and his own foolhardy im-
portance.

That was the last remark the man made. A fist
flew and connected with his face, smashing his
nose, and the fight was on. Chairs and tables were
overturned, sending glasses, mugs, and alcohol in
all directions. As strong as was his desire to stay
and finish off the overseer and Noel Cardwell himself, Aidan knew that this was his best chance to
escape. To carry six hundred dollars through the
streets of New Orleans was a risky proposition, and
right now, getting out of here was more important
than knocking Cardwell on his arse.

If this man he'd known as a pampered, over-
dressed peacock had developed enough ambition
and energy to follow Aidan and Farrell all the way
to America, he couldn't take any chances.

They had to get away. Tonight.

Noel looked around at the distasteful wreckage of
the pub where he'd endeavored, and rightly so, to
corner Aidan O'Rourke. The ne'er-do-well Irish
scum had always been known to like a good fight,

and Noel had retreated to his corner, expecting some burly oaf to do him the favor of taking O'Rourke down. Or at least to see him arrested by the constables for disorderly conduct. But no constables or police arrived, and when the brawl began to wane, he realized that the subject of his search was not even present. He stood and looked around the small pub. Men staggered to their feet, nursing split lips, black eyes, broken noses, and other injuries, but Aidan O'Rourke was not among them.

Damn it all. The benighted bog-trotter had slipped away during all the commotion.

Cardwell thumped a fist on the table. O'Rourke had gotten away from him again, and therefore, so had Farrell Kirwan. Noel had made the grueling trip from Queenstown across the ocean, a miserable journey during which he'd been confined to his quarters with unrelenting mal de mer, made worse by an intolerably proud and righteous sea captain who barely acknowledged him. Then, as if that weren't insult enough, he'd finally arrived in this hot, swampy city only to be forced to frequent every low-end pub in town in search of his quarry. Now, after at last locating O'Rourke, he'd sat here for hours, watching the proceedings from a dark corner, waiting for the right moment to confront him, suffering the association of men who weren't fit to shine his boots, only to have O'Rourke vanish like a wisp of smoke.

Goddamn it all. Noel thumped the table again.

As he sat there, one of the men O'Rourke had gambled with approached the table, holding a white handkerchief to his face. His nose was misshapen and swollen, and his shirtfront bore the bloody evidence of its recent injury. "Beg pardon, sir."

"Whatever do *you* want?" Noel asked, tired, and offended by the man's presence. Across the room, the bartender had begun righting tables and sweeping up broken glass.

"If you're looking for O'Rourke, sir, I know where he is."

Noel looked up. "Oh, *do* you."

"Yes, I know several things that might be useful to you."

Noel pushed out a chair with his boot. "Sit down, then." The man sat. "And you are?"

"The name's Seth Fitch. I'm the overseer at Magnolia Grove plantation."

"Ah, yes, of course. I am Lord Cardwell." It wasn't exactly true, yet, but it would be eventually. That the man practically genuflected upon hearing the title was most gratifying. Instantly, Noel sensed a kindred spirit in Fitch. Or at least one who recognized the difference between the classes and the natural order of things. Little more than a greasy yeoman himself, at least Fitch was a notch above the other riffraff in this place. Plus, he obviously held Noel in proper esteem, and it salved Noel's ego after the earlier scene with O'Rourke. He pushed his bottle of brandy and a glass across the table to the man. Fitch nodded and poured himself a healthy measure.

"It's a damnable state of affairs when a man of your position is assaulted by baseborn thugs," Noel said with mock sympathy.

"These foreigners come to America, believing that cock-and-bull story about equality. And they expect to be treated so." He snuffled noisily through his broken nose, which was crusted with dark, dried blood. Gingerly, he poked a handkerchief-wrapped finger into each nostril, bringing out more blood. Noel averted his gaze from the disgusting display.

"You say you know where I can find Aidan O'Rourke?" he prodded, eager to move the conversation along and be done with this doughy-looking oaf with a nose like a boiled, squashed beet.

"While we were playing cards, he said he's staying at the Grand View Hotel. It's just down the street."

Noel nodded. He'd passed it during his odyssey to the various pubs.

"You say you know other things about him?"

Now Fitch turned coy. "I do."

God, how much would it cost him to find out, Noel wondered, and would the information be accurate? Doing his own investigating was tedious. It required him to visit places he wouldn't see even in his nightmares. Only one thing kept him from turning for home, regardless of his father's edict, and that was Noel's ultimate prize: Farrell Kirwan. He craved her in a way he'd never wanted anything or anyone before. He *had* to have her. But if he could hire someone to do the dirty end of this job, he certainly would.

Noel clenched his jaw. If he could hire someone . . .

Suddenly an idea came to him.

"Fitch, how would you like to work for me? I could use a good man like you, someone who knows the city. And now you know what O'Rourke looks like, as well, which would give you a great advantage. You're not married, are you?"

"Well, not exactly. I have a pretty little slave gal, Silky, who keeps house for me, and, well, you know."

Noel liked the way these ignorant colonials thought. Farrell Kirwan would have no recourse in a place such as this when she came to know the weight of her master's hand. She would have to do as he commanded. The pictures that flashed through Noel's mind heated his blood and made him shift on his chair.

"Perfect, then. You are a free agent, so to speak."

The man goggled at him. "I don't know, your lordship, I've been with Mr. Thibodeaux, the owner, for six years. I don't know that he could replace me. My job overseeing the slaves and the plantation is very important."

Noel refrained from pointing out that anyone, absolutely *anyone,* could be replaced, from kings to chimney sweeps. "Yes, yes, I'm sure it's an important position." He leaned a bit closer and lowered his voice to a confidential tone. "But what if I told you I'll double whatever he pays you, and give you bonuses for special assignments?"

Fitch snuffled again and swallowed. "What did this O'Rourke do that you want him so bad?"

Noel sat back and tapped the brandy cork on the tabletop. "A fair enough question, Fitch. I'm the owner of a large estate in County Cork in Ireland."

"Oh!" Fitch leaned closer and whispered in a confidential tone, "That's where O'Rourke said he was from."

Hoping that Fitch was smarter than he seemed, Noel nudged away second thoughts about his employment offer and continued. "Yes, I know where he's from. On that estate, I have tenant farmers who pay rent. At least they're supposed to pay, but the lazy bog-trotters are always whining about failed crops and being hungry." Noel sniffed. "Naturally, I don't deal with them directly."

"Naturally, sir."

"I hire a rent agent who collects the money and keeps track of the accounts. If a tenant doesn't pay three months in a row, he and his family are evicted. It's a harsh system, I suppose," he threw in regretfully, "but I'm not running a charity. At any rate, when the rent agent went to evict Aidan O'Rourke's family, O'Rourke killed the poor man, right there in the yard before a dozen witnesses. Then off he ran in the middle of the night and boarded a ship for America. I have followed him all this way to bring him back to pay for his crime. Murder is not countenanced in Great Britain."

"Well, I can tell you they don't like it here, either, your lordship."

The blatant toadying might get tiresome later on—but then again, maybe not. Right now, it soothed Noel's vanity like the strokes of a warm, soft hand. "Then what do you say, Fitch? Will you help me bring this killer to justice, and stick with the job until it's done, however it must be finished?"

"Double my current pay, your lordship?" the man reaffirmed.

"With bonuses."

"I'm your man, sir." Fitch extended a hand with dried blood on it. Noel hesitated for only a heartbeat, then shook it.

CHAPTER TEN

"FARRELL! Wake up, for God's sake!"

Farrell did wake up to feel Aidan's hand shaking her shoulder, none too gently. Rudely jerked from a sound sleep, she was startled and disoriented. She sat up, and saw him moving around the room, grabbing their belongings to stuff into a burlap bag she'd never seen before.

"God, what's wrong now?"

"We've got to leave this place."

"What, tonight?"

"*Right now.* Get out of the bed, will ye?"

She had no idea what time it was, but she clambered out, her hair falling around her in long, loose strands because she'd fallen asleep before she could braid it. "What's happened? Is there a fire?"

"Cardwell is here in New Orleans. Just down the street at the Lass of Killarney."

Her heart began thundering in her chest and her throat seemed so dry, she couldn't swallow. "Oh, dear God, are you sure?"

"I talked to him face to face. He says he intends to bring me back to Ireland for murder." He looked around the room, obviously searching for anything else that might belong to them. Turning back to her he demanded, "Christ, aren't ye dressed yet? We've got to go!" Worry had drained the color from his face, and that frightened her even more. Aidan never *looked* worried.

She made frantic grabs for her clothes. "Yes, but where to?"

"Another hotel for the night, maybe. Then before daybreak, we'll slip off to catch a boat upriver to St. Louis. There's a stagecoach station up there that can take us west."

"Have we got the money to go?" She turned her back to him and shimmied into the dress she'd worn earlier.

"I've got six hundred dollars. Enough to get us there and give us a little start."

"Six hundred!" The amount was almost more than she could conceive. "Did you steal it?"

He spun her around, and she saw true anger in his features. "Damn it, woman, have a little faith in me, will ye please? I won that money in a card game, and if you're thinking it was just a romp across a field, think again. It was hard, gut-twisting work, and dangerous to boot. Men don't *like* losing that much. Even before Cardwell appeared, I was worried about whether I'd have my throat cut in the street before I got back here."

"I'm sorry," she said, properly chastised.

He gave a short nod, acknowledging her apology.

"How would he know where to find us? Cardwell, I mean." She hopped around on one foot, trying to put on her stockings with no thought of sitting to do it. "Did he follow you here?"

"I don't know, but there are others in the pub who know we're staying at this hotel. He'll learn one way or another."

Slipping her feet into her worn shoes, she buttoned her bodice at the same time.

He looked at her. "For the love of Mary, hide your hair. Even in the dark it's like a red flag."

She grabbed her shawl and draped it over her head and shoulders like a Skibbereen widow. He threw two dollars on the desk along with the room key. With one last look around for any forgotten belongings, he picked up the burlap bag, grabbed her hand, and led her to the door. He opened it slowly, just a crack, and looked into the hall.

"All right," he whispered. "Down the back steps. Quick and quiet."

Down the back stairway they went and out the hotel's alley door into the steamy New Orleans night. They stayed close to the buildings, hiding in the shadows.

It wasn't until they were rushing along the sidewalk that Farrell realized her left and right shoes were reversed.

Neither of them saw the figure that stepped from the alley after them.

The riverboat trip from New Orleans to St. Louis would have been enjoyable had Farrell not been so keenly worried that Noel Cardwell, that thoroughly despicable blackguard, might be chasing them up the Mississippi River. Aidan tried to calm her fears but she could see the concern in his face, as well. Often during that steamy journey, he put a hand on her shoulder and drew her against his hard, lean frame.

"God's with us, Farrell," he whispered again and again. "It'll be all right. Trust me."

Farrell wanted nothing more than to toss her cares to the wind that moved so sluggishly along the expansive ribbon of water, but that was more easily contemplated than actually done. She and Aidan were in great peril, and only a child or a fool could believe otherwise.

When they finally reached St. Louis two days later, Farrell's nerves were frayed and she was exhausted. Aidan led her from the docks to a dingy boardinghouse, recommended to him by a deckhand. After a quick, unspectacular supper, they adjourned to their room, with Farrell once again ensconced on the bed while Aidan took his rest in a chair.

Dawn came in feeble fingers of murky light that

shone through the dusty curtains and striped the soiled gray walls with silver. Her skin damp with sweat, Farrell quickly straightened her clothing and made ready to catch the stage.

"There's no rush," Aidan reminded her. "We've two hours yet."

She glanced up and blinked. He smiled slightly and closed the space between them. With a gentle brush of his fingertips, he moved the hair from her eyes. Then he tried to tidy her tangled locks.

"Have ye a hairbrush?" he asked.

"You know I don't. I can manage," she protested.

"Aye, I know ye can. Did it never occur to you, then, that I might enjoy doing for you?"

Farrell could think of no response to that, and she was still pondering the revelation when they sat down to breakfast in a bustling eatery up the street. He enjoyed doing for her? This took her by great surprise. No one had ever "done" for her, and his admission made her feel warm and jumpy inside, a sensation that was as unsettling to her as it was pleasant.

Over the next few days as they began the arduous stagecoach journey west, Farrell had reason to recall those words of Aidan's countless times. He remained close to her side, protective, and made it known by his presence that she was his wife, not to be trifled with.

The ocean voyage had only *seemed* like hell.
The stagecoach must surely be an affliction sent by
God to give people a better taste of the true hell,
Farrell thought. If it wasn't, she could offer it up
for her sins. She and Aidan ought to be able to
avoid purgatory altogether in exchange for this.

The roads were rough, but even worse were the
conditions on the coach. Eighteen people, counting
the drivers and those passengers seated on the roof,
all squeezed onto the four-wheeled vehicle, was
most certainly worse than the miserable conditions
aboard the *Mary Fiona*. Day after day they bumped
along, stopping every ten or fifteen miles to change
horses at the stage, the place from which the mode
of transportation derived its name.

The dust was constant, as were crying children
and vomiting passengers—the ride was as nause-
ating as a ship's at sea—rain, suffocating heat, vile
food, exhaustion, and a myriad of discomforts that
Farrell had never once imagined. Two hundred dollars bought a ride, not a seat. If a passenger got off
at a stop to answer the call of nature, chances were
good that when he returned, he would have lost his
place to one of the unfortunates consigned to the
roof and be forced to take that person's place until
the opportunity came to steal another seat inside.
The passengers on the opposite side of the coach
sat so close, their knees bumped those across from
them. A fat man sitting beside Farrell fell asleep

with his head lolling on her shoulder until Aidan
reached across and pushed him off.

Aidan. He was Farrell's only solace, his
strong shoulder providing a cushion for her cheek
when exhaustion claimed her, his work-muscled
arm steadying her when the coach pitched violently, which it did more often than not, sometimes bouncing her off the seat entirely. During
the brief stops, it was Aidan who escorted her to
a private place and stood guard with his back to
her so that she could take care of personal business. It was also Aidan who made certain that
their seats weren't taken, which would have ban-
ished them to precarious perches on the roof. It
was Aidan who urged her to eat when she grew
so weary she could barely put the food to her
mouth, let alone swallow.

Farrell lost all track of time. The days and
nights blended into a nightmarish blur of chilling
darkness and dusty heat, the humidity of the east
soon giving way to a blistering dryness that sucked
every bit of moisture from the passengers' skin and
throats, leaving their lips cracked and bleeding.

Late one evening during a brief stop at a stage
to change horses, Aidan left her to speak with the
stage keeper's wife. When he returned, he held a
small tin canister in one hand. "Look up, little red
one."

When Farrell complied, he carefully smeared a

greasy, nasty-smelling ointment over her smarting lips. "What—" She reared away to sputter, "What is that awful stuff?"

"Never mind that. The stage keeper's wife tells me it will heal your dry lips."

"It's awful."

He sniffed at the tin. "Aye, it is," he agreed with a smile, then put it on his own lips. "But it might help."

Then he accompanied her into the brush to relieve herself. While she fumbled with her skirts, she heard an odd rattling sound. The next instant, Aidan snatched her, none too gently, into his arms, his body colliding so sharply with hers that she would have been knocked off her feet if not for the strength of his grip.

"God's teeth!" he shouted.

With a vicious push he shoved her aside, grabbed a rock, and threw it with all his strength at the ground. Then, with another profanity, he began dancing about like a Skibbereen lad gone daft on poteen at a wake, his boots violently pummeling the dirt.

"Ye poisonous bastard, and Satan take you!" he yelled, still stomping around. "Jesus, Mary, and Holy Saint Joseph! Stand back, Farrell! It's a viper."

Farrell staggered back a step, her heart up so high in her throat, it bumped the back of her tongue. "Take care with the thing, Aidan!"

She saw the snake strike at him. Aidan barely avoided the deadly fangs. "Spawn of the devil!"

She shrieked a wordless warning.

Terror flooded her body, turning it ice-cold. She'd understood before they left St. Louis that there were dangers galore in this godforsaken wilderness, venomous snakes and marauding Indians, to name only two. But somehow, until this moment, she'd never honestly considered the possibility that she or Aidan might die out here.

Now the reality of it struck home. Aidan. With one cruel stroke of fate, she could lose him. For reasons she hadn't time to consider, the thought nearly took Farrell to her knees. She didn't know if it was mere cowardice on her part, because she would face terrible circumstances, indeed, should she lose him. Or was it a deeper, more powerful emotion that made her fear for him so?

"Get away from it, Aidan! Stand clear of the thing."

Finally Aidan stopped leaping about and stomping his boots. "It's dead, lass." His chest heaved with exertion. "It's dead, and the devil take it."

A sob erupted from her chest, and she pressed violently shaking hands to her face.

"Farrell! What is it? Did it bite you, then?" He strode to her and took her by the shoulders. "Answer me. Did the thing bite you?"

She didn't know what came over her, but sud-

denly she was angry. She doubled her right fist and
swung at Aidan's shoulder.

"No, it didn't bite me, ye great addlepated fool!
How dare you risk life and limb that way? How
dare you?" She hit his chest with her second swing.
"You're not a strutting cock without a care. You
have a wife and responsibilities! You have no
right—no right, do you hear?—to put yourself at
risk that way, without a thought for me."

He caught her wrist just as she attempted a third
blow. "Farrell, now, nothing happened. It's all right,
céadsearc, I'm fine. The filthy thing tried, but it
didn't get me." His arms came around her, hard and
warm, leaving her no choice but to press full-length
against him. He clamped a hand over the back of
her head to push her face to his shirt. She inhaled
the scent of him; neither of them were particularly
clean after all these days on the road, but it was a
smell she recognized and it comforted her.

Pain moved into Farrell's chest, cutting off her
breath. She made fists on Aidan's shirt, her body
shuddering. He stroked a big hand over her back.

"Whisht, now," he whispered near her ear.
" 'Tis over. I'm here. Just a wee snake, is all. It'll
take more than that to get the best of Aidan
O'Rourke. Don't take on so, please."

A sob tore up her throat, and suddenly she was
weeping. Not softly, not delicately ladylike. The
dry, wracking sounds she emitted were so awful

that they startled even her. It wasn't like her to fall apart and carry on. Fits of crying were for infants and the elderly. But somehow, she couldn't seem to stop. All the tension and trials of the last months had finally caught up with her.

Aidan let her cry, swaying softly in the moonlit darkness with her cradled against his long body. Occasionally he murmured to her, but she was crying so hard, she couldn't make out his words. Dimly she was aware of other voices and Aidan barking out a husky reply.

When exhaustion finally calmed the storm, Farrell leaned limply against him and said, "You frightened me half to death, Aidan O'Rourke. Half to death, do you hear? Don't ever do anything so foolish again. Promise me."

He pressed his lips to her hair. "Foolish! Should I have let the thing sink its fearful fangs into you, then? I'll protect what's mine. You'll be waiting a long time before you wrest such a promise from me."

With that, he turned her toward the coach and ushered her back to her seat. Once inside, Farrell was strangely glad that he kept one strong arm clamped around her shoulders—strangely glad that she could remain pressed against his strength and count on him to hold her erect. Once Liam had assured her that Aidan would die for her.

Now she'd seen the proof of that with her own eyes.

Shortly thereafter, the stagecoach resumed its pitching race across the vast expanses of nothingness, the horses' hooves sending up constant billows of dust. Farrell lost track of time, her mind closing down to the misery. When she looked into the faces of the other passengers, she saw her numbness reflected in every expression. They stopped to drink, eat, and attend to personal needs, but those brief moments were the only reprieve. Otherwise, the punishment was relentless.

If a person had unwittingly used grease or pomade in his hair, the dust stuck to it and grew to a patch rich enough for cultivation. There were no washing facilities at all, no bathing, and they could do little more than wet a handkerchief in a horse trough to wipe faces and hands.

The other passengers complained about the primitive stage stops—one-story sod huts with dirt floors—but they weren't much worse than the cottages where Aidan and Farrell had grown up.

Part of the time, Farrell wished to God that she'd never agreed to make this trip. The people she'd met along the way had strange, twanging accents, except for the Germans and Swedes, who struggled with English even more.

Still, despite the trials of the journey, as the days turned into weeks, Aidan's hope began to rub off on her. His family had always thought that his constant desire to see beyond the next day was his biggest failing. If he didn't know how to make do with what he had, he'd never be content, his brother Tommy had said. Yet, something inside Farrell stirred at the possibilities that Aidan raised when they talked. There had to be something beyond the abysmal poverty they knew in Ireland, poverty that ate away at her pride and her soul. If Oregon proved to be half as grand as Aidan hoped, she would have a life where her children wouldn't starve, and she'd have clothes, not rags, to dress them in. That, almost more than anything else, gave her determination to go on. As they jounced along, she realized that this was the first time she'd envisioned having Aidan's children.

The closer they got to Oregon, and the more breathtaking the open plains, the more she felt the heat grow between them. With even less privacy than they'd had on the ship, the yearning only seemed to grow stronger. Sometimes weeks passed when she forgot about Michael's death and Aidan's part in it.

She caught herself watching him, fascinated by the shape of his brows and the thick, dark lashes that framed his eyes. His hands were big and callused from years of hard work, and could probably punch a hole in a wall. But she had felt their gentleness, too, when his fingertips grazed her cheek, her hair, the tender underside of her breast. Remembering that, her face flushed as hot as a flatiron.

Aidan studied Farrell, as well. It took his mind off the lardy, stinking traveling salesman wedged next to him, and the screaming child who sometimes occupied his lap. Everyone took a turn with the child, especially when the mother rode on the roof. When he'd planned this trip, he'd had no idea how difficult it would be. He kept waiting for his wife to begin complaining, and God knew she'd have every right. But just as on the walk to Queenstown, she uttered not one protest. He wasn't sure if she was saving up every grievance for one great venting of her spleen at the end of the trip, but he didn't think so. She sent him no poisonous looks and though she occasionally appeared distressed, it wasn't directed at him. There was a strength in her that awed Aidan, and sometimes even surpassed his own, though he would be hard-pressed to tell her so outright.

They passed through the Great Plains, grassy, rolling wilderness that stretched from horizon to horizon with no fences or boundaries. The vistas only stoked the fires of his hope until it flamed into impatient ambition. Unlike in Ireland, where a man was trapped in his station and could not escape, out here he had a chance to build an empire in this new land and raise fine, strong sons to inherit his holdings. With a woman like Farrell beside him, he could accomplish just about anything. For all her grit and determination, she was as fair and fresh as a rosebud. And, he imagined as he studied her firm curves, as ripe as that rosebud on a summer morning. His few teasing tastes of her had challenged his resolve to wait for their consummation more times than he wanted to think about. Of course, now, he had no choice.

At last the landscape began to change subtly. From vast seas of rolling grass, to mountains the likes of which they had never seen, they arrived at a town in Oregon called The Dalles.

"We're in Oregon?" Farrell asked, sitting up straighter on the seat. The town looked busy and prosperous, and from the blue-uniformed riders they passed on the road, it seemed to include some kind of military installation.

"Yes, indeed, ma'am," Frank Pittman, the salesman, replied. "We came into Oregon Territory miles and miles ago. We'll be pulling up to the stop in a bit. This is my third trip out here, so I know what I'm talking about."

Sure, and didn't he know about everything? she wondered irritably. He'd been talking almost non-stop since they boarded in St. Louis, and seemed to be an expert on nearly any topic someone brought up.

"Where will you folks be going from here?"

She exchanged a glance with Aidan, who sat opposite her. He had warned her not to discuss their planned destination, Oregon City. There was no telling who might overhear them and repeat it to someone else.

He interjected, "We're going to stay in town a few days and consider our options. We've nothing special in mind."

Off Pittman went again, relating his opinion on the subject from a seemingly inexhaustible source of hearsay and personal experience, when they pulled up to the stop.

Stiff and feeling far older than her twenty-two years, Farrell followed Aidan out of the coach, grateful for the support of his hand at her elbow to keep from falling.

"Will ye look at this, Farrell?" he said, looking at the churning waters of the Columbia River and the high rock walls that bracketed it. "Have you ever seen anything like it? Didn't I tell you it would be grand?"

Aidan didn't realize just *how* grand it would be until an early morning two days later, when he and Farrell stood on a barge that two burly ferrymen piloted through the churning waters of the Columbia River. It was a treacherous ride, but they had an advantage, one of the men told them, because they weren't trying to take a wagonful of goods downstream, like those who would be coming by wagon train later in the summer. "Those things are

lost in the river all the time, and so are them trying
to keep the stuff on the rafts."

When their barge entered the place where the
river breached the Cascade Mountains, Aidan could
hardly believe his eyes. From the desertlike conditions of the eastern part of the territory, the terrain
turned misty, green, and cool, reminding him so
much of Ireland, he was filled with an over-
whelming sense of homecoming. The sky grew
overcast and the temperature dropped to a gentle
degree.

"Holy Mother of God," he intoned and crossed
himself. "We've come home, Farrell. It's not a
strange place at all. It's home." His heart swelled
with emotion that he couldn't keep out of his voice,
and tears blurred his vision. "It's home." Waterfalls
cascaded down the sides of high, rocky cliffs; trees,
dark green and ancient, stretched skyward; and
everywhere a plant could grow, lush greenery and
wildflowers sprouted.

"I can scarce believe it," she said, awestruck
and clinging tightly to his arm. "I'd begun to think
the stories you were telling me about this place
were invented by hawkers to sell fares and wagons."

Keeping his eyes on the view, he wrapped his
arms around her and planted a brief kiss on the top
of her head. "It's going to be all right. We made it,

we're shut of the damned Cardwells, and it's going to be all right."

"Excusez-moi, Lord Cardwell. I em so sorry to interrupt your meal, mais zat, um, gentleman in the foyer asks to see you." The majordomo of the fashionable New Orleans hotel where Noel was staying spoke to him in a confidential tone.

Noel looked up to see Seth Fitch standing in the entrance to the hotel dining room, practically tying a knot in the hat that he twisted in his hands.

"Thank you, Dubois. I'll take care of it."

"Très bien, monsieur."

Noel turned to his dining companions, George and Dolly Gray. "Please excuse me for just a moment. I've a bit of business to take care of. Tiresome, but important."

Dolly waved him off, her large diamond ring sparkling like a star in the candlelight. Her multiple chins jiggled like aspic when she chewed or spoke, and she was often breathless, presumably due to a tightly laced corset. "Now don't you bother yourself, your lordship. George and I will be just fine, won't we, George?"

George spoke around a mouthful of buttered bread, revealing the partially chewed mass. He had not denied himself the pleasures of the table. His watch chain stretched tight to reach across his considerable but well-dressed belly. "Fine, of course."

Noel pushed back his chair and tried not to shudder visibly. The Grays were crude and ignorant nouveaux riches whom, under any other circumstances, Noel would not have given the time of day. But the estimable fortune they'd acquired during the California gold rush made them sufferable. His own finances were in a precarious state, especially now that he'd hired Fitch, and the Grays' ignorance worked to his advantage. They believed him to be practically royal and a very distant cousin to Queen Victoria. The fools thought that anyone with a title must be related to the crown somehow, and he didn't trouble to correct them. After their chance meeting in the lobby, they had been his nearly constant companions. They would not permit him to pay for his meals, and asked him along on their outings to the opera and the theater.

God, if only they weren't such loutish bumpkins, he thought, crossing the dining room. Of course, they wouldn't be such gullible benefactors if they were more sophisticated.

He reached Fitch and motioned him to a quiet corner of the lobby. "For God's sake, Fitch, what is the matter?" he asked.

"I'm afraid I've got some bad news for you, sir." Fitch's hat was practically ruined by his sweaty-handed, worrying grasp.

"Well? Spit it out, man. Can't you see that I'm otherwise engaged?"

"The O'Rourkes have gone. Left New Orleans."
Noel clenched his jaw. "Where did they go?"

"They caught a riverboat to St. Louis. I talked to some of the men in the Lass of Killarney and I learned that O'Rourke said he was going to the Oregon Territory."

The place sounded vaguely familiar, but Noel had no great knowledge of American geography beyond the eastern seaboard and this part of the Gulf of Mexico. "Where is that?"

"It's about two thousand miles west, on the Pacific Coast."

"What?" he barked. Catching a curious glance from the desk clerk, he went on in a lower voice. "By God, when did they leave? How are they traveling?" He drilled Fitch with questions, and although the man had most of the answers, none of them was to Noel's liking. Not at all.

"All right, then. Stay in touch. I'll let you know what our next move will be." He had no idea what that next move might be, and the realization that O'Rourke, and worse, Farrell, had slipped away from him so easily made his blood boil. He had to find them. His father's wishes be damned—this had become a personal grudge that would be satisfied.

Somehow.

He returned to his companions and drank a full glass of wine in one swallow, then poured another.

"Troubling news, was it?" George asked.

Noel waved languidly. "Oh, you know how vexing business can be sometimes."

"Huh, do I ever! Why, before the gold rush, me and Dolly piddled along for years in that dry-goods store in Sacramento. If I'd had to show old Mrs. Grant one more bolt of that damned chambray— Well, anyhow, when word leaked out about the gold strike at Sutter's mill, we raced over there to stake our claim. We grubbed in the dirt like pigs, but look at us now." He thumped his chest. "Happy as pigs in mud—golden mud, that is, haw-haw-haw!"

Dolly brayed at George's clever joke while Noel downed another glass of wine.

"That's right—I'd forgotten you're from the West. You're both so cosmopolitan, it's hard to remember that you aren't from a large Eastern city," Noel said. The lie came a little more easily with four glasses of wine sloshing around in his belly.

Dolly giggled at the compliment. "And you're such a fine gentleman, your lordship."

He bent over the woman's chubby hand and placed a kiss just above the diamond. As he did so, the germ of an idea began to take shape in his mind. "Madam, you are too kind." He held out both hands to them. "Please, we've become such good friends, we three, I wish you would call me Noel."

George grabbed his hand and pumped it. "By Jesus, Noel, you're all right. A top fellow."

Noel managed a smile that he certainly did not feel. "Now, tell me more about the west. It sounds like a fascinating place, maybe one I'd like to visit."

Chapter Eleven

THE furnished house that Aidan rented for himself and Farrell in Oregon City was a tidy place with a real bedroom, a kitchen, and a parlor. It even had flowers blooming beside the front door. Dr. John McLoughlin, who had founded Oregon City in 1829, was a man of prestige and many interests in the territory, and owned this property. Aidan had told Farrell that he would never be a tenant again, but even he realized that they must live somewhere until they could settle on their own land. McLoughlin, nothing like Arthur Cardwell, had offered to help them find a suitable parcel. It was August now, though, and they had only another month or two before the rains would begin. There wasn't enough time to build a cabin before winter came.

Aidan and Farrell had bought food, and some household and personal necessities. They were little things—candles, soap, thread and needles, a few clothes that fit—but important. Finally, after two nights in yet another hotel, they had come home. The owner of the general store had sent a lad with a wagon to deliver their purchases, and they were stacked around Farrell as the evening sky began to dim.

In the parlor, she twirled and laughed like a young girl, making her skirt flare, her arms outstretched. "Aidan, isn't it just lovely? All these rooms! Wood floors and rugs, a feather bed, not just a pallet, decent food and a kitchen with a real *stove* to cook on! We have so many riches, I think I've died and gone to heaven."

Aidan closed the front door behind him and smiled. "It's good to hear you laugh again, *céad-searc*. I know the last few months were pure misery." He gestured at their surroundings. "You deserve this and more."

She dropped her arms and looked at him intently. She didn't know how he felt about her, and she wasn't sure any longer how she felt about him. That she was attracted to him she could not deny. After all, what woman would not be? But things had changed between them over the course of their trials. "I swear to ye, Aidan, even though I promised myself and vowed to Brigit that I'd survive the trip, often I was sorry that I came, and I was furious with you for taking me from Ireland. I was ready to give up."

He stepped around a fifty-pound bag of flour and came close enough for her to smell the soap he'd washed with. "I admit I never guessed how hard it would be, myself. Many was the time that I regretted dragging ye off on what you called a fool's errand. And it could have ended badly, at least a dozen different times." He lifted her hand and kissed the back of her finger that bore her silver wedding ring. "Are ye still sorry?"

His voice took on subtle, husky shades and he captured her gaze with his. It was almost frightening, the heat and depth of emotion she saw there. A woman could get lost in eyes like his and never find her way back. She could fall in love with a man who had such eyes and never be the same.

"No. I'm not sorry."

He turned her hand over and kissed the center of her palm, making gooseflesh rise on her arm.

"And are ye still furious with me?"

She drew a deep breath when his tongue touched her palm. "No."

He looked at her over her hand and put his arm around her waist to draw her to him. "I'm glad. Shall we start over, then?"

"Start over?"

"Aye." He backed up and bowed slightly. "Hello, pretty lass. I'm Aidan O'Rourke. And who might you be?"

She laughed. "And how many girls in Skibbereen heard those very same words?"

"Now, now, we're not in Skibbereen. We're in America, and a fine place it is, too. But ye look like an Irish girl I used to know. What did you say your name is?"

She gave him an arch look. "This is silly. You know my name."

"But I want to hear you say it."

"I'm Farrell Kirwan."

"Hmm. I've heard that ye're married."

" 'Tis true, I am."

"Yet you don't use your husband's name? Well, join me at the table over here for a wee dram of good Irish whiskey and tell me about it."

She followed him to the table and sat. She didn't know what kind of game he was playing, but she went along with it, wondering where it would lead.

After taking two cups from a shelf on the wall, he sat with her and pulled the cork from the bottle. "I'm sorry we have to drink from teacups, but I don't know where things are kept at this inn." He poured a measure for both of them.

She smiled, intrigued. Through the open windows, the wind pushed heavy clouds across the sky and rustled the dark fir trees around the house. Chirping birds flew past, looking for their nests before nightfall and the start of rain.

"In the name of Erin," he intoned, and held up his cup.

"In the name of Erin," she responded and took a careful sip of her drink, recognizing the whiskey's distinctive flavor that no other country on earth produced. "Where did you find this? This isn't your da's poteen."

"No, one of the saloons in town, Kelleher's, is owned by a man from Dublin. He has it shipped in, thank God. That poteen from home won't last forever." He bolted back his drink and set down the cup. "Now, then. You were going to tell me about your husband."

"I was?"

"Yes. Ye tell me you're married but you've given me your maiden name." He gazed at her. "What is your married name?"

"Farrell Kirwan . . . O'Rourke." It was as if he'd willed the truth from her.

"Aye," he said, seeming satisfied. "Just so." He poured another drink for himself. "What kind of man is this O'Rourke?"

Ah, now she realized what he was doing. He wanted to know how she felt about him. "He's a good man, I think. Better than I might have thought originally." She considered him over the rim of her own cup. She had come to realize that Aidan was not the irresponsible philanderer she'd believed. Or at least not the one he'd once been. Time and again he'd proven himself to be ambitious, honest, considerate, and protective of her. His handsomeness had made her follow him with her eyes more times than she could count. She didn't much care for his gambling, but she understood why he'd taken part in those card games—to get the money to bring them here. She added, "Marrying him wasn't the

entire disaster I expected it would be." She put a
finger over her lips, realizing how unflattering her
comment was.

He almost sprayed a mouthful of whiskey over
them both when he laughed. "God, but you're kind,
woman!"

"Oh, mercy, I'm sorry," she said, laughing, too.
"I didn't mean it to sound that way."

"So maybe what ye meant was that being my
wife is better than you expected."

She smiled at him and dropped her gaze. "Yes,
maybe that was it."

It was true. Liam had never made her feel giddy
with her heart thumping in her chest. He'd never
made her breath come fast. Liam, dear as he'd been
to her, was a man of few words and she'd always
felt as if she were interrupting his lofty thoughts. If
he'd had any. She'd never really known what he
was thinking. She had only known that he wasn't
at all like her father, and she'd assumed he was the
man for her.

With Aidan, she found she could be his equal
with words. And, as he was proving to her right
now, they could laugh together. Over the last many
months, they'd had precious little time to simply
have fun, but judging by the laughter in his eyes,
he wasn't a man to count himself too proud to have
a frolic now and then. That was a great gift considering the hard life they'd known.

Aidan reached across the small table and took her left hand again, fingering her wedding ring. He knew she didn't love him. But her clumsy words gave him hope that maybe one day, he would drive his brother out of her heart and make room there for himself. She'd told him what attracted her to Liam, and for the life of him, he still couldn't understand it. A woman needed a man who would put a roof over her head and make something of what fate and God handed them, no matter what it was. And Aidan was determined to give her every luxury, every possible thing he could, to make her life better than it had been before.

He kissed her knuckles, then turned her hand over to press his mouth to her wrist. Beneath his lips, he felt her pulse in the vein throbbing beneath her creamy skin, strong and quickening. "Maybe," he murmured over her wrist, "being my wife is *a lot* better than ye expected."

He touched his lips to the soft, tender flesh inside her arm, unbuttoning her cuff as he went to give him access. Was that her hand he felt brush over his hair? he wondered.

At last he looked up at her, at her eyes, faintly luminous in the gathering darkness, her mouth, full-lipped and trembling, asking—no, needing to be kissed. He had denied himself for months, holding back, taking small tastes of her that only made his abstinence much more torturous. But abstained he had. For what if she became pregnant and he lost her, just as Deirdre Connagher had been lost?

Now no such obstacle stood in his way. No obstacle but her acceptance of him.

"Will ye have me, then, Farrell?" This he'd not asked her that night in Tommy's cottage, although he knew she would have refused. He and the others had simply herded her along like a lamb, and though circumstances were dire and he'd done what needed doing, he regretted it. "Will you take me as your husband?" His second question left no doubt as to his meaning.

"Yes," she uttered in a small voice. "Yes, please."

At those words, a snap of electricity arced through his body and desire overtook him. He left his chair and pulled her into his arms in a swift, fluid movement. When he took her mouth with his, he was gentle, not wanting her to think he was nothing but a swinish lout. He teased open her lips with his tongue and touched it to the roof of her mouth. She responded, shyly at first, and then with more eagerness.

Picking her up, he carried her to the bedroom where she'd already made up the bed. The sheet and blanket were turned back, as if in invitation.

Putting her on her feet, he kissed her again, small nibbles at the temple, at her jaw, on each side of her mouth where the dimples hid when she wasn't smiling. Her hair smelled sweet, of lavender, he thought, and her slender throat was as smooth as a rose petal.

With an impatient moan, she reached up and wrapped her hands in the lapels of his coat and pulled his mouth to hers. That single action ignited his urgent need, and it licked through his body like the flames of whiskey set ablaze. He fumbled with the buttons on her bodice, working hard to keep from ripping them open in his eagerness to once again touch her fair softness. His own fly buttons strained against his rising desire.

Finally, she stood before him in her simple white underwear, and he was certain he'd never seen any creature so beautiful. Reaching out, he pulled the carved ivory pins from her hair and it came down in a shimmering fall of dark cinnamon that caught the last light of the day in its luxurious strands. She unbuttoned her camisole and let it fall from her shoulders, revealing smooth, sweetly rounded breasts. She was innocent, but not coy or shy, and that only turned up the fire under his own need. When she began to untie the tape drawstring of her drawers, he stayed her hand.

"Wait, let me," he whispered. She stopped and he pulled on the end of the tape. Slipping his hands just inside the waist of the garment, he savored the warmth of her skin beneath his touch before sliding her last covering over her hips. His heart thundered so hard against his ribs, he was sure that she could hear it.

She stepped out of the drawers, and for a moment, she stood before him in the twilit room, allowing him to see what he'd had only a glimpse of in New Orleans. Emotion warred with his own raging hunger and formed a knot in his throat. He was glad for the whiskey—he'd never been afraid of making love to a woman, but now he was more nervous than he had been his first time.

"You're beautiful, ye know. I don't think—" He swallowed hard. "I've never seen anything or anyone as lovely as you, Farrell Kirwan O'Rourke."

She sat on the edge of the bed, and watched as he pulled off his clothes. He'd never undressed so quickly in his life. He joined her on the bed and pulled her into his arms, raining soft, urgent kisses over her body.

Farrell tried to grasp and hold one of the sensations that flowed through her, but she couldn't catch any particular one. Aidan's ministrations left her unable to even catch her own breath. His mouth, demanding yet gentle on her breast, made her twine her fingers in his dark hair to hold him there. But when he tugged on her nipple with his lips and tongue, bolts of sensation she'd never experienced shot straight to her belly to begin a demanding, insistent ache between her legs.

While he continued to pour warm, moist kisses

over her, he ran the flat of his hand down her side, over her hip, and up the insides of her thighs, skimming the swollen ache, but not really touching her there. The teasing graze was sweet torture, and with no conscious effort on her part, her hips began lifting slightly to make contact.

"I think this is what ye want, *a muirnín,*" he whispered. He trapped her right leg between his and let his fingertips delve the slick moistness of her.

A moan escaped her, one that she could not have stopped if she'd wanted. She felt him smile against her neck. "Was I right?"

She answered with a wordless affirmation, and he stepped up the speed of the strokes to her sensitive flesh. Against the leg he held between his own she felt the hot hardness of him, throbbing and leaving a smear of wetness on her skin. Instinctively, she reached down to touch him and he sucked in a rasping breath. He pulled back while she held him fast and an inarticulate noise sounded in his throat. Then he pushed forward and pulled away again, his own hand upon her stilled. "Jesus," he groaned.

"No," she pleaded, "don't stop, please." She wiggled beneath his hand and he began the massage again, now faster and faster still. His own hips moved against hers, while she kept her grip on his erect maleness. He whispered in her ear, urging her on with words that she felt rather than heard. Nearly sobbing with the fierceness of her need, she plunged toward a breathless knife point of exquisite torment. Then wave upon wave of spasms crashed through her, consuming her, making her buck in his embrace and weep against his shoulder.

He pulled her hand away from his engorged flesh and parted her legs. Hovering over her in the darkness, he muttered, "You're my wife, aye? You're Farrell O'Rourke."

"I am," she replied, dazed and overwhelmed, with little tremors still shuddering through her. At this moment, she couldn't even remember why she had objected to marrying him.

"I swear I'll be tender with ye. Do I have your trust?"

"And my heart."

His emotions churning like the fires in his body, Aidan eased himself between her thighs and bumped against the sentinel of her innocence. Pushing a bit harder, he heard her suck in a breath, and he maintained steady pressure until he was completely sheathed within her warmth.

"Are ye all right?"

She nodded on the pillow, and with a kiss on her lips, he began moving inside her.

He hoisted himself to the full length of his arms and pressed into her, withdrew, and pushed forward again. After a few strokes, she began to complement his movements with her own. Aidan was certain that he would burst before this sweet agony ended. Farrell wrapped her arms around his waist as if trying to pull him deeper. His movements grew shorter and faster until, oh God, he felt the convulsions build and at last white heat poured from him into her. He dropped to his elbows and pressed his forehead to hers. His breath coming fast, he kissed her once before letting out an exhausted sigh. She'd said he had her heart. Had she really meant that? he wondered. Or had he only imagined it, as he'd imagined making love to her so many times?

"I have waited all my life for this moment," he said at last, and keeping them joined, rolled them both to their sides.

"All your life—but Aidan, ye didn't mean to marry me."

"Well, I didn't think I would. You'd been mooning after Liam since you were a lassie." He pulled her closer, tucking her forehead against his chin. "And yes, I knew some women before you."

He felt her shoulders shake with a chuckle. "More than a *few,* according to the talk around the *clachan.*"

"But every one I kissed, every one I, well, was with, I always imagined each was you."

She pulled back a bit, trying to see his face in the low light. "Oh, go on with you."

He touched her cheek with his fingertips. "It's true. I was so eaten up with jealousy when I thought you would marry Liam, I didn't think I could bear it any longer. I was planning to leave Skibbereen."

This confession was astounding. His words were sincere in the darkness and revealed a side of Aidan that Farrell never knew existed. After a pause she said, "I'm glad ye didn't."

He interlaced her fingers with his. "So am I."

Then she pondered the question that had been plaguing her curiosity since they'd landed in New Orleans. "I was wondering . . ."

"What?"

"Well, I was wondering why you never, um— after all, we were alone in the hotel in New Orleans and you didn't, you could have—" She broke off, too embarrassed to go on.

"Ohh. Ye want to know why I didn't make love to you before tonight?"

She heard the smile in his words and nodded against his chin.

"I'd meant to. That was why I talked Morton into wagering his cabin on the *Mary Fiona,* so I could be alone with you and make you my wife. But then you were called away to tend Deirdre. When she died and her babe with her, and I had to lift them over the side to put them into the ocean, I made a promise to myself. That I wouldn't take the chance of getting you with child until we were in a safe place." He kissed her forehead. "Until we were home."

Tears filled her eyes. She was beginning to realize that almost everything she thought she'd known about Aidan had been wrong. She hadn't known him at all. "And now we're home?"

"Not quite yet. But close enough."

Outside, late summer rain began falling, and under a roof ten thousand miles from the land of their birth, Farrell O'Rourke fell asleep in her husband's arms.

Early the next afternoon, Farrell was standing in the kitchen making soda bread for dinner. It was her third try. Although she was thrilled to have a stove to cook on, getting used to it was another matter. The first loaf turned out with a golden crust but a gooey middle. The second was charred as black as a cannonball.

Ordinarily, she would have felt a grinding guilt over wasting the flour and buttermilk. In Ireland, they would have eaten that bread, burned or raw, no matter what. But today she felt only a twinge of remorse over the lost food, hummed to herself, and thought about the night she had spent with Aidan. They had dozed and awakened to make love until dawn. He'd done things to her that should have embarrassed her just to remember them, but the images that moved sweetly through her mind didn't bother her, either. She hummed on, forming the soft dough into a dome-shaped loaf.

Just as she slid the bread into the oven, Aidan came through the back door.

"I've got some grand news," he said. She could see he was excited—his blue eyes shone like dark stars and he was grinning from ear to ear. He looked different to her today. More rested, she thought, even though he hadn't slept much.

She wiped her hands on her apron. "What is it? Did ye find us a good parcel of land?"

"Even better. I met with Dr. McLoughlin, and he knows of a man who's looking to sell his sawmill. It comes with property and a house already built."

"Sawmill—whatever is that?"

He went to the stove and shook the empty coffeepot. "You know, it's where they make trees into lumber for buildings or crates or, well, lots of different things."

She went to the hutch and took down the teapot and tea cannister. "But I thought we were going to farm. That's what we talked about. That's why we came here. For the free acreage."

"I know. But if we farm, we'll probably have to clear the land and build a log cabin and live with dirt floors again. It will take months and months. The sawmill and the house already exist. All we have to do is move in."

She paused in her spooning of tea into the pot. "Well, it's not free, is it? Where will you get the money to pay for it?" She waved the spoon at him, as a thought occurred to her. "Oh, *no*. You'd better not be planning what I think you're planning," she warned.

"And what would that be?"

"You're going to get into another card game. Aidan, ye can't. You just can't risk what little we have on such foolishness."

He shook his head. "No, no, lass, you've got it all wrong. The owner—his name is Geoffrey Brother—his wife died recently, and he has no other family out here. He wants to go back to Ohio, where he came from. Dr. McLoughlin confided that he thinks the man has a broken heart and will just pine away."

"So he's giving you the property? Really, Aidan, I'm smarter than that." She poured boiling water from the kettle over the leaves and put the lid back on the teapot. She didn't mean to sound so harsh, but all these months she'd believed she'd finally get a chance to connect with the earth again. To grow good crops and not have to worry about giving up the harvest to pay the rent. Now Aidan had come home and thrown the plan out the window.

"Of course he's not giving it to me. But he's been successful and he's not hurting for money. He's willing to carry a contract. We'll send the payments to him in Ohio."

"Do you know anything about sawing logs, or sawmilling, or whatever it's called?"

"No, but Mr. Brother has a work crew that will stay on. He can give me the details before he leaves and I can learn the rest on my own."

She leaned a hip against the kitchen table. "Aidan, this isn't what we planned at all. You were so eager to work the soil, to see your own vast acres under plow."

"I'll plant your kitchen garden, Farrell, don't worry about that. But this is better than farming, and your life will be easier as a businessman's wife than a farmer's, *a ghrá.*"

"You might not think I'm so 'darling' if this doesn't go well. We've been through so much already."

He came to her and took her upper arms in his hands. "Ye trust me, don't you?" He kissed both cheeks. "You did last night."

His comment made a flush creep up the front of her throat and over her face. She nodded. "Aye, I trust you."

He arched a dark brow at her. "Can ye say it as if you mean it, then?"

"Didn't I follow you all these months and miles, because I believed in you?"

"Is that why you came?" He looked very pleased.

"Yes, I suppose it is."

"All right, then. We're to have supper tonight with Mr. Brother at his house. It will give you a chance to see the place."

"Supper tonight?" She cast a regretful glance at the oven where the soda bread was baking. "I guess I'd better see what I have to wear." She untied her apron and left the kitchen, wondering what in the world was in store for them now.

CHAPTER TWELVE

AIDAN looked at the machinery inside the mill with awe and a little intimidation. A creek-fed water wheel supplied the power to cut logs with a system of belts, gears, saws, and terms that were as foreign to him as anything he'd heard yet. Geoffrey Brother referred to a host of people and animals—*mule, dog, Swede, donkey, bear fighter*—but Aidan saw no individual or animal anywhere. The place smelled of grease and fresh-cut green wood, not an unpleasant combination.

"In the summer we run the mill twelve hours a day, from five-thirty to five-thirty," Brother told him over the racket of the machinery. "I've got a small crew, about seven men, and though I'm not a wealthy man, I've done well enough."

Aidan nodded, following him through the noisy place.

Suddenly a bell rang out, loud enough to be heard over the din of everything else. "It's quitting time," Brother added, looking at his pocket watch and then at the mill foreman manning the bell. "Let's go on, then. We've left Mrs. O'Rourke on her own long enough."

Farrell had remained in the house to be served a cup of tea by the housekeeper. Accustomed to hard work and lots of it, Farrell had never been waited upon until she'd arrived in America. Mr. Brother also employed a cook, and one of the mill workers who did odd jobs around the business maintained the house's yard, as well.

This was a beautiful home, a huge home, with a lush green lawn that sloped down to the Willamette River. The view from the parlor window offered not only an unbroken vista of the water, but the massive forest of trees on the other side. As Farrell watched, a slow-moving barge floated by and ducks waddled around on the grass. It was peaceful and yet majestic.

After remarking so to Mrs. Hill, the housekeeper, Farrell was told, "Oh, yes, the late missus loved this place. She chose the furniture and decorated the rooms herself. I can't believe she's been gone almost a year." She dabbed at her eyes with the corner of her apron. "Please forgive me—she was so dear to me and she leaves a great gap with her passing."

From what Farrell could gather, Ann Brother had died suddenly, perhaps from apoplexy. At least that was what her doctor had said. Mrs. Hill made a noise of disgust. "Doctors! You can't believe a single one of them. If they don't know what's wrong with a body, they just make up something that sounds important so *they'll* sound important. Miss Ann was barely thirty-five years old—apoplexy is an old woman's ailment."

At last the weepy servant returned to her kitchen and Farrell was left to investigate the parlor while the men toured the mill. She was afraid to sit anywhere, afraid to touch anything. She'd never seen such a wondrous place from the inside, except for Greensward Manor. And she'd been so miserable there, she'd barely taken note of her surroundings.

A lovely patterned carpet had a place of honor at the center of the room, and the furnishings, artfully arranged, were of good quality. Although she had no real experience with such matters, Farrell had no trouble telling the difference between these finely finished, well-tended pieces, and the few serviceable but crude ones they'd had back home.

A pianoforte stood against one wall, a magnificent thing that she stared at in wonder. She'd heard of the instrument, but never seen one. They were expensive, and only a wealthy few could afford them.

And books: one wall was lined with bookcases, filled with different-colored volumes of various sizes. *Pride and Prejudice, Ivanhoe, Lives of the Poets, The Pilgrim's Progress*—she was not familiar with the titles but she was curious. She was also grateful that her mother had taught the village children to read so that now the titles on the book spines were more than just a jumble of symbols.

For a moment, just for a single moment, she imagined sitting in this room in the evenings, a crackling fire burning on the hearth, while she and Aidan sat here reading and talking and drinking tea from flowered china cups that had no chips in them. It was an enchanting daydream.

But she could just as easily imagine a house such as the one they were now renting, with a kitchen to cook a big meal for her hungry man, who'd spent his days in the fields, making things grow, tending animals, and building fences. They could still read and chat in the evenings—books were not only for the wealthy. That image was every bit as appealing. More so, in fact.

Just as she put a finger on the top of a book to pull it from the shelf, she heard male voices in the hall and jumped back, feeling like a guilty child.

"Ah, Mrs. O'Rourke. Please forgive us for leaving you alone so long," Mr. Brother said, standing in the parlor doorway. His face clouded when he added, "I hope you haven't been too bored while I showed your husband the mill. I'm sorry that there is no hostess to entertain you." Aidan had told her that he was about forty, but he was as gray in the face and hair as a much older man. Perhaps his wife's death had aged him.

"Not to worry, sir. I've been enjoying the view

from your window. It's most pleasant." She gestured lightly about the room. "As is your home."

She caught a glance from Aidan, who stood behind Brother and seemed very pleased by her comments.

"Thank you, madam. I believe Cook is about to serve our supper. Shall we retire to the dining room?" He held out his arm to her and she joined him, with Aidan on her other side.

A dining room in a house, she thought. A room in a house that was used solely for eating. It was a staggering notion.

Supper consisted of baked salmon, potatoes, and garden vegetables, accompanied by wine. For dessert, they enjoyed a tasty, moist cake and coffee, served in dainty cups, just as Farrell had been envisioning earlier. Having come from a place where even bread was a delicacy and sugar a rare treat, she had to resist the temptation to lick the crumbs from between the tines of her fork. Glancing frequently at their host, she could scarce believe that anyone could have so much and consider leaving it behind.

During the meal, the conversation shifted from the mill itself to Mr. Brother's plans. "I came out here from Ohio as a young man and worked for the Hudson's Bay Company. I met Mrs. Brother at church and was instantly smitten. Although she was quite young, we were married three months later and had fifteen wonderful years. Unfortunately, we had no children and I have no real ties here now that she's gone." His voice began to quiver and he paused, apparently to collect himself. "Oregon has become my home, but I'd rather spend my last years in the company of my family. I have brothers and sisters still in Ohio. I'll be going by boat around the Horn and it's a long journey, so I must get my affairs settled here soon." Farrell thought she'd never seen a man so grief-stricken. He wasn't that old but sounded as though he'd come to the end of his life.

He turned to Aidan. "Dr. McLoughlin speaks well of you. He tells me you're an ambitious young man, eager to make his mark in the world. I'd much rather see the mill go to someone like you than a man who would just see this as another addition to his holdings."

Aidan cast a sidelong look at Farrell. "Well, sir, I do appreciate your circumstances and your consideration. But there is a matter of funds . . ."

Brother twiddled with his dessert fork. "Yes, I understand that. I'm not a wealthy man, but I'm well fixed. If you're interested in pursuing the opportunity, let's say that we'll meet again tomorrow to discuss the details. The hour grows late for me and I'm sure that Mrs. O'Rourke isn't interested in such mundane business matters."

"Aye, of course, sir." Aidan flicked a meaningful glance at Farrell. "My wife has plenty to do with her own concerns." Arrangements were made for the men to talk again the following day.

Actually, Mrs. O'Rourke was *very* interested—after all, this would affect her life, as well—but she didn't want to contradict Aidan in front of Geoffrey Brother.

"In the meantime, I'll draw up a list of the equipment, what I think it's worth, and what the business itself is worth."

Brother saw them to the front door, the two men shook hands, and good-nights were exchanged.

Walking home, Aidan could barely contain his excitement over the potential business deal, but he made an effort to rein it in. So far, he'd been unable to tell what Farrell thought of the matter.

He studied his wife's profile in the twilight. The last light of day was very complimentary to her face, to the softly rounded cheeks and slim, well-shaped jawline. "How did ye like the house, Farrell? Could you imagine living there?"

"Maybe. But it seems awfully lavish for just two people."

He tucked her hand in the crook of his arm and grinned. "Well, it won't always be just the two of us. I expect we'll be having some sons."

She turned to look at him, a spark in her green eyes. "Oh, sons is it? And what about daughters, then? Will ye have nothing to do with them if that's what I give you?"

His grin widened. "Of course I will. They'll have fine bedchambers in our new house, and books, and music. I saw that pianoforte in the parlor. It's a lady's instrument, they say."

"But . . ."

He knew she wasn't sold on the idea of the mill and the house, but he might be able to work on that. "We came here to make a better life, not just for us, but for our children. Wouldn't ye rather see them grow up in a fine home than live one on top of the other in a little cabin? To have an easier time of it than we did?" He bent to pluck a pink wildflower from the side of the road.

"Of course I would."

He teased her ear with the late-summer bloom. "I think we stand a good chance of giving that to them. And Mr. Brother hinted that he would probably leave behind much of the furnishings and so on. He said he didn't want to ship them to Ohio and suffer reminders of his late wife."

"I can surely understand that, just from the standpoint of packing up all that stuff. I wouldn't want to do it."

"So you'd agree to the arrangement for our children." She nodded with only a moment's hesitation that he could see. He stopped in his tracks and turned her toward him. "Then would ye let me do it for *you*, for the joy it would give me?"

"Joy?"

"Remember I told you in St. Louis that I like doing for you? Will ye let me?"

She smiled and shook her head at him. "You're too charming for your own good by half, ye know. And mine, as well."

"That means you agree."

"Aye, Aidan."

He searched her pretty face and swept her into his arms. "You're a fine woman, Farrell Kirwan O'Rourke."

"Ah, well, I've a fine man for a husband." He kissed her then, long and leisurely, stirring up memories of the night before, which made Aidan want to step fancy for home. Instead he put her hand back in the crook of his arm and began walking again at a leisurely pace, reminding himself that even a married lass needed a wee bit of romancing. He pointed to the deepening sky.

"Have ye ever seen such a brilliant sparkle of stars? They remind me of the way your eyes shimmer in candlelight."

Even in the dim light, he saw a blush of pleasure on her cheeks. "Aidan, this sounds like some of the blarney I used to hear about back home, the stuff that made the colleens weak in the knees. You'll not be turning my head with that."

He just grinned and laid his hand over hers. She could protest all she liked, but he could tell when he'd set spark to tinder.

Her slender fingers felt so small and finely made, sandwiched between his larger ones and the starched sleeve of his shirt. He brushed his thumb over the protrusion of her wrist bone and felt her shiver. His grin broadened, because by that he knew he wasn't alone in remembering last night.

His thoughts returned to the mill and the fine life he could give her there. Her heart set on farming, Farrell was indulging him and he knew it. But as they neared the little house that was their home for now, he swore to himself that he'd make sure she never regretted it. He would win her love yet.

Even if he had to work eighteen hours a day to do it.

Noel Cardwell had never set eyes on drier, uglier terrain in all his days. Granted, in the distance he could see mountains covered with trees, but in this immediate area, on the outskirts of Sacramento, the sun had leached the soil of moisture, and only the hardiest of scrubby bushes had managed to take root.

Yearning for the greenness of home, Noel lamented his long absence and silently cursed Aidan O'Rourke for being the cause of it. Even the peat bogs of Ireland had been more appealing to the eye than this godforsaken landscape.

"There she is, Noel. That was our general store, where it all began." George Gray pointed out a grubby little storefront bordered by a sagging, gap-planked sidewalk. "It looks like the new owner has made some improvements."

Their open carriage, driven by Seth Fitch, paused in the road so that they could all view the Grays' former place of occupation.

Noel was hard-pressed to be civil at this point. He had been saddled with these clodhoppers since New Orleans. On yet another appalling ocean voyage, he'd traveled around Cape Horn, a harrowing experience in itself. This time he'd had the Grays with him and had almost welcomed the seasickness—it had given him a reason to stay in his cabin and away from them. The only thing that made them at all tolerable was that they were still footing the bill for all of his expenses. Not only did he find this to his liking, it enabled Noel to pay Seth Fitch to continue his search for Aidan O'Rourke, the reason Noel had traveled west to begin with.

"We've come far since those days, haven't we, Dolly?" George inquired of his powdered and highly perfumed wife.

"Oh, my, and haven't we?" She held a parasol over her head, but the autumn sun still revealed the gray roots of her hair, telling Noel that she'd used a concoction of some kind to alter its natural color. "To think we were just small-town hicks back then. Didn't know a thing. But not anymore! Just look at us—we've seen the world, traveled on a sailing ship around the end of South America. Now we have *sophistication.*" Noel did his best to disguise a laugh with a loud cough and hoped it was convincing. "And best of all," she went on, "we've made friends with dear Lord Noel Cardwell." Discreetly, she patted his knee with her chubby, beringed hand.

Lately, Dolly had begun making some very obvious overtures when George wasn't looking or was out of the room. It was rather trying, but Noel had no trouble fending her off while keeping her on a string. Sometimes he thought with private amusement that he should have been born a woman. He would have married very well and had a string of wealthy lovers on the side. "Ah, lovely Dolly, it is I who have been enriched by our friendship."

They completed their carriage tour of Sacramento, the California state capital, and now they were all going to dinner.

When they arrived back at their hotel to change to evening clothes, Noel had a chance to talk with Fitch in his room.

"Well, man, what have you learned, anything yet?" Noel asked as he threaded the studs through his shirtfront.

Fitch remained standing in his presence. It wasn't necessary and Noel had never demanded it of him. But he liked it. "I've had a message from a private investigation agency in San Francisco.

They have an operative in Portland and they think
they've located O'Rourke."

"Really? He's in Portland?" Noel had learned a
little about the major cities on the West Coast, and
Portland was about six hundred miles north.

"No, but in Oregon City, nearby."

"By God, this is fabulous news, Fitch, fabulous.
Can you book passage for us on a boat north?"

"Yes, sir. As soon as the ticket office opens in
the morning."

"Excellent." Noel pulled his wallet from his
coat pocket on the bed and extracted a ten-dollar
gold piece. "Take this and find some pleasure for
yourself. You've earned it."

Fitch gazed upon the coin as if it had been
hand-wrought by President Pierce himself. "Yes,
sir, your lordship! Thank you, sir!"

"Well, didn't I promise bonuses?"

"You did, sir."

"Off with you, then. Just don't have so much
fun that you forget to book that passage." Fitch
bowed his way out of the room, leaving Noel to
consider the situation.

At last.

Aidan O'Rourke was within his reach at last,
and he could finally rid himself of the tedious
Grays. Noel sank into an upholstered chair next to
the bed and considered his prospects. He had
enough money to see himself and his manservant,

which was how he'd come to view Seth Fitch, to Portland. He'd have only a bit of capital left, but with some discreet inquiries, it shouldn't be too hard to connect with the right circle of people who would love to entertain a titled gentleman as their guest.

Not only was O'Rourke close at hand, more importantly, so was Farrell. He'd heard that she'd married that Irish scum, which struck him as odd. In Ireland, she'd been engaged to the other O'Rourke brother, Liam. Maybe she wanted no more of Aidan than Noel did. The rumor of marriage might not be true, but even if it was, a widow would be unencumbered in any event. In fact, he might be doing both her and himself a favor by dispatching her husband. He smiled to himself at the prospect. After he had performed this deed for her—not that he would do so personally—how could she refuse him? She might be so grateful, she would be willing to do anything to repay him for her outrageous assault and for ridding her of her loutish husband.

That certainly opened up some interesting possibilities. He poured a drink for himself from the bedside brandy decanter while his imagination went to work with a flame-haired woman who had a temper to match. He swallowed the drink in one gulp. He'd tame that temper and enjoy the process immensely.

She probably would not, but that didn't matter to him. He'd teach her a lesson about insulting her betters, one that she would not forget.

The next evening at dinner, with passage secured, Noel broke the news to the Grays that their own personal lord would be moving on. God, their jaws nearly fell into their blancmange. Despite his joy at leaving their company, their disappointment was most gratifying.

"Oh, no," Dolly mourned, her small blue eyes filling with tears.

"This is disappointing, Noel," George agreed, but perhaps not for the same reason as his wife. "We've had such jolly adventures together."

Noel nodded with feigned regret. "We have, it's true. But business calls. I've put this off as long as I can to remain in your wonderful company, but now the situation has become critical and I can't delay any longer."

"Then we must drink to your success." George signaled the waiter to bring them a bottle of their very best and oldest brandy—well, old for America—and the pair drank toast after toast to him, until they were so besotted, Noel worried that they would begin singing, right there in the hotel dining room. It was bad enough that Dolly was blubbering like the shop girl that she was. George had moved his chair next to Noel's and slung an arm over his shoulder, slurring compliments in his face. In a way, it was all quite flattering, but Noel wanted to go before the management asked them to leave. That moment appeared imminent, with the headwaiter casting baleful looks at their table. With his white towel draped over his arm, the man started across the dining room.

Noel stood and bowed slightly. "I shall wish you good night, then, and good-bye. My ship leaves early in the morning and I won't have a chance to see you before I go." He made all the right comments, all the proper, gentlemanly thanks, and managed to get away before he became part of the scene that was about to occur.

Later that night, after he had gone to bed, he heard a cautious tapping on his door. Surely it wouldn't be Fitch at this hour. The man knew better than to bother him. At least Noel thought he did. Noel ignored the tapping and rolled over. The knock sounded again, louder this time.

"Bloody Christ!" he muttered, throwing on a dressing robe over his nightshirt. He went to the door and opened it to find Dolly Gray standing on his threshold, dressed in a red Japanese kimono.

"Dolly! What are you doing here?"

"Shhh!" she whispered and pushed him into the darkened room, closing the door behind her. She brought with her the lingering fumes of brandy along with her perfume. "I just had to see you one last time. I couldn't let you leave without telling you . . . telling you . . ."

Noel fumbled around and lit his bedside lamp with a match, throwing harsh light on Dolly's tear-puffy face. "Telling me what?"

She flung herself into his arms. As round as she was short, it was like holding on to a big ball. "That I love you! I've loved you from the first moment we met. You're so suave and debonair and cultured. You're just the kind of man I've always hoped for."

Noel was horrified and yet perversely amused. "But Dolly, what about George?"

She dismissed her husband with an impatient wave of her hand. "He doesn't know the first thing about what a woman needs." She pulled back to look at him with her wet eyes. "But you, I know you would. I know you'd do more than just climb on and grunt a few times, then roll off. Oh, Noel, we'd be so perfect together, me and you." Without warning, she grabbed the back of his neck and dragged his head down to her smacking lips.

"Dolly, I think you might have gotten the wrong—"

She shook her head, refusing to hear any protest he might be about to offer. "I'd do anything for you, darling. Anything at all." To prove it, she dropped to her knees like a beggar.

With those words and her action, he felt his erection spring forward, and a hot white light flashed on in his head. Despite the woman's completely revolting manner and appearance, her total self-abasement affected him like an aphrodisiac. She was willing to degrade herself for him, to let him use her however he chose. And he could not resist.

"Anything?" he asked, just to hear her reassure him.

"Oh, God, yes."

He put out his hand and helped her to her feet. "Then come here, little dove, and prove it."

He led her to his bed and took off his robe. Then he pulled his nightshirt off over his head. He heard her gasp of delight and she reached out greedy hands to touch his flanks.

"No, no, not yet." He lay down and said, "First let us see how clever you are with those lips and that tongue. Then we'll explore parts of your body that I'd wager George has never considered during his grunting sessions."

CHAPTER THIRTEEN

In a month's time, Aidan and Farrell moved into their new home near the mill. Geoffrey Brother and Aidan had been able to reach an agreement that was satisfactory to them both. Farrell didn't know all of the details, but she suspected that they would be working for a long time to pay off this purchase. Or rather, Aidan would be working. She had understood what she would be required to do as a farm wife. As the lady of a house, she was not as well versed.

Their first night under this roof, she and Aidan had run through the halls like children, opening cupboards and drawers to see what was in them, whooping and laughing and acting like fools in general. But they had had a wonderful time pretending to be the lord and lady of the manor, even though that was a station neither of them craved.

Farrell's independent explorations revealed three bedrooms, including the master, the dining room, a study, a good-sized kitchen, a root cellar, and the attic. The attic was filled with old furniture draped in sheets, empty picture frames, and miscellaneous knickknacks. Worried that it was a fire hazard, Farrell wanted to get rid of the stuff up there, but Mrs. Hill carried on so, she abandoned the plan.

Mrs. Hill had asked to stay on after the sale. She'd worked in this house for nearly twenty years, she said, and after all that time, didn't know what else to do with herself. Aidan was more than amenable to the idea, but Farrell, less so. If she had a housekeeper, what was she supposed to do with her time? At least he hadn't argued about letting the cook go. She wanted to prepare their meals, and Aidan couldn't justify the expense of another servant right now.

Servant! Farrell thought with a shudder. Somehow it all seemed wrong. This wasn't what she'd envisioned when she thought of that new start he'd talked about.

Brother had told them that he had regular, loyal customers who would probably be happy to remain with Aidan. So far, that had proven to be true, and Aidan was up every day before the sun so that he could not only learn and oversee the operation of the mill, but could also call upon those customers as a gesture of goodwill. He didn't come up to the house until after the mill closed for the day, then when he did, he closed himself in the study to go over the books and try to get a sense of the expenses and income of the business.

Mrs. Hill had wanted to serve him his supper

in the study, but Farrell put a fast halt to that. If he wanted to eat, he had to come to the table and eat with *her*.

At the end of the long day, he'd fall into bed, worn out, then start the whole thing over again before dawn. He worked like a man possessed, and when she objected, he told her he'd be a fool to let such an opportunity pass him by. In Ireland, as dear as their homeland was, they'd starved and suffered centuries of subjugation. He had the chance to turn everything around for the two of them and give Farrell the best that money could buy.

Farrell regarded his explanations with a shadow of doubt. They already had so much more now than they'd had in Skibbereen, it seemed greedy to wish for more. But she also understood what drove Aidan—or thought she did.

Now it was November, and the days had grown short. The good thing about it was that nightfall came on at around five o'clock and Aidan couldn't work in the dark. So at least he was in the house some nights. On many others, he met with other businessmen and potential customers. Often he didn't get home until she was already in bed.

One night he came to bed and began nuzzling her neck, pulling her closer to him with both hands on her buttocks. He smelled wonderful, like fresh wood and a touch of whiskey, and his bare skin was warm against hers. But she wiggled away.

"What? What's wrong?" he asked.

She rolled over and faced him in the moonlight. "I haven't seen you all day. You were gone before I woke and I ate supper by myself again. Now ye come in here like a wraith, wake me up, and expect me to make love with you? I wouldn't mind except that it's like this every day. I didn't know I'd be living this 'better life' you promised me by myself."

Aidan withdrew to his own side of the big bed, feeling her coldness. "I'm sorry, lass. It won't always be this way. I'm just trying to make a success of this mill and it takes long hours. Ye have the house to keep you busy, don't you?"

"Mrs. Hill won't let me change anything. Whenever I try, she starts weeping and carrying on about the late Mrs. Brother, and how she liked things thus, and how she liked things so. It's as if the house belongs to Mrs. Hill instead of us."

"You have to take charge of the help, Farrell. That's your job. You have to let her know who's boss." He rolled to his back and put his hands behind his head. "My job is to get the knack of the business part of this, get new customers, keep the crew in line. I still have a lot to learn."

"Aye, that's the truth, Aidan. You do."

A silence fell over them in the darkness. He loved Farrell with his entire soul. He had for years. But, so far, knowing that she might still adore Liam, he hadn't been able to tell her with words. He wasn't sure if he'd heard her correctly the night they'd consummated their marriage, when she'd said that he had her trust and her heart. He couldn't bring himself to ask her about that either. He knew she wanted security and stability. All he could think to do was work harder to give her a life of ease. Maybe then he could win her love.

"I'm sorry, lass," he repeated. He leaned over and kissed her forehead. "I'll say good night, then."

She waited so long to respond, he wasn't sure she would. He lay down and closed his eyes.

"Good night."

"God, what a primitive backwater this is," Noel said to Fitch as they arrived at the dock in Portland. Compared to some of the other American cities he'd seen, this was nothing but some wood frame buildings and trees, trees, trees. The post office was a log cabin, and then there were more trees. He'd heard the stories of people packing up their belongings in wagons and making the six-month journey across the country to travel to Oregon. It was a perilous trip, it was said, and many died of disease and accidents along the way. Why in hell would anyone risk life and limb to come *here*? he wondered.

As they waited to disembark, he gave his henchman his instructions. "Our first order of business is to find out who the influential people are in these parts. If possible, I'd like to meet some others like the Grays." He didn't come right out and tell Fitch what amazing dupes they'd been, because in many ways, Fitch was also a dupe. But despite some truly grating moments, his association with George and Dolly had worked out well, especially at the end. He had left the woman in the hotel sobbing over his departure, after he'd used her like a common doxy in every possible way, and without the cost. In fact, she'd given him her massive diamond ring as a farewell gift, which he'd sold for cash. It had been most delightful.

"Then we must find O'Rourke. Find out where Oregon City is." He let his gaze stray to the muddy riverbanks. "I certainly hope it's more cosmopolitan than this place."

Farrell stood in the dining room, removing the china from the cabinet and putting it in an empty tea crate she'd found in the attic. She packed the dishes in wood shavings she'd gotten from the mill to keep them from breaking.

"Oh, no! You aren't going to put the china in the attic, are you? The poor missus loved it." Mrs. Hill was already groping in her apron pocket for her handkerchief.

Startled by the woman's trumpeting, Farrell jumped and nearly dropped the plate she held. She clenched her teeth to keep from saying the first rude thing that came to mind, that she didn't care what the "missus" had liked, and that if the housekeeper missed her so, she could go sit by her grave on the back acres. Instead, she replied, "Mrs. Hill, this is *my* home now, and my china. I know that ye grieve for your former mistress, and I'm sorry that you lost her. But my husband is working to pay for all this because it doesn't belong to Mr. Brother anymore. He sold it all to us. I thought you understood that when you asked to stay on—when you asked *us* to keep paying you. Now, Mr. O'Rourke has bought new dishes for me and I'd like to put them in the china cabinet."

Mrs. Hill ran from the room, sobbing into her apron—*again*—and Farrell clenched her teeth *again,* this time so hard that she began to get a headache. Or maybe she'd been getting a headache anyway. She'd been feeling poorly lately, irritable, and with an appetite that waxed and waned. Sometimes it seemed she couldn't get enough to eat and other mornings she woke up too sick to even look at food. She was sure it had to do with the commotion in her life.

And she was beginning to get the feeling that the housekeeper had asked to stay on not because she didn't know what to do with herself, as she'd said, but primarily to keep an eye on her dead mistress's belongings.

This was not going to work, Farrell decided, fed

up with the woman's daily emotional collapses. She didn't need a servant, and she surely didn't want one who treated her like a meddlesome guest in her own home. She'd rather take the woman's salary and use it on seed and other farming equipment in the spring. This house sat on Geoffrey Brother's donation land claim of three hundred twenty acres, the same kind of claim that Farrell and Aidan had planned to file before the business with the sawmill came along. The land had been cleared but now lay fallow, and she intended to farm it. And she'd tell Aidan so, the next time she saw him.

For now, though, Farrell decided to go lie down. She wasn't the type to give in to every little physical complaint, but suddenly, she was so sleepy, she couldn't keep her eyes open. It *had* to be due to the commotion.

A week later, Farrell went to answer a knock at the back door. Aidan had agreed to let her terminate Mrs. Hill, and it was a relief to be able to answer her own door, rearrange the furniture, and do anything else to the place she wanted. She'd asked for Aidan's help with the heavy pieces but he kept putting it off.

When she opened the door, she saw one of the mill workers standing there. "How do, ma'am. I'm Tom Fitzgerald. Your husband sent me up—he said you want some furniture moved?"

"Oh, yes! Please come in. I can shift the little things but some of the pieces are too heavy." The big, carrot-haired young man stepped into the kitchen. Farrell knew she saw Ireland in his face, but heard it only in his name and not his voice. "Forgive my asking, Mr. Fitzgerald, but were ye born here?"

"No, ma'am. I was born in County Mayo."

"Were you, now?" she asked, pleased.

"Yes, but my family came to America when I was just a baby. I don't remember anything about Ireland."

"Ah, that's a shame. It's a beautiful place."

He grinned. "That's what my ma told me. You sound like her, too. The rest of the family is in Heppner raising sheep. That's east of here about a hundred and fifty miles. It's nice to hear the accent again."

Farrell laughed. "You must hear it every day from Mr. O'Rourke."

His smile faded slightly. "Yes'm. Every day. Shall we see about that furniture?"

She couldn't help but notice the change, both of subject and Tom Fitzgerald's attitude when she mentioned Aidan. "Have you worked at the mill long?" she asked, leading him to the parlor.

"About three years, now. Mr. Brother hired me when I was just sixteen. I appreciated it. He was a good man to work for."

And Aidan O'Rourke is not. Maybe it was Farrell's imagination, but it seemed that Tom might have finished his sentence that way if he'd been talking to someone else. Something was going on.

"Good to his men, was he?" she prodded.

"Oh, yes, ma'am. And we always gave him our best work because of it. Some bosses, um, some people think that if you drive workers like cattle, they'll move faster. But that can lead to trouble—mistakes, accidents, hard feelings among the crew."

"Yes, I'm sure that's so."

Tom helped her move the sofa so that it faced the fireplace, and put the matching marble-topped round tables on either end.

"There, that's better," she said, happy with the result. "Thank you for your help, Tom. I'm glad I had the chance to meet you."

She walked him to the back door. "Same here, ma'am. Let me know if you need anything else."

"I will." She spied the soda bread from breakfast still sitting on the table. She'd finally figured out how to bake in an oven. "Oh, here, I have something for you." She cut a slice and gave it to him. "To remind you of your mam."

Genuine pleasure lighted his face. "Thanks, Mrs. O'Rourke. I haven't had soda bread in a long time."

She watched him bound down the steps and walk back toward the mill, savoring his bread as he went. He seemed like a very nice young man.

But she was worried by what he'd revealed about Aidan. Her husband had bought her a satin dress and fancy table linens, and he often brought her silly little gifts. And God above, he'd even bought two suits for himself and had taken to wearing one every day. He looked very handsome dressed nicely, but what good was any of it if he lost the man inside whom she'd come to love?

Yes, she had to finally admit it to herself. Farrell was in love with Aidan. He was tender, considerate, loyal, funny—in fact, he was everything that his brother had not been. Looking back, she wondered why she'd been so blind and insistent about Liam. She saw him now as Aidan had described him, and as Liam had described himself. Methodical and dispassionate, as steady as a rock, but just as dull.

Aidan was a good man, probably the best she'd ever met.

She let her gaze drift to the roof of the mill in the distance and remembered Tom Fitzgerald's barely subtle comments.

Aidan, she thought, Aidan what are ye doing?

After she closed the back door, Farrell felt her own soda bread coming up and she knew something wasn't right. After retching into the slop bucket, she rinsed out her mouth and caught her breath. This had to be more than just worry and nerves. Then she stopped to think, and counted backward. Her jaw dropped as she stared at the three fingers she'd ticked off. She'd missed three monthly cycles—well, Jesus, Mary, and Joseph, she was pregnant. In fact, she had probably conceived the first time she made love with Aidan.

She smiled to herself, and thought of how she would tell him. Over supper tonight, maybe. Yes, that would be good. She'd cook something special, a roast chicken and some potatoes—thank the Holy Mother that they finally had enough to eat.

A child. Aidan's and hers. This might be just what he needed to make him remember what was really important.

Aidan hurried up to the house at four o'clock to wash and change clothes. He'd received a message from Dr. McLoughlin, asking him to a attend business dinner at his home. The man was not well these days, but occasionally he brought a gathering together.

"Farrell?" he called, walking through the front door. "Farrell, ye need to dress for supper."

"What?" She came out of the kitchen and met him in the back hallway. She wore an apron with chicken feathers stuck to it.

He laughed and gave her a casual kiss. "I've seen ye like this before, *a muirnín.* You've been wringing necks again."

She arched a brow at him. "Yes, and I'm very good at it, so you'd best watch your step."

"Well, you need to get dressed. We've been invited to supper."

"But—tonight?"

"Yes, I got a message from Dr. McLoughlin. He apologized for the short notice, but he wants me to come for supper to introduce me to some new customers. We need to be there by six o'clock."

"But what about the chicken and potatoes I'm roasting? And the pound cake I'm making for dessert? I was planning something special."

He was already heading upstairs to their bedroom. "They'll hold, won't they? Maybe you can take them out of the oven and finish them when we get back. Besides, this is more important." There was a crash downstairs in the kitchen. "Did ye drop something?" he called.

She came into the bedroom while he stripped off his shirt. "Would you like me to demonstrate how I wrung that chicken's neck?" She sounded angry, and he knew to tread carefully.

He rummaged through the bureau, looking for his cravat. "Did Tom Fitzgerald come up to help with the furniture?"

"He did."

He glanced over his shoulder at her. "What, was he not properly respectful to you?"

She reached into the wardrobe for a dress.

"He's very nice. He told me about his family and their sheep farm in Heppner, and talked about Mr. Brother. He said that he was a good man to work for."

"Sure and everyone and their donkey is moaning about Mr. Brother this, and Mr. Brother that. I think all Mr. Brother did was spoil that crew so I can't get a decent day's work out of them. I'm trying to remedy that, but I'm worried the damage may already be done. Most of them have got ten thumbs and they're slower than the Second Coming."

"Aidan!" She worked at the buttons of her bodice.

" 'Tis true. I've got orders coming in right and left. I don't want to just deliver them on time. I want to beat that time. I'm not asking anything of them I wouldn't demand from myself. When I think of how hard we had it, and how we slaved in those fields—"

"Like whipped curs, ye mean? Or maybe like those people we saw chained together in New Orleans."

He ducked, trying to see his image in the mirror to comb his hair. "God, what bee slipped under your bonnet, Farrell?" He looked up at her and she was putting away her dress again. "Don't dawdle, lass. We don't have much time."

"I have a headache and I'm not going. You go and have your business meeting. I'll be here when you get back." She left the room then and went downstairs. For such a small-boned woman, she had a heavy step sometimes. He could hear her heels thumping through the hallway.

Aidan winced. She was angrier than he'd realized. Ah, well, a ruined supper plan wasn't the end of the world. He'd buy her a little gift tomorrow, and she'd forget all about it.

He rode the horse that had come with the mill to Dr. McLoughlin's house. Inside, he was ushered into the parlor where he was given a drink by a serving woman and presented to several businessmen and their wives. As he worked his way through the introductions, he spotted a man who looked vaguely familiar. There was nothing remarkable about his balding head and squat roundness, but still—

"I feel we've met before, but not around here," he said to the man. "Are ye newly come?"

"We *have* met before, O'Rourke. I'm Seth Fitch, and you won a sizable amount of money from me in a card game in New Orleans."

"Of course, now I remember!" If nothing else, his Southern accent gave him away as an outsider, just as Aidan's Irish accent marked him. He pumped the man's hand. "Whatever brings you to these parts? Surely not another sugar cane contract."

"Oh, no, I left that position. I'm in business for

myself now, with a few select clients."

"Are you? Well, that's good news. So you'll be staying in the area?"

"No, no, I'm just here on a special assignment. I don't imagine I'll be here long. But I was hoping I'd have a chance to meet your wife."

Aidan gave him a sharper look. "Oh? Why is that?"

He smiled. "You'd told us all what a beauty she is that night at the Lass of Killarney. I was hoping to see for myself."

Despite the tension that night, he knew he'd done no such thing. He never would have discussed Farrell's appearance in a place like that. It would have been insulting to her. "What special assignment are ye working on?" he asked, changing the subject.

"I'm just investigating some business opportunities."

Aidan couldn't put a name to what he felt, but a cold hand of apprehension gripped his heart and then faded.

Supper and the meeting went smoothly enough, but he found himself talking less and listening more. With Fitch in the room, he was on guard and he didn't know why. There was just something about him that Aidan didn't like.

Something very bad.

CHAPTER FOURTEEN

WHEN Aidan came around the bend in the road that led to his house, he was grateful for the light pouring from the windows. All the way home, he'd kept glancing over his shoulder, trying to peer through the cold and damp November darkness to see if he was being followed. Now and then, when the clouds parted to let the moon light his way, he'd speed his mount, ducking under the canopy of tree branches that lined the road. Then he would slow it again and listen. It was quiet here and it would be hard for someone to follow him on horseback without him hearing it.

He had nothing on which to base his cautiousness and unease except Fitch's presence at that meeting. It had gone well otherwise. Aidan had met several men who were interested in doing business with O'Rourke Lumber Mill. The territory was growing, his prospects were good, and the future more promising than he'd ever dared hope when he undertook this operation. He'd expected to have to work for years to attain even half the success he saw looming ahead.

Yet, as he led the horse into the stable and

lighted a lamp hanging from the doorframe, Aidan realized there was another side to this good fortune. He'd begun to worry about losing it, about something going wrong. The success of his business was not only vital to his sense of accomplishment, but he also saw it as critical to winning and keeping Farrell's heart. He'd promised her so much and he had to make good on those promises.

Aidan unharnessed and dried his mount with a piece of sacking, fed him, and then, with a last look around, went to the back door. Farrell wouldn't appreciate him tracking mud into the entryway, and she was already put out with him over supper. Just inside the kitchen, he kicked off his boots.

A faint aroma of roast chicken still lingered and he felt a twinge of regret that he'd had to miss it. She had a talent for cooking that he hadn't suspected. In Ireland, the food had been so basic and the options so few, there hadn't been much opportunity to learn to do anything beyond baking soda bread—when they had the flour—and preparing potatoes in one of three ways, boiling, frying, or baking them.

Carrying the candle she'd left burning for him on the table, he went upstairs to their bedroom. Farrell was still awake and sitting up in bed reading. Her lovely red hair hung in a braid over the front of her shoulder and she'd propped the book on her bent knees like a young lass.

"Hello, *céadsearc*," he said from the doorway. "Am I allowed to come in?"

She looked up at him and he could see she still harbored a bit of annoyance with him. "If you've a mind to visit for a while before you're gone again."

He walked in and put the candle on his bedside table. "What are you reading?"

She flipped to the title page. "It's called *The Life and Strange Surprizing Adventures of Robinson Crusoe, of York, Mariner.*"

"You're reading about an Englishman? And a seaman? I'd have thought you'd had your fill of both."

"This one is shipwrecked."

Her brief answers confirmed his suspicions. "You're still displeased, aye?" he asked, sitting next to her.

She sighed and put a scrap of ribbon in the book to hold her place. "I wanted to spend the evening with you. I had something to tell you."

He loosened his collar. "Well, I'm glad you didn't go with me tonight." Realizing this didn't sound very good, he was about to tell her about Seth Fitch, then changed his mind. It might frighten her, and he didn't want to do that. He would have to keep a sharp lookout himself for the man. Instead he finished, "You'd have been bored."

She looked at him. "Do you think me not smart enough to follow a conversation that doesn't have to do with housekeeping or babies or the quilting bees at St. John's Church?"

He realized he was only digging himself a deeper hole. "No, I didn't mean that. Besides, I thought you were glad that we have a parish now so we can attend mass and see the neighbors. You have some friends like Marigold Lewis and—and—" He tapped his forehead with his fingertips, trying to remember the other women she'd met.

She gave him a look of utter frustration and closed the book with a loud clap. "I *am* glad, ye great dunderhead! But I expect to see you, as well!"

Didn't she understand that he was working this hard for her? He sat on the bed. "I'm sorry, little red one. I know I've been busy, but it will all pay off for us. I promise. And I haven't broken a promise to you yet." He locked his little finger with hers where her hand rested on the coverlet. At least she didn't pull away. He remembered something she'd said when he walked in. "Ye wanted to tell me something? What?" She turned her face away and a moment or two passed. "What is it?" he urged.

When she looked back at him, tears streamed down her cheeks. "It's important. More important than your *damned* meeting."

He'd heard her swear only one other time, and it was when she was very angry. Her tears were a harsher punishment than her anger, though. "What is it, then?"

"I—we—there's going to be a child."

He squinted at her and shrugged, perplexed. "A child?"

"Yes, a child! You and I, we're going to have a baby."

He stared at her with wide eyes and a huge grin. "A baby? Really?" Now she was crying in earnest, and he felt like the world's greatest cad.

"Would I joke about such a thing? I planned a nice dinner and I was going to tell you after. But you left."

No wonder she was so upset. He took her into his arms, and though she was stiff at first, she relaxed against him. "I wish you had told me before I went out the door. I never would have left ye if I'd known."

"I didn't want to just blurt it out like that. It's—it's *special*."

"Aye, it is, very special." He looked off across the room, imagining a red-haired lad. "A son."

She gave him a slight frown. "I didn't say that! It might be a girl, ye know."

"It might be," he agreed, but thought to himself, *A son!* "You're sure?"

"I'm sure."

"Then you must rest," he said, pulling back to look at her tear-streaked face. "Do you think we can get Mrs. Hill to come back?"

Making a rude noise with her mouth, she said,

"I don't want that woman back here, and I don't need anyone. Did our mams have housekeepers? No, they had their children without even enough to eat or peat for the fire. I'm sturdy. I'll do."

He shook his head, baffled. "Farrell, I don't understand why ye resist every bit of peace, ease, and comfort I try to give you. Don't you know that I only want to make your life better? Happier?"

She sat up a little and looked into his face. God, but she was a beauty with those green eyes and delicate copper brows. "We both grew up barely seeing a farthing from one year to the next. I learned to live without and to be thrifty. I can't forget all that overnight. Besides, satin dresses and pretty china are lovely, but they aren't what will make me happy."

"What is it, then?"

"I want to farm that claim out back."

"What? When?"

"I'd hoped this spring, but I might be otherwise occupied now."

"I can plow it for ye come February. How can I know what you want if you don't tell me? Besides, you can have both, can't you? Nice things and a farm?"

She nodded, a bit unwillingly. "Aye, I guess. But I'd like a husband at home, too."

"Once we're established, I promise I'll be home more often." Aidan supposed that a frugal wife was better than one who spent him into the poorhouse. But now, more than ever, he had reason to work hard. His child would not grow up ignorant entirely, or be educated in the hedges. There would be real school and perhaps, God willing, university. It made him a little nervous to think about it—an O'Rourke going to university. His own parents had not even been able to read or write.

He lay down beside her and pulled her closer. "Just the same, I don't want you to wear yourself out. Um, when do ye think the babe will come?"

"In the spring, around May, I think." She yawned. "I've been so sleepy lately, I can barely keep my eyes open."

He lay with Farrell sleeping in his arms till the candle burned low. He eased her to her pillow and moved the book from her lap so that he could undress for bed. Morning would come early for him, and now more than ever, he had reason to be up before the dawn, pushing the crew to keep the mill running at top speed.

A baby.

"I love you, *céadsearc*," he whispered to her sleeping form, and drew the blankets to her chin.

"I tried to find out about her for you, your lordship, but O'Rourke wouldn't say anything. To hear him, you'd almost think he has no wife. But I've talked to people who have met her. They say she's got fire-red hair, and they've verified her name—Farrell."

Seth Fitch reported to Noel Cardwell in the room he'd taken at the Linn City Hotel, just across the river from Oregon City. As always, Fitch remained standing, like any good butler or manservant who recognized his place in the social order.

Noel paced the room, his hands behind his back, as he studied the pattern of the rug beneath his boots. "And you say he has his own business? Not a farm?"

Fitch filled him in on what details he had about O'Rourke's enterprise. "He's doing well, it seems. But he's also making some enemies."

Noel looked up, interested. "Is he? Tell me more."

"I've lingered in the taverns around town. Some of his employees are not too happy with the change of the mill's ownership."

That didn't surprise Noel. The working class always had some whining complaint, about their pay, their employers, their working conditions. The ungrateful good-for-nothings. God knew he'd heard it all often enough in Skibbereen.

"What about other merchants and businessmen? Any complaints there?"

"None that I know of. In fact, I've heard mostly good things about the man, that he's honest and ambitious. Dr. McLoughlin speaks well of him, too."

Noel made a sour face at the name. Although John McLoughlin was a wealthy prominent citizen in the Oregon Territory, Noel had learned that the Canadian-born man had defied a direct order from his own employer, Hudson's Bay Company, by providing aid and comfort to emigrating settlers. It had been a British-controlled territory and their aim, naturally, had been to discourage such settlement of Americans. Instead, softhearted McLoughlin had extended credit to them, cared for their sick, fed, clothed, and housed them. He even gave them seed for planting and donated land for public use, including five different churches, a school, and a jail. Eventually he resigned from Hudson's Bay Company and relinquished his British citizenship by becoming an American. And this after he'd received a knighthood from Queen Victoria herself. God, what Noel wouldn't give to kneel before his queen and receive the tap of her scepter. The man's actions were beyond Noel's comprehension. So of course he would think well of Aidan O'Rourke, and Noel knew he could expect no assistance from him in bringing the bastard down.

"McLoughlin will be no help," Noel said aloud. "But this discontentment among the mill employees could work in our favor." He went to the window and looked out at the river rolling past and the large, snow-covered mountain on the gray, eastern horizon. "In fact, it might be smarter to take advantage of their unhappiness and win McLoughlin's favor separately." It could serve as a screen between himself and the outcome of his plan, but he didn't voice the idea. In the end, he would sacrifice anyone, including the dog-faithful Fitch, to attain his goal and keep himself above suspicion. Farrell would be his, just as soon as he dispatched her troublesome husband.

"Shall I mingle with the mill workers, your lordship?" Fitch asked.

"Yes, see if you can learn anything else. But for God's sake, be discreet. There's no point in arousing undue curiosity. We can't know who might decide to play both sides against the middle, befriending you and then betraying you to O'Rourke."

Fitch nodded. "Yes, sir."

"In the meantime, I'll see about getting an introduction to McLoughlin. Perhaps that famed generosity of his can work to my advantage."

The next month or so went smoothly enough. Farrell's clothes were getting to be too small and she spent part of her time letting out the waist seams of her dresses. But she knew there would come a point when she'd have to stitch up new things to wear for later on, when she grew much bigger. Fortunately, her queasy stomach had finally calmed down and she was feeling altogether better, Brigit be thanked.

One morning she sat in the parlor, working on her alterations, chatting and having tea with Marigold Lewis, a woman close to her own age whom she'd met at church. Marigold's husband had recently presented her with a charming little pony cart that she drove all over town. The little beastie that pulled it was a sweet, gentle animal but strong enough to do the job, and it gave Marigold the mobility that Farrell craved. Unless someone came to get her, or Aidan was available to take her, Farrell had to walk everywhere. That hadn't been a problem in Ireland—her excursions rarely took her farther than a mile or two from home. But this was a big territory. Things were more spread out, and it rained as much here as it did in Ireland. Of course, the cart offered no shelter against the weather, but Marigold, possessing an ingenuity that Farrell recognized and respected, had suspended a tarp over the seat of the cart to cover her on rainy days. Farrell had learned long ago that resourcefulness could mean the difference between surviving and not.

"Maybe I should talk to Aidan about getting one of those wee carts. I could go to mass for some of the feast days, if I was of a mind, and I wouldn't feel so alone up here. Maybe it could be my Christmas present—for the next five years!"

They both laughed, and Marigold's long, bony face lighted with enthusiasm. "Definitely, that would be wonderful. That little cart has made my life easier, I can tell you. I do my errands in town and go calling—oh, all kinds of things. And now that you're expecting, you shouldn't be walking too far. My doctor said it isn't good for the baby." She had two children of her own.

"Really?" Farrell had never consulted a doctor in her entire life.

"Yes, a little exercise and fresh air is enough."

Just then, as if in response, Farrell felt a flip-flop low in her belly. She let out a quiet gasp of delight. Putting her hand over the place, she waited. There it was again.

"What?" The other young woman looked alarmed. "Are you all right?"

Farrell laughed in surprise, her mouth open in astonishment. "The baby moved."

Marigold pressed a hand to her chest and laughed in relief. "Oh! I remember the first time that happened to me."

Farrell was so excited she threw down her sewing and rose from the sofa. "I can't wait to tell Aidan." She would hurry down the quarter mile to the mill and find Aidan to tell him. Giggling, she ran to the kitchen and grabbed her shawl from its hook by the back door. With her hand on the knob, she was ready to leave.

"Farrell, wait!" Marigold hurried after her, her heels tapping on the hardwood floor in the hallway. "You can't do that."

"Why not?"

"Well, dear, it isn't at all fitting. Think a moment of where you're going."

Farrell nodded. "Oh. Of course, you're right." She couldn't do this. It wouldn't be appropriate. If Aidan were a farmer out in the fields with just his horse, that would be different. They would have no witnesses but the earth and sky. Oh, and the horse. But the mill was big, noisy, and dirty, full of men shouting to be heard over the din, and not a place where a woman went to tell her husband about something so private. She'd been inside the mill only twice and those visits had proved to be quite enough.

Though she might burst with the anticipation, she'd wait until suppertime. She took off her shawl and went back to the study to take up her sewing again. After Marigold left, she spent most of her day wearing a private little smile and cherishing her secret.

That evening, Farrell and Aidan were sitting at the dining room table, enjoying poached salmon, when she said casually, "I felt the baby move today."

Aidan who had been a bit preoccupied until that moment, snapped up his head to look at her. "Ye did?"

She knew she wore a sly smile. "Aye, three times. Twice while Marigold was here, and one more time after."

He grinned and reached over to squeeze her hand. "He's a little mischief-maker with his fists, aye?"

Farrell lifted her brows and pointed her fork at him. "*She* might have just been shifting in her sleep. That's what Marigold told me."

He returned her sly look, one that said, think what you like.

"Aidan, that reminds me. Marigold has a gorgeous little horsecart that she can take everywhere. Her pony is as gentle as an old dog and she whisks around fine. I haven't asked for much, but that's something I'd truly like. I could get about on my own for visiting and such."

"Not now, little red one. Maybe after the babe comes."

"Why not?"

"I don't like the idea of ye out there alone in one of those little contraptions. Gentle or not, the pony could pull up lame too far from help. Or worse, the cart could overturn and you could hurt the baby, or be injured yourself. I don't like the sound of it."

"But—"

"After the babe is born and the weather improves, we'll talk about it again."

She put down her fork. "Aidan, you're away so much and I'm lonely here, especially at night."

He gave her a horrified look. "Christ, woman,

ye wouldn't go about at night in the thing, would you? No man worth his boot polish would allow his wife to do something so foolish and dangerous."

"Well, no, I suppose not," she agreed.

"Hmph." He made a satisfied sound. "I wouldn't think so. I promise I'll try to be home more often now that you're advancing in your— your condition."

She smiled, obviously pleased with that. "Then after the baby is born—"

"Yes, then. But you won't have a cart. Maybe a phaeton or something else more substantial."

After dinner, Aidan led Farrell upstairs to bed, anxious for sleep himself. These were long, hard days. But Farrell had other ideas. Some women, he'd heard, had no interest in making love after they became pregnant, and wouldn't even allow their husbands to cast eyes upon them when they were barefoot. Not his wife. She permitted him to see her sweetly rounding body in the candlelight, and she was shyly eager to be with him, to touch him.

When she joined him in bed, the sweet scent of her surrounded him, making him feel as if he were walking through a garden, rife with wild lavender. He didn't know if it was a perfume she wore, the soap she used, or just an essence entirely her own that emanated from her skin, but the fragrance intoxicated him. One thought moved through his mind, that he wanted her—needed her. Just the idea of burying himself in her moist heat made his body harden.

At first he had worried that he would hurt the child, but she'd assured him that he wouldn't and had taken charge of matters. Now, once more, he found himself helpless on his back, with her straddling him and driving him beyond the bounds of any passion he'd ever known before. Her hair, Christ help him, fell like a silken curtain streaked with fire, warm where it pooled on his chest, electrical as it slid like a caress over his skin.

Aidan knew he was a lucky man. He had everything he'd ever dreamed of, everything he'd ever hoped for. He lifted his hips to enter her, praying as he did that all would go well when she bore his child. Then with one shift of her own hips, she drove the worry and every other thought from his mind as spasms of excruciating pleasure shuddered through his body, one upon another.

Afterward, as he gathered her close in his arms, he wished to feel the baby move, but the wee thing was evidently asleep.

No matter, Aidan thought as sleep closed over him. He already held the entire world in his arms. How could he yearn for anything more?

Aidan came downstairs for breakfast to find Farrell doing laundry in the tub she kept on the back porch. She'd left the door ajar and he paused in the entrance to the kitchen to watch her. He could see steam rising from the water as she rubbed one of his shirts on the washboard. Her apron was tied about her waist, revealing the soft swell of her belly. Although it was a chilly autumn morning, the work was hot and made loose tendrils of her hair curl like burnished copper springs around her face. She'd rolled up her sleeves to her elbows, and the muscles in her pale, slender arms flexed with the effort of the job. He didn't like to see her working that hard, especially in her condition. And yet . . . there was something arousing about the picture she made, a sturdy, finely made Irish lass, carrying his child beneath her heart, and framed by the pewter-gray sky.

"Ye look quite fetching out there, Mrs. O'Rourke," he said, coming out to talk with her.

She looked up at him, and he saw that either the hot water or the brisk air had put roses in her cheeks. The sparkle in her green eyes, he knew, was hers alone. "Do I now?" she asked, a coy note in her voice. "So you have a taste for washerwomen, then?"

"Maybe. I used to like milkmaids and shepherd girls, too."

Sticking out her tongue at him, she slashed the water with the edge of her hand. He jumped, but not quickly enough, and he was wet from chest to knees. "Used to. Now it's just washerwomen."

"Ah, no, not all of them. Just one," he replied. He closed his arms around her growing waist, and nuzzled her neck.

"You'll have no clean shirts if you don't let me finish here," she said, without much conviction.

"I'd rather have my breakfast—in bed."

She gave him a scandalized look, and then laughed. "You are wild and unrepentant, Aidan O'Rourke."

"Aye, that I am," he agreed, letting his hands run up and down her damp arms, raising gooseflesh as he went. "And that's why you love me." He threw that out and held his breath, not knowing how she would respond.

"That must be why. D'ye think I'd wash just any man's shirts if I didn't?" She turned into his embrace and kissed him, her warm breath fanning his cheek.

His blood turned to fire. She hadn't come right out and said she loved him, but Aidan, starved for any sign of devotion that she might give him, grabbed onto her response like a drowning man reaching for a lifeline. He pulled her away from the tub and held her against the length of his body. "Damn the clean shirts. I'd rather have you instead."

She stepped back and looked up at him with a mischievous glint. "But you'll have to catch me." Squealing, she ran back through the kitchen and down the hallway. He gave her a bit of a head start to add to the fun, but when she got to the top of the stairs, she was winded. He picked her up and carried her to their bedroom, kicking the door shut behind him.

CHAPTER FIFTEEN

TEN days before Christmas, Farrell stood in the kitchen peeling potatoes and onions for the supper stew she was cooking when three of Aidan's mill workers came to the front door. One of them she recognized as Tom Fitzgerald. He introduced the others to her, Pete Dorsett and James Cole. As strong and broad as Tom, they nodded at her and mumbled a greeting.

"If you're looking for Mr. O'Rourke, he'll be down at the mill," she said, wiping her hands on her apron.

"Yes, ma'am, he sent us up. He asked us to bring this to the house." He gestured over his shoulder and she saw a horse-drawn wagon with crates in the back.

"What is that?"

"I don't know, but we're to unpack them and bring them in. Oh, and before I forget—" He reached into his pocket and handed her an envelope that bore her name, written in Aidan's hand.

She watched as they pried open the crates and carried in a large dining room table, twelve chairs, and one smaller item that was wrapped in burlap.

"What in the name of Saint Patrick—" she began, rubbing her arms to warm them in the cold December breeze that blew through the open door. By the time they were finished, they'd set up the new furniture and carried the old set to the attic.

"Is there anything else we can do while we're here, Mrs. O'Rourke?" Tom asked.

"No, not that I can think of. Would ye like some hot tea or coffee before you go back? Cakes? Maybe a sandwich. It's a raw day outside."

Tom shifted uneasily. "Um, no, ma'am. But thank you. Mr. O'Rourke said we weren't to dawdle."

"Oh. Well, thank you for your help. I hope all of you and your families have a happy Christmas."

As they went down the front stairs and climbed back into the wagon, she heard one of them say, "She's a sight nicer than her old man, that skinflint bastard. Too bad he ain't got the kindness that old Mr. Brother had. Firing Jacob just for taking a little drink—"

There was a shushing sound when one of them turned and realized she was still standing in the open doorway. Slowly, she closed the door, embarrassed and disappointed that her husband was viewed so poorly by his own employees. Just from things Aidan had said to her, she suspected that they had good reason to grumble, and that bothered her even more.

She wandered into the dining room to look at the new furniture. It was beautiful and she knew it must have cost a lot of money. But there had been nothing wrong with the table and chairs they'd bought with the house. The table hadn't been as big but it was a nice piece. What was Aidan up to? she wondered. What compelled him to spend money on these trappings and drive his workers so hard that they called him names and complained bitterly about him?

Remembering the burlap-wrapped bundle left in the parlor, she went down the hall and untied the cord that held the rough covering in place. "Ohhh," she said aloud, and sat on the floor beside it, her annoyance forgotten. Inside was a lovely cradle with a soft feather tick and a satin blanket. She ran her hand along the edge of the dark, polished wood, wondering again about the man she'd married. "Oh, Aidan." Tears filled her eyes when she imagined their sweet child sleeping in this cozy bed. She did love him, she realized, she loved him so. And she was happy being his wife, happy with everything, except the way he worked himself.

The note, he'd sent a note. She reached into her apron pocket and opened the envelope.

Dear Farrell—
    I hope ye Enjoy the early Christmas presents I am sending to the house. I think

the Cradle will fit nicely next to our bed.

And since I Have delivered you some nice gifts, I am hoping you will not Be too angry with me for missing supper tonight. I have a meeting with one of my Customers about a rush order. Please know that it is important, for nothing else could take me from your side.

I will Make every Effort to be home before you are asleep. I love you, *céadsearc*.

Your Husband,
Aidan

Important. Farrell lowered the note to her lap and she sighed. He loved her, he said, but that accursed mill took him from her. It even prevented him from expressing his love for her to her face. She was beginning to detest it. It took Aidan away from her at night, it had made him acquisitive, and although he was good to her, his employees found him to be an unkind taskmaster. Of all people, Aidan, who had suffered under the yoke of another man's oppression, should know better and have empathy.

"Sometimes he makes me think of old Lord Cardwell himself. Maybe he bought that blasted table and chairs so we can have grand parties, the kind we all sneered at back home," she muttered aloud, then realized what she had said and how disloyal it was. But what was she to think? His obsession with work and success was growing worse with each passing week.

She hoisted herself from the floor, a task that had become more difficult lately with the shift of her weight. That stew she was cooking wouldn't go to waste as had some of her other suppers. She'd finish it and if Aidan got it for breakfast, he'd damned well better not complain.

Just as Farrell sat down to eat, she felt the first twinge. Ah, it was just the babe settling more comfortably, she thought. She took a bite of the stew and was pleased with the way it had turned out. She smiled to herself. Maybe Aidan wouldn't *mind* having it for breakfast. Looking down the length of the lovely dining room table, she thought of the men who had brought it. Aidan was driving them, but who or what was driving Aidan? What made him want to buy all of these—

She felt another twinge, followed by a pain sharp enough to make her drop her spoon. Dear God, what was that?

She got up from her chair and felt a flooding warmth between her legs. When she looked down, she saw a large bloodstain on the upholstery of the new chair.

"Oh, no," she mourned, "oh, please no!"

She tried to remember if she'd heard of any

practical cures to prevent miscarriage, but nothing came to mind. All she could think of was to lie down.

She worked her way up the stairs, carrying a candlestick in one hand and gripping the railing with the other. In the bedroom, she took off her clothes and was horrified by the amount of blood she found. After a frantic search for her carving of Brigit in her skirt pocket, she left her clothes in a heap on the floor, pulled her nightgown on over her head, and climbed into bed to lie on her back with her feet propped up on the footboard, hoping and praying that she could stop this.

Frightened and yearning for a familiar face, a hand to hold, for the first time since leaving, she wished with all her heart that she were back in Ireland. In the *clachan* they'd been poverty-stricken and they'd had nothing, except each other. Yet, in that they had been rich. What good was it to lie on fine white sheets, only to live through the loss of her child alone?

Another wrenching cramp twisted her womb and another. She prayed to Brigit, she prayed the rosary, she appealed directly to God. Tonight, though, she felt truly forsaken. The prayers did not comfort her and they did not stop the bleeding or the cramping.

Tonight, she was utterly deserted.

． ． ．

Aidan rode up the drive at about ten o'clock. He hadn't seen the perfidious Seth Fitch since the night at Dr. McLoughlin's and he was glad for that. Maybe it had been his imagination that the man was up to no good. Maybe he'd done whatever business had called him here and was gone. But Aidan doubted it.

The lights still burned in the house, which surprised him. These days Farrell could barely stay awake beyond half past eight. He hoped that the furniture he'd sent up this afternoon had appeased her. He'd promised to spend more time with her, but he'd not yet found a way to do so. He didn't worry about her health—she had convinced him that she was strong. But he knew that she would be lonely here with no one to talk to most of her day. Visitors were not that frequent and except for church on Sundays the mill kept him so busy, he usually didn't have time to take her out.

After stabling his horse, he went up the back stairs and into the kitchen. What he found stopped his heart in his chest. Farrell's wooden laundry tub sat in the middle of the floor, filled with bloodred water and what looked like sheets. A bloody trail across the floor, smeared and diluted as if someone had tried to mop it up, led out through the hallway to the stairs. He ran toward the staircase but paused at the doorway to the dining room. There he found the new table and chairs, a plate of unfinished stew, and a chair seat also soaked with blood.

Panic dried his throat to chalk and his heart pounded back to life, banging against his ribs. "Farrell!" He flew up the steps two at a time and pounded down the upper hall toward their bedroom. "Farrell!" he called again.

He didn't see her at first. The bed was stripped and empty, the tick bloodstained. Then he saw a bundle on the floor wrapped in blankets, huddled like the most unfortunate wretch he'd ever seen trembling in a Skibbereen doorway during the famine. He dropped to his knees and took her by the shoulders. "God, Farrell, what happened? Are ye alive?"

Her face was the color of cold ashes in the fireplace. Next to her was the cradle he'd sent her. And in the cradle, under the satin blanket, lay a little figure with just its head showing. A cross had been drawn on its forehead with what looked like oil.

He sat back on his heels, aghast, feeling as if a horse had kicked him in the chest. He couldn't breathe, and though he groped for words, none would come. "Oh, Jesus," he intoned at last. "Jesus and God and Holy Mother Mary."

"I tried them all," Farrell croaked. "None of them helped." The tone of her voice frightened him.

It sounded like someone else's, an old woman's, hoarse, papery, bitter. "None of them."

"Come on, lass, ye can't stay here on the floor. You need to lie down."

She turned slitted, furious eyes on him, like those of a cornered mother cat. "You leave us alone," she fairly hissed. He wasn't sure if it was a demand or an accusation. "I'll do, and it won't be any different than usual."

He pulled away and stared at her. "Are ye blaming me for this, then?" he asked quietly.

"I'm blaming you for always doing exactly as you've pleased, and never mind what I wanted. I blame you for leaving me to suffer through this by myself because everything you have to do is so much more important than what little I've asked of ye. Yes, you've given me fine china, and furniture, and useless stuff I have no need for. What I needed was you!" Her voice broke and her gray face crumpled. "And where were you when our child died? You were out being Mr. High-and-Mighty."

"Farrell—"

"You shut up! You'll listen to me this time, by God, you will!" she screamed at him. "Can ye not see what you've become? You're no better than Lord Cardwell, the man you cursed often enough. Well, your workers curse *you* and rue the day that you bought out Mr. Brother. Did you know that? It's true. I heard it myself."

Her accusations were like knife slashes to Aidan's heart. "Farrell, let me help you to bed. You're tired and sick." He tried to take her arm to help her to her feet, but she yanked it from his grasp.

"No, I'm *sick and tired* of the way we've been living! And be quiet, damn you, because I'll have my say. You give me a note that says you love me, yet you leave me alone night after night, telling me that somehow it's all for my own good. For someday. But I don't need all the fancy trappings you've given us—I need *you* and I've told you so. Should I have written it on my forehead?" She gestured at the dead child. "This baby needed you here, not chasing around the countryside, grubbing every dollar you can get your hands on. You must choose, Aidan. You must choose me and a simpler life, or the mill. Because you can't have both."

He looked at the tiny little soul under the satin blanket and tears blurred his eyes. It was impossible to tell if the child was a girl or a boy, but it didn't matter. His heart ached for all three of them. He tried to take her into his arms, but she pulled away again. "Come along, *céadsearc,*" he said in a low, reasonable voice. "Ye must lie down and rest. I'll see to the babe."

She looked at him with wild, grief-filled eyes, and for a moment he feared for her sanity. "You must choose, Aidan," she insisted.

He sat beside her on the floor. "I should have

hired someone to help you. To stay with you when I had to be out."

Suddenly she slumped against the wall and stared at him. "Have you understood nothing I've said? *Nothing?* Go away, Aidan. I don't want to be under the same roof with ye."

He understood why, but her words lacerated him. He considered her, the color drained from her face, almost from her hair. This was the worst thing he'd ever experienced, and he'd seen a lot of suffering and death. The woman whose heart he'd tried to win despised him, and the child they had conceived was lost. For the first time in his life, his hope, the one thing that had sustained him through good times and bad, had burned out.

"I'll take you to Dr. McLoughlin," he offered quietly. "I know he'll let you stay for a few days, and though he's getting on himself, he and his wife can look after ye till you're feeling better." It was the last thing he wanted, to be away from her, but he knew they couldn't stay together right now. She would have none of it. "Are you agreeable to that?"

She dropped her gaze to the cradle again, her chin quivering, and with a shaking hand tucked the blanket around the child. "All right."

Allowing Aidan to help her to her feet, she leaned against him. For all her strength, she felt as frail as a child. He helped her to gather a few things, but when he stooped to pick up her little figure of Saint. Brigit, she snapped, "Leave it. I don't want it anymore."

Aidan knew with a sickening certainty that if she'd ever loved him, even just a little, she surely hated him now.

"Drink the beef tea, child. You've had a fearful shock and this will give you strength." Dr. John McLoughlin loomed over Farrell's sickbed, a giant of a man at six feet four. He picked up the cup from her bedside table and put it into her hands. "No matter what the future holds, you must be well enough to meet it."

His snowy mane, which was rumored to have turned white after an accident that occurred when he was a young man, had earned him the nickname Great White Eagle from the Indians he'd dealt with in the territory. Farrell could see why.

She had been here at the McLoughlins' house for two days, most of which she had slept through. Although she was beginning to recover physically, her spirit was crushed. But dutifully, she took a sip of the beef tea, not because she wanted it, but because the doctor and his wife had been very good to her and she didn't want to disappoint him.

"Will ye sit for a minute, Doctor?"

He pulled a chair up to her bedside. "You're young and strong. You come from good, sturdy stock. You will get better. And there will be children in the future."

She swallowed the lump in her throat. "I want to thank you for your kindness, taking me in and all. Aidan—my husband is always busy and it would be too hard for him to look after me."

"Yes, he's a very determined young man. Very ambitious. But he's been by here every day to check on your welfare."

"He has?"

"Oh, yes. You were sleeping, though, and he didn't want to bother you." He paused. "He looks worse than you feel, you know. If he doesn't take better care of himself, I'll have two patients to see to."

Farrell gazed out the window next to her bed. "He works too hard. He works everyone else too hard."

The doctor sighed. "As I said, he's ambitious. But he's not ruthless. Sometimes those two go together and make an ugly pairing. Aidan has a good heart."

"I know he does."

"And he's scared."

She turned to look at his piercing gray eyes that were nearly as pale as his hair. "Scared? Aidan? And sure but he didn't tell you *that*."

"No, no, he didn't have to. Misfortune can drive a man to desperate acts. I was Canadian-born, but my grandfather was from Ireland so I know about her history. And of course, we heard about the potato famine here. News like that travels. Aidan is fearful of the two of you starving again." He tapped a finger on his chin. "Something else is bothering him, too, but I don't know what. Whatever it is, he's determined to succeed at something." He reached out and patted her hand. "You just get well so you can go back and help him understand what that something is. He needs you."

She thanked him and he left her alone to ponder his words. Aidan needed her? In this, she thought the doctor was wrong. Yes, Aidan had been kindness itself at times, tender and thoughtful. He'd even told her that he loved her, a hurried scribble on a piece of paper. But she had never sensed that he needed her.

She loved him, and worried that just as in all other aspects of their lives, she was in love alone.

"This is Jacob Richards, your lordship. He used to work for O'Rourke. He was the mill foreman." Seth Fitch made the introductions at the back table of a Linn City saloon where the three men sat. Fitch had decided it was best to meet on this side of the river, just for security's sake. Noel had concurred.

God, Noel thought, if he had to frequent one more of these dingy places and rub elbows with ignorant rabble—well, it was for a good purpose, and if luck was with him, this entire country and his visit to the common side of life would soon be behind him.

"Richards," Noel acknowledged. "How is it that you don't work for O'Rourke any longer?"

"The egg-sucking son of a bitch turned me out."

Noel lifted his brows at the vehemence of the statement. "Really? What reason did he give you?"

"He claimed I was drinking on the job."

"And were you?" Noel pushed the whiskey bottle to him that stood on the sticky table.

"Hell, no! It was a filthy lie. I barely touch the stuff." Richards poured himself a healthy measure. He had the bloodshot eyes and telltale bloated, red face of a man who had a long-standing association with the drink.

Swirling the contents of his own brandy glass, Noel said, "I see. Would you be interested in getting some of your own back?"

"How do you mean?"

"I have a job that needs doing, and I need a man with your connections and knowledge of O'Rourke's operation to accomplish it." It wasn't true—Noel's purpose in involving Richards had nothing to do with those blandishments. But my, my, didn't Richards just *bask* in Noel's line of bunkum.

The man leaned back in his chair. "Well, I might be able to help you," he agreed expansively. "It all depends on what you have in mind and how much you're willing to pay."

Noel smiled. "And isn't that the crux of any agreement, Richards?"

CHAPTER SIXTEEN

FARRELL was dressed and sitting by the fireplace in the McLoughlins' parlor when she looked out the window and saw Aidan pull their wagon around to the front of the house. Her heart gave a joyful leap at the sight of him. She had missed him these past four days, although she had not forgiven him for anything. Watching him come up the walk, she still admired the broad shoulders and straight back, but he looked as pale and drawn as the leafless December trees. The thin winter afternoon sun settled over him like an old gray shroud.

The serving girl answered his knock, then discreetly left the room to give them privacy.

Aidan drew up a footstool and sat before her. He began to reach for her hand, then didn't. "How are ye feeling, Farrell?"

"The doctor says I'll be fine in time, and this morning he told me that I'm free to go home if I want." This close, she could see how tired and worn-looking he really was. The firelight played up his haggard features. Red-eyed and with a bristle of day-old beard, he looked uncared for.

"And do you want that?" he asked.

She found she couldn't look at him too closely. The bitterness in her heart had not faded in the few short days that she'd been here. In fact, she wasn't sure she'd ever recover from the loss of their child. "I don't know."

He nodded, as if he'd been expecting nothing more from her.

"Have ye been working hard?"

He shrugged. "Aye. There's not much else to do. Now." He took a deep breath and went on, as if from a speech he'd rehearsed in his head many times. "Farrell, I'm sorry for, well, for everything. That night—the night I brought you here, you told me I must choose between you and the mill. I've had a lot of time to think about everything while you've been gone." He hung his hands between his knees. "I never should have taken ye away from Ireland. It was wrong of me. I should have seen you settled there in another town where none could find you, just as you'd asked, and then left for America on my own." Farrell's heart chilled in her chest. "I thought we could build a life, and I've given you everything I can think to give, but—" He shook his head. "I didn't do what I should have to begin with, so now I want to make it right. I'll give you an annulment, and that will be my final gift to you. I'll swear we never consummated the marriage and you can go home to Ireland. I'll pay your passage and provide money so you can live your life there, in safety, then send you more as long as you need it."

Icy-handed and dry-mouthed, she asked, "This is what you want? *This* is your choice?"

He closed his eyes for a moment, then looked at her. "It's for the best. Too much has happened between us. I thought I was doing you a favor by bringing you to America. But I wasn't. Stay here until spring, when the sailing is better, or—or if you'd rather, we can find a boardinghouse where you can live until then." He searched her face, as if waiting for a particular response. But she couldn't speak.

So much for Dr. McLoughlin's notion that Aidan needed her. Maybe Aidan was right. Maybe there were too many hurt feelings to ever get over. So he'd chosen the mill. She shouldn't have been surprised, but she was, and oh, God, so *crushed*. How strange, she thought woodenly, that his dreams had not broken his heart, as his family had predicted, but hers instead.

Once again, Liam's words came back to haunt her. *I love ye, lass, but in God's truth, I don't love you well enough.* Neither, it seemed, did Aidan.

She swallowed the hard lump in her throat, the one that threatened to cause tears to begin flowing. "All right, Aidan," she said at last. "I'll come home—I mean, back to the house, until I decide what I want to do. Just let me collect my things here and thank the McLoughlins."

When they got back to the house, Aidan remained in the kitchen while Farrell walked through the rooms. She saw that he'd replaced the tick in the bedroom with a new one and removed every trace of what had happened that night. The floors were clean, the bloodstains washed away. Even the cradle was gone. It was as if nothing had happened here. As if the baby had never existed. Grief welled up within her again, as strong as ever. It seemed that he would just sweep away all vestiges of Farrell and their child.

Apparently, he had been sleeping in one of the other bedrooms. There, the bed was unmade. Clothes were flung here and there, and his other good suit lay in a heap in a corner. Dirty dishes and a half-empty whiskey bottle stood on the floor next to the bed. God, what a mess, she thought.

She made her way back downstairs to the kitchen, where he was drinking a cup of tea. "The ladies from church came to help clean up. They send their condolences."

"Thank you." Afraid to ask, she finally had to. "Where—what did you—" She took a deep breath and tried again. "What about the babe?"

"I buried it out in back. I'll take you there if you'd like."

She let her hand trail over the worktable. "Later, maybe."

Aidan left his tea mug on that table and went

out then, saying he had business to attend to. Of course. When had he not?

Christmas was only a few days away, and as the sun set on this Friday afternoon, people in town were hurrying home with gifts and provisions for Christmas dinners. But Aidan had one goal as he rode over the frosted landscape to Kelleher's saloon, and that was to get roaring drunk. It had been his goal every night since Farrell had first gone to the McLoughlins'. This afternoon, that seemed to be an especially important task, since he couldn't face staying in the house with Farrell there, knowing that she would soon be gone.

It had all seemed so logical when he'd worked it out in his head, this gut-wrenching decision to send her away. But when he'd first set eyes upon her that afternoon, it had taken all the strength he had to keep from dropping to his knees in front of her, begging her for another chance, and blubbering like a child in her lap. Then he'd mustered that waning strength to make his little speech. She'd already been pale, but when he'd uttered his words, any color left in her face faded away.

He tied his horse to the rail in front of Kelleher's and walked into the saloon. After stopping at the bar to get a bottle and a glass, he found a table in the back and flopped into a chair. The questions that had plagued him all the way into town were still buzzing around his brain like a bee trapped in a jar. Had he done a stupid thing with Farrell? Had he done the right thing? Was there yet hope? Did he even know anything at all anymore? He'd been utterly miserable the entire time she was across town—how would he feel when he knew she was gone forever, ten thousand miles across the world?

He uncorked the bottle, poured a drink, and bolted it in one swallow, hoping to numb the pain in his heart and to silence those questions before they made his head burst. He drank three in quick succession, gasping for a breath between each. The kindly fire of the alcohol was beginning to dull his brain when, across the saloon, he spotted Jacob Richards's woozy, bloated countenance. Aidan knew he'd made an enemy of the man when he'd discharged him. It was perfectly acceptable for a man to sit in a saloon and soak his troubles when he had just told the only woman he'd ever loved to seek an annulment, hoped that she wouldn't, and was scared to death that she would. It was just fine to get stinking drunk when a man felt like he was the biggest idiot and most successful failure on God's earth. But he couldn't have someone gone with the drink working in a place with machinery and saw blades. If Geoffrey Brother had ignored the problem, or hadn't recognized it, that wasn't Aidan's fault.

Then he noticed that Richards was sitting with

Seth Fitch, that scheming spalpeen. An alarm bell went off in his head—something wasn't right, but he didn't know what. They saw him as well but didn't acknowledge him. They merely put their heads closer and spoke in tones too low for him to hear. Now and then, one or the other would glance up at him.

Suddenly, the idea of getting drunk in this place didn't seem like a good one to Aidan. Oh, he yearned for the oblivion of the whiskey, but he worried that in his intoxication, his oblivion might become permanent when one of those men smashed his head in. He wasn't about to die at the hands of such low men. Fitch meant him no good, and he'd probably enlisted the aid of Richards, who also bore him a grudge. Surely this had to be about something besides some money lost on a gambling table, but he didn't know what.

He put the cork back in the bottle, tucked it under his arm, and threw two dollars on the table. Then he left through Kelleher's back door, intent on heading back to the mill where he could drink in peace.

The next morning, Farrell was already up and sitting at the kitchen table when Aidan came downstairs. Outside, dawn was just beginning to light the gloom of the overcast sky. He wore one of his suits, but he moved carefully and without the usual bounce in his step, as if he feared his head might roll off his shoulders. She had heard him come in late and had known from the sound of his gait that he was drunk. He'd bounced along the hallway walls, shushing himself when he thought he'd made too much noise. If it hadn't been so sad, she would have laughed. But there was nothing funny about this.

"You're up early," he commented. "Did ye sleep at all?"

She rose from the table and wrapped her shawl around her shoulders. "I want to see the baby's grave."

He looked at her with red-edged eyes and she saw the heartache in his gaze before he glanced away. How had they come to such a dreadful pass? she wondered.

"Ye're sure?"

She glared at him.

He nodded. "All right." He walked to the door and opened it, then waited for her to pass. She detected the scents she'd come to love about him, including a whiff of fresh-cut wood. She might hate the mill that stole him from her as surely as she would hate another woman who tried to take him, but she loved the clean smell of its perfume.

She walked down the steps and he followed her. "It's this way." He led her over the wet grass to a small grove of bare-branched hazelnut trees, half-way down the lawn to the river. They were planted in a semicircle and seemed to embrace and protect the charge that had been laid at the base of their trunks. She could see where the earth had been turned, but she wasn't prepared for what she found when she got to the little mound. She sank to her knees, and a sob rose in her throat.

"Oh, God," she mourned. "Oh, God."

He knelt beside her, heedless of the mud grinding into the knees of his suit pants. "I'll order a headstone, but for now, I thought this would be all right. She'll watch over the babe."

On top of the tiny grave sat Farrell's little figure of Saint Brigit, the one she'd abandoned the night she'd gone to Dr. McLoughlin's house. She bowed her head and sobbed, her heart breaking as she rocked on her knees.

"I'm sorry, Farrell," she heard Aidan say, his voice shaking. "I didn't know what else to do. D'ye want me to take it away?"

She felt him beside her and she wanted to fall into his embrace. But they'd wounded each other so badly. "N-no. It's fitting, Aidan." She stretched out a tentative fingertip to the head of the little figure Aidan's father had carved for her so many years ago. "It's fitting that she take care of the poor wee thing. I couldn't."

. . .

Late that night Farrell lay in the bed she shared with
Aidan, listening to every creak and groan the house
made in the chill wind that blew under the eaves
and whistled around the windows. She knew that it
was far past ten o'clock, and although she'd been
tired and sleeping a lot since the miscarriage, tonight she was tense and wide awake.

Aidan was still not home.

She supposed that what he did now was his
business, but she felt fairly certain that he wasn't
working late in the mill office. She had gone to the
front window several times and looked out at the
building, quiet for the night, searching for a light
in even one window. But she saw not even a candle
glimmer.

At last, when she was about to put on her shawl
and go looking for him around the yard, she heard
the door open downstairs. His unsteady footsteps
sounded across the hardwood floors and she heard
him utter a sharp curse when he bumped into something and knocked it over. He was drunk again.
Then he was on the stairs, and she lay rigid under
the quilts, wondering if despite everything he'd said
he would now try to come back to this bed. He
reached the top step and staggered down the hallway. Though her room was dark, she felt him standing at the doorway, as if trying to see her in the

bed. She smelled the alcohol on him, even from here.

Then he turned and stumbled back to the other bedroom where he'd been sleeping. In a few moments, she heard him snoring.

She rolled onto her side and wept for them both.

"They've parted? You know this for certain?" Noel stared at Fitch across a table in the Linn City saloon that had become their meeting place.

"Yes, your lordship, that's the story going around. Richards has seen O'Rourke with his own eyes at Kelleher's every night, putting away the better part of a bottle. Servants' chatter says that Farrell O'Rourke has been staying with the McLoughlins."

This was working out better than Noel could have hoped for. He'd imagined Farrell and Aidan O'Rourke to be a happily married, parvenu couple in the new home that must seem like a castle to people accustomed to living in a thatched-roof hovel. But apparently there was trouble in their fool's paradise, and that would make things so much easier for Noel. Once he'd had O'Rourke disposed of, he could step in as a magnanimous, kindhearted old acquaintance, ready to take Farrell back to Ireland. Thank God this miserable odyssey was almost over. She might even be glad to see him, after all was said and done.

"Richards has turned out to be a valuable asset, for all that he's a drunken sot. All right, then. Wait right here, Fitch. I'm going to write a message for you to deliver to O'Rourke." He rose from the table to walk back to his room, then turned. "And Fitch—good job."

The man beamed and bobbed like the well-trained lackey that Noel had made of him. "Yes, sir. Thank you, sir."

"Mr. O'Rourke?" Tom Fitzgerald knocked on the door to Aidan's office and poked his head inside, letting in the din of the mill beyond. "Someone to see you, sir." Aidan noticed that Fitzgerald had been a bit happier since he'd been promoted to mill foreman. He'd taken Farrell's words to heart about how his men felt. What good would it do if they despised him? He'd come to realize what he'd always known—a resentful, unhappy worker wasn't likely to produce much. Fitzgerald was a good man, and Aidan was willing to reward his efforts.

Aidan signaled to him to let the visitor in. He looked up from his account books and found himself face to face with Seth Fitch, who closed the door behind him.

"I have a message for you from an old acquaintance." He threw an envelope on top of the open ledger. He didn't trouble to hide his cold hostility, and Aidan knew his instincts about the man were right.

Aidan looked at the paper where it lay. "Oh? And who would that acquaintance be?"

Fitch gave him a lizardlike smile and walked out again. Aidan picked up the envelope and opened it.

O'Rourke—

You and I have some business to attend to. Meet me at your sawmill Saturday night, eight o'clock, if cowardice does not overcome you first.

Cardwell

So Cardwell was the special client Fitch had mentioned. Astonished and furious, Aidan wadded up the note. Had Cardwell really come this far, all these thousands of miles, just to confront him for the death of a man he knew Cardwell cared nothing about? If he had, he was stark, raving mad. Meet him, hell, Aidan thought.

Then, reconsidering, he smoothed it out again and put it in his pocket. He was sick to death of Noel Cardwell, that foolishly decorated popinjay, following him around the world. And fop or no, he was a dangerous man with enough hired lackeys to do his bidding. Maybe it was best to get this over with once and for all.

He looked at the note again. The arrogance of this bastard, he thought. Aidan decided that he would meet him at the appointed time, for good or ill. In the back of his mind, all this time he'd worried that Noel would take him back to Ireland to face murder charges. But he'd finally come to recognize that Noel had no authority in America. Even if he had, Aidan had never run from a fight in his life, and he was going to run from this no longer.

He looked up at the wall clock. It was not quite five, and if he moved quickly, he'd still have time to run an errand in town before the stores closed. He might be willing to meet Cardwell, but he wouldn't walk into a possible trap empty-handed.

He closed the ledgers and locked them in his desk. Then put on his coat and strode out into the chill winter evening, determined to be ready for whatever fate brought to him next.

Farrell stared morosely into the flames of the fire she'd lighted in the parlor. The clock had just chimed seven o'clock and she didn't know if Aidan would come up from the mill or not. She had seen him this morning in the kitchen, and he'd looked terrible. Oh, he'd washed, combed, and shaved, but plainly he'd been paying for his drinking. Beyond the obvious signs of his dissolute activity, she thought she saw a yearning in his eyes, an aching, silent appeal to her that had been so strong, she'd almost gone to him to rest his head on her shoulder. But he'd turned and left for work, and aside from the most painfully polite of greetings, they had not spoken. How could she stay here under these circumstances? Yet there were things that she sensed were going unsaid, and without talking to him first, really sitting down and talking, she didn't feel as if she could go.

She couldn't speak that morning at the grave. She'd been so overwhelmed with grief, she could think of nothing else. But strangely, the visit had comforted her too. She'd begun to believe that she might heal from her loss, with the help of Saint Brigit. But what she really wanted was Aidan's help.

The idea of going back to Ireland frightened her. The trip over here had been bad enough, but she'd had him with her. To go alone, to be stuck down in steerage, would be miserable. And where would she go? What city? She didn't know anyone outside of Skibbereen. Both sides of her family had spent generations there and none had ventured to other places. Would she end up working for a man like Noel Cardwell, in a big house where she would be as inconsequential and open to abuse as a dog in the yard? It wasn't that she feared hard work— she never had. And she didn't crave special privilege or esteem—she hadn't even liked having a housekeeper. But such a life would be so dreary, and worse than farming in Skibbereen. Still, she didn't know how to do anything else but keep house and work the land.

Most important of all, she loved Aidan O'Rourke to distraction and it would tear out her heart to leave him. Sighing, she left the parlor and went upstairs to straighten the room where he slept. Standing in the doorway, she surveyed the mess. At first, she'd been unhappy enough to let him stew in his own rubbish—the dirty dishes, the rumpled bed, the pile of clothes. But she was still his wife and she would see to his needs.

She went to the window and opened it a crack to air out the stale smells. It was then that an odd glow of light caught her eye. What was that? A lamp? A torch.

Her eyes flew open wide. The end of the house was on fire. She ran downstairs to find the back porch and the side wall engulfed. Flames crept to the ceiling and smoke filled the kitchen. She reached for the bucket of water that stood by the doorway to the hall. But when she threw it on the wall, it made no difference.

Driven out of the room by smoke and heat, she ran to the front door, wondering what to do next. At the rate it was burning, the entire house would be ablaze unless a miracle occurred.

Inside his coat, Aidan clutched the Colt Navy revolver he'd bought in town. The shopkeeper where he'd gotten it had loaded it for him and given him a general overview of how to fire the thing. Aidan had never held a gun in his life. The English did not permit Irishmen to own firearms, but if it came down to it, he'd figure it out quickly enough.

He stood in a doorway to the mill. He'd set a lantern on a barrel next to him. It was the best place he could think of to watch for Noel and Fitch—sure, he'd bring Fitch, and perhaps Richards, too. Aidan would see them coming and have the advantage of a bit of cover if he needed it. He didn't know what might happen after that, but as far as he was concerned, this whole thing would be settled tonight.

Aidan heard the murmur of voices in the distance. Out here, there was no possibility that they could be simply passing travelers. There was nothing else here but the house and the mill. He had shut down the operation early to make certain that no one was left behind who wasn't involved with his meeting with Noel.

Out of the darkness, just one man revealed himself, and that was Noel Cardwell.

"So, O'Rourke, I've found you at last."

Aidan had hoped to never see those dead blue eyes again. "What do ye want, Cardwell? If you've followed me all these thousands of miles over the accidental death of Michael Kirwan, I'd say you're not right in the head. Given the chance, I think you'd kill a man"—he searched the darkness beyond where he thought he saw Fitch—"or more likely, have a man killed, without much thought beyond what the cost might be. So what is this about?"

Cardwell laughed softly. "For one, you deprived *me* of the satisfaction of doing in Kirwan. No doubt you've heard that he was stealing from the Cardwell estate. My father was extremely unhappy to learn about that."

Aidan's smile was grim. "Ah, yes, I'm sure he was. So you must answer for your rent agent's thievery."

"In part, yes. He sent me to America to find you and bring you back. Of course, I'm not about to do that. I've read a term on proclamations posted about this uncouth wilderness that I believe fits aptly: wanted dead or alive. I don't need to bring you back, just some physical evidence of your death. An ear, perhaps, or knowing my father, your head in a basket."

Aidan adjusted his grip on the gun handle. He'd been right earlier—Cardwell was insane. "I can tell ye, that won't be happening, either. What's the other part of your complaint? That I'm far away from Ireland and not bothering you or anyone else?"

Noel's eyes narrowed. "You took something I want, and she is the one who will return to Ireland with me. Now that you and Farrell will be separating, gaining her trust should present less of a problem. Poor soul, a stranger in a foreign country with no husband or other friends. I'm sure she won't mind posing as the grieving widow if I rid her of you."

Aidan's heart froze in his chest. So, now they had come to Cardwell's true purpose. Farrell. God, this changed everything. How much did this viper know? More than he should, it would seem. "Ye know I won't let you do that," he said, his voice deadly quiet. "I'll drop you where you stand before I see her carried off by you. She is my wife and we are bound, now and forever." He made this announcement not only to Cardwell and any of his toadies who might lurk in the darkness, but to himself and the world. Farrell and he were *meant* to be together. He would not give her an annulment, and he must have been out of his own mind with grief when he'd suggested it. He loved her, and he'd fight for her to the death if he had to. "If I hadn't left Ireland, I would have broken *your* head on a rock for what ye did to her. I saw her the night she ran home, her dress torn from neck to waist, you filthy degenerate."

Noel took a step forward. "As I said, you can easily be gotten rid of, and in the doing, I'll accomplish two deeds at once. I'll regain my father's favor, and I'll bring back a very handsome mistress." His eyes looked like black, empty sockets under the shadow of his brow bone.

"And since you seem to know everything, if she and I have separated, where d'ye think she is?"

"I know she's with Dr. McLoughlin. A very nice man, but his serving girl is better at providing information."

Aidan kept his expression carefully blank, one of the most valuable skills he'd learned from card playing. At least Cardwell didn't know where Farrell really was, safe at home.

From the far side of the mill, Aidan picked up the scent of wood smoke. He dared not look away from Noel, but he lifted his nose to sniff the wind.

"Yes, that's smoke you smell. Jacob Richards had a score to settle with you, as well, so we let him set the fire. While I'm about getting rid of you, I decided I'd destroy this little empire you're trying to build, as well. That has always been your trouble, O'Rourke. You've never recognized your place in the social order, as Fitch does. It was an outstanding stroke of luck that he lost money to you in New Orleans. He's almost as hungry for your blood as I am."

Seth Fitch stepped out of the shadows with a shotgun, which he threw to Cardwell. God, what was that in Fitch's other hand? It looked like a snake that he uncoiled. But one crack across Aidan's arm corrected his misconception. The pistol he held went flying into the darkness.

It was not a snake that Fitch held. It was the

kind of weapon a former plantation overseer would own.

It was a bullwhip.

"Inside, O'Rourke." Noel picked up the lamp and prodded him with the shotgun. Fitch flicked the tail of the whip right next to Aidan's ear. At that close range, the snap sounded like an explosion and Aidan could hear nothing but ringing on that side of his head.

"You've slipped away from me before and I've come too far to let that happen again. This time, I'm going to make sure that you get what's coming to you because I'm going to see it done."

"Not man enough to take on the job yourself, aye, Cardwell?" Aidan goaded—foolishly, he knew.

This time the whip flicked the top of his ear and he felt the sizzling burn of torn flesh.

"You might learn your place yet before this night is over," Fitch said.

"But it's an unfortunate place, O'Rourke," Cardwell added. "You're going to die in a tragic accident. By the time they find your bones in the charred rubble, I'll be far away from here with Farrell."

CHAPTER SEVENTEEN

FLAMES ate up the front of the house at an alarming rate, and Farrell caught a whiff of kerosene in the air along with the burning wood. She stood on the front lawn, horrified, watching as the house was consumed by fire so hot, the skeleton of its frame gleamed dark red through the flames. Sparks and hot cinders floated skyward, and the whole fire roared with an evil sound, as if the ceiling of hell had cracked open and reached up to take the house. Bits of burning fabric and paper fluttered over the roof, carried along on the hot air currents. The yard was lit up as brightly as day. Farrell wore only a thin dress and no shawl, but fear and heat from the fire drenched her with perspiration.

From the bend in the drive, she heard horses and wagons, and voices raised in alarm. Neighbors who'd seen the flames had come to help, already forming a bucket brigade at the nearby creek, the same one that powered the mill. Seeing them, her gratitude made her throat tight.

"Mrs. O'Rourke, are you all right?" She recognized Tom Fitzgerald among the many who were pulling up. He jumped down from his horse and tied it securely to a tree far from danger.

"Yes, yes, but Tom, I don't know where Aidan is. Have you seen him since closing?"

"No, ma'am, I—" He broke off to stare over her shoulder, and she followed the path of his gaze. Then she froze, her jaw open as terror flashed over her in waves.

"Oh, my God." Flames were eating up the mill just as quickly as they were taking the house. "Tom, this is no accident! Someone has set these fires, trying to kill us both! What if Aidan is down there?"

"Don't you worry, ma'am. I have Pete Dorsett and James Cole following. They should be here any minute. We'll find out what's going on." He sprinted back to his horse and pulled a shotgun from its leather scabbard next to the saddle.

Farrell ran from person to person in the bucket brigade, all working on the house fire. "Damn the house!" she said, shouting over the inferno. "Ye must save the sawmill! Please!" It was a curse to her, but it was also Aidan's pride and joy, and she loved him so much, she'd save it for him if she could.

She reorganized the bucket brigade, leading them to the mill. As they raced over there, Tom, James, and Pete passed them at a full run, each carrying a firearm. Farrell took her place in the line, opting to stand close to the blaze so that she could keep an eye out for Aidan. Minutes dragged by like hours. Farrell's hands blistered from passing the heavy buckets of water. She also noted a cramping protest in her womb, a remnant of her miscarriage, but still she kept on, doing her best to ignore the pain. Her agony lay in her worry for Aidan.

The house, now completely engulfed, gave an eerie wail. The tongues of flame cut through the roof and Farrell glanced up in time to see it collapse inward on the rest of the structure with a roar. She was certain that all the furniture in the attic served as fuel.

The mill did not seem to be faring any better. "Faster with the buckets! Keep them coming!" she screamed over the racket. "Ye must save this mill!" But where was Aidan? Even if they could put out the mill fire, if he was not safe, none of it would matter.

Over the din of the fire, she heard *crack! crack!* Moments later a group of men rounded the corner of the building. Aidan, his face a mask of black soot, led the way. Breaking ranks, Farrell dropped her bucket and ran to him, throwing herself into his embrace and sobbing incoherently.

"Aidan, oh my dear God, Aidan! Are ye safe?"

"Aye, *céadsearc,* but it was nip and tuck for a while." Tom Fitzgerald and the other men passed them, with Seth Fitch and Jacob Richards bound at the hands. The mill workers prodded them along at gunpoint. "Those men were working for Noel Card-well."

"Noel! Holy Mother, Noel is here?"

"He's inside. Tom shot him just as he was about to kill me. If he and the others hadn't come when they did—" He left the sentence unfinished, but it was all too clear what nearly happened.

She saw the drying blood that left a gory trail down the side of his neck from the missing tip of his ear. "What have they done to you?" She whirled to look at the two trespassing arsonists. "Did they do this?"

"It's all right. I'll be all right."

Suddenly, the mill gave a great, heaving groan, like a living thing suffering the throes of death.

"Look out!" someone shouted. "It's going down!" Everyone ran, including Aidan and Farrell, who sank onto the wet grass far enough away to be safe. The roof collapsed in a raging blizzard of hot sparks and flying embers.

Aidan looked at the house, also on fire but now just a flaming wreck. "They fired the house, too? I suppose they would. Thank God you're safe. Card-well thought ye were still with the McLoughlins."

"Me? What do I have to do with this?"

"I'll tell you all about it later. We have a *lot* to talk about."

"Yes, we do." Overhead, the skies opened up and cold rain began falling.

He stared at the hissing, steaming fires. "I've lost everything."

"Ye haven't lost me. I'm still here."

He pulled up a yellow-green blade of the dormant grass. "Ah, but you've never stopped loving Liam."

"Is *that* what you think?" She gripped his sooty chin in her blistered hand. "Don't you know, don't you realize how much I love you already? Why do you think I craved your company at night? Just for someone to talk to? No! I wanted to be with you. And why else would I have urged everyone over here to try and save the mill?"

"You did that?"

"Of course. I hated the place, but I knew how much it meant to you, you great dunderhead!"

He gave her a wry smile. "I should have known. Whenever ye call me a great dunderhead, it's done with love."

"Well, it is!"

Now he laughed, actually laughed, and it was good to hear. "I know."

"We'll have a good life, Aidan. Ye promised me that, and I'm holding ye to it. You can't just change your mind about that whenever the mood strikes you."

"So you'll stay and be my wife, even though, great dunderhead that I am, I tried to send you away?"

"I'll stay. But don't ever, ever do that again."

He sighed. "I really thought I was doing you a favor, you know. I wanted to die the day I sat in the McLoughlins' parlor and said that to you." He took her hand. "And Farrell, I want you to know— Christ, I'm so sorry I left you alone that night. I should have been here. I feel like it's my fault the child was lost."

She swallowed hard, her throat tight at the mention of the baby. "I don't know that it's anyone's fault. I just needed you to be with me, and ye weren't."

He put his arm around her shoulders and pulled her close. "I promise that will never happen again. I was a fool, even if a well-intentioned one. I know how wrong I was."

"It'll take some time, I think, but we'll heal." The rain poured down upon them, soaking them to the bone, streaking the soot on them. "Where are we going to live now?" she asked, looking at the ruined house.

"Well, we're not destitute. I've cash buried in the field, enough to get us started again. But no more sawmills. We'll farm this acreage, just as we'd planned. Are ye good with that?"

She smiled at him, and though they sat in the rain and people still milled around them, she gave him a moist, passionate kiss.

"I'll do," she replied.

. . .

The hotel opened its doors to them that night, though they came in looking even worse than they had the day they'd stepped off the *Mary Fiona*. This time, though, they were respected and known members of their community, and the desk clerk, upon learning of their horrible misfortune, and at Christmas besides, offered them every service he could think of. And damn, if they didn't look like the holy family with no place to go, Aidan agreed. Farrell jabbed him in the ribs with her elbow, and warned him of his blasphemy, but she laughed anyway.

"I'm sure we look far worse than they did. We're wet and smoke-stained and bloody. At least they had a nice donkey."

Aidan placed the same order he had at L'Hôtel Grand De Vue—baths and supper for both of them.

This time, Aidan stayed behind to lather every inch of Farrell's skin. He washed her hair, massaging her scalp and neck until he evoked groans of pleasure from her.

"Mmm, that feels wonderful," she intoned. "Ye might guess that this hasn't been one of my better weeks."

It was true, the week had been disastrous and heartbreaking. But her spirit wasn't broken. He could hear it in her voice, and her arch tone made him laugh.

"That's one of the things I love about you, Farrell. You can always make me laugh."

She turned in the tub to look at him. "Why, that's how I feel about you. You let me have fun."

When he'd dried her and wrapped her in towels, he put her in the upholstered chair and knelt before her. "I'm sorry for everything that's happened. At least the things I could have helped. But I thought that I'd win your love by giving you the security you'd never had as a girl. That was why I worked so hard. And the harder I worked, the more I feared losing everything and you." He put his forehead on her knees. He couldn't keep the emotion out of his voice. It had been a bad week for him, too, and tonight had brought him as close to death as he'd ever been. "Farrell, please, will you marry me?"

"Oh, Aidan." She stroked his dirty hair. "But I am married to you. You've told me so yourself."

He raised his head. "No, I mean will you marry me in a proper church wedding at St. John's? You'll have a nice dress and friends to see you turned out, just as you should have almost a year ago."

She searched his eyes and her expression softened so, she began crying. And looking at her, he feared he might cry, as well. "That would be lovely. How about on our first anniversary in February? We'll plan it for then."

Aidan had never wanted to be a wealthy man. But he realized that as long as he had his Irish bride, he would always be the richest man in the world.

EPILOGUE

July 1881

AIDAN took Farrell's hand in his as they climbed the last rise in the road that led to the valley. Around them the hills swelled and dipped gently, green and lush beneath the high summer sun.

He looked at her against the backdrop where they'd grown up. Despite the passage of twenty-six years and a lifetime spent raising four lovely daughters, three fine sons, and forging a home from raw land, his wife was still the most beautiful woman he'd ever seen. Over time, her hair had softened from its fiery cinnamon to a pale copper, and a few silver threads wove through her braid to glint like moonlight.

Aidan knew he was hardly the same man who'd left this land, either. He was older, yes. To reach fifty-four years had seemed incomprehensible when youth and foolishness had made his blood run high and hot. But he was a better man now—tempered and improved by this woman who had never left his side, though the saints knew he'd given her good cause more than once.

Clearing the rise, he felt his heart suddenly begin to pound in his chest, and it wasn't due to the walk to Skibbereen. The place where they'd been born and had once expected to die spread before them. Farrell's hand tightened around his.

"God in heaven," she whispered, a kind of wonderment in her voice. "Will ye look at that?"

"Aye, look at that," Aidan echoed. They moved closer, approaching the glen with the hushed respect and awe saved for a graveyard.

Since they'd walked away from here that desolate winter of 1855, he'd nurtured the memory of how this place had looked. Not the day that Michael Kirwan had come to tear down his cottage, and paid with his life for the deed, but before famine had moved like a dark cloud over Ireland. The memory Aidan held bore a timeless sense of substance and belonging, a frozen, evergreen moment when youth had been his, and trouble lay on the far side of the future.

Now only rocks remained, in piles that had once been cottages, and in the zigzagging walls that snaked over the country's valleys and meadows. Farther up the hillside, a flock of plump sheep grazed peacefully on what had been Jack Mc-Cready's field.

"It's all gone, Aidan, the houses—everything. And we waited so long to see it again." He heard the sense of loss in Farrell's voice.

"Aye. Nothing stays the same, but somehow . . . somehow I thought this would." If he closed his eyes, it was easy to remember his da, Sean, still alive, younger than Aidan himself was now, coming home with a heavy sack of cut peat on his broad shoulders.

The rest of the family had scattered over the years, to Dublin, to Boston, and New York, and Chicago. But although some of the nieces and nephews had made it to America, Aidan and Farrell had never seen any of them again. Oh, they had talked about visiting in letters they sent back and forth, but time passed, and one thing or another had gotten in the way.

While Farrell stood in the yard, shading her eyes as she gazed across the deserted valley, he made his way to the remains of his brother Tommy's cottage. The square of the foundation still stood, as did one wall, but grass grew on the floor. The hearth, positioned in the center of the cottage as tradition dictated, yet bore a few stones blackened by the eternal turf fire that had burned there. Turning, he reached out and beckoned her wordlessly. She joined him, and they stood side by side.

"This is where I took you to wife, remember? God, but you were angry."

Farrell looked up into Aidan's eyes, still dark blue, still intense. Lines framed their outer corners and fanned toward his temples, but they gave his face more character than it had had when he was a young man, handsome as he'd been. "Oh, yes, I was. I didn't know if I could ever forgive you for what you'd done."

"But you did, *céadsearc*—in time, for which I am most grateful." He fingered the thin, plain silver wedding band on her finger, then lifted her hand to his lips. "Are you sorry that you left Skibbereen?"

Farrell had yearned to visit since the day she'd stood on the deck of the *Mary Fiona* and watched their homeland grow smaller and smaller. She scanned the hills again, searching for something that matched the image in her memory, and found nothing. "I never thought we'd come back—it looks familiar but not the way I remembered. It seems smaller, somehow . . . I don't know how to explain it."

"*Go mbeannaí Dia duit,*" Aidan murmured, as he had all those years ago. May God bless you. Then to her, he said, "Come on, Farrell. Let's go home. Back to America."